LETHBRIDGE-STEWART

BLOOD OF ATLANTIS

Simon A Forward

CANDY JAR BOOKS · CARDIFF
2025

The right of Simon A Forward to be identified as the
Author of the Work has been asserted by him in accordance
with the Copyright, Designs and Patents Act 1988.

Blood of Atlantis © Simon A Forward 2016, 2025

Characters and Concepts from 'The Web of Fear'
© *Hannah Haisman & Lincoln Estate,* 1968, 2025
Lethbridge-Stewart: The Series
© Andy Frankham-Allen & Shaun Russell, 2015, 2025

Doctor Who is © British Broadcasting Corporation, 1963, 2025.

ISBN: 978-0-9954821-0-4

Range Editor: Andy Frankham-Allen
Editor: Shaun Russell
Editorial: Hayley Cox, Lauren Thomas, & Philip Bates
Licensed by Hannah Haisman
Cover by Richard Young & Will Brooks

Printed and bound in the UK by
4edge, 22 Eldon Way, Hockley, Essex, SS5 4AD

Published by
Candy Jar Books
Mackintosh House
136 Newport Road, Cardiff, CF24 1DJ
www.candyjarbooks.co.uk

A catalogue record of this book is available
from the British Library

All rights reserved.
No part of this publication may be reproduced, stored in a
retrieval system, or transmitted at any time or by any means, electronic,
mechanical, photocopying, recording or otherwise without the prior
permission of the copyright holder. This book is sold subject to the
condition that it shall not by way of trade or otherwise be circulated
without the publisher's prior consent in any form of binding or cover
other than that in which it is published.

PROLOGUE

THERE WERE times when the mass of the ocean could weigh down upon a man.

The trick – Mikhail Artyomovich Zaretsky's job – was to visualise that space without allowing any of the pressure to penetrate. To be in command of himself as much as the eighty men under him. Give a man a blindfold of rolled steel and ask him to fight under several hundred fathoms of water. Even at their current depth of barely ninety feet, such a man had to possess a skull like the hull of his boat, be able to feel the pressure without letting any of it interfere with the smooth running of operations inside.

No man was born to such gifts. Zaretsky could not recall the moment when he had come by them. There was no single moment. Rather, the knowledge had seeped into him through a conspiracy of training and instinct, permeated his soul almost, to become not second nature but more. It changed him, adapted him to the world below the waves.

It was, to his mind, a kind of evolution.

'Contact, bearing three-five-two degrees. Range thirteen thousand yards.'

Captain Zaretsky visualised the warship, mapped it onto his mind's-eye view. The British Leander-class frigate executing a slow turn. A touch over six nautical miles, moving away at ten knots, but no less a threat.

Her helo had been up for approaching three hours, sowing the field with her listening seeds, perhaps nearing bingo fuel. Possibly the *Aphrodite* was manoeuvring to recapture her aircraft.

'Sonar buoy in the water! We are being pinged!'

Litvin, always so excitable. The way he clasped a hand to his headphones, one might think he had heard his mother screaming. Zaretsky shared a steady gaze among his junior officers, distributing calm like breadcrumbs to birds. Trust answered back from every pair of eyes.

The seventh buoy in the water. The Royal Navy feared something lurked below, but the search efforts seemed precautionary, suggesting suspicions rather than firm knowledge.

'Bearing?'

'Bearing twelve degrees. Range eighteen hundred yards.'

A little on the close side. But the buoy's ping would get a weak return.

'They're trying to startle us out of hiding. Trying to stir some activity.' The new anechoic tiles were doing their job. 'Let us trust our new coat, hmm?' Zaretsky performed a few brisk calculations. The sonobuoys were scattered too widely to provide the British with a triangulation, but the safe lanes for his boat grew narrower and fewer with every buoy dropped. 'Helm. Take us down to three hundred feet. Just so Mr Litvin can relax a little.'

A murmur of laughter did the rounds of the CIC. Litvin soaked it up in good spirits, before returning to his usual intense stare. Like Zaretsky, he had a talent for seeing the sounds.

Slipping below the thermocline would effectively drop them out of the buoy's range. It would ping away at apparently empty space, its signals bouncing off a screen formed from the simple change in water temperature. In their metal bottle there were no seasons, but the summer retained its uses outside.

His boat had little enough depth to play with in this stretch of the Aegean. But there was room. Another three hundred feet to spare between their hull and the seabed.

Litvin frowned. No, it was more of a wince. Like a man hearing scratches on his favourite classical records. 'Captain, I'm getting–' He shrugged. 'Strange echoes.'

Strange echoes? What picture was Zaretsky supposed to paint with that?

'Mr Litvin, more information, if you please.'

The sea rumbled. Thunder in a world without sky.

The boat shook, like a present rattled in the hands of a child. Zaretsky grasped the periscope handle to help keep his footing. 'Steady!'

His officers all grabbed available handholds.

Something scraped the hull. Some angry god raked steel fingernails down a blackboard. There was no image other than the fanciful and impossible. Zaretsky's mental picture of the surrounding space broke down. He could visualise nothing because there should be nothing there. No rocks, nothing. His boat should have clear water all around.

He rushed to the chart table. The deck pitched under him and threw him against the table. He struck the edge, slapped his hands on the map.

Shrieking, grinding, metal on – what? Rock, or more metal? Poseidon digging into the boat with his trident. Gutting the boat like a fish.

Lights blinked and flickered across the consoles. Across the frightened faces of too many men.

Litvin tore off his headphones and pushed away from his station. He stared and stared. But now his eyes seemed to see something. Not mere sounds translated into images in the mind. But something real. Something that moved, ranging across the instruments in front of him.

Zaretsky could not recall the moment when it appeared. There was no single moment.

It crept into the boat and spread. Permeating everything.

Consuming the metal and the courage of men.

There were things worse than pressure and water to find their way through a hull. And into a man's soul.

CHAPTER ONE
Green Death

THE ZODIAC bounced over the waves like a skimmed stone with a will to keep going and going. It was a punishing ride, even across calm seas.

Owain Vine ignored the battering as best he could and focused ahead. He felt like a modern Ahab, keeping eyes peeled for the monstrous white whale. They'd had the rig in view for an age now but they were beginning to get their first proper look, able to pick out details on the structure.

Blimey, she was big.

Monster wasn't far off the mark. A giant steel dinosaur rising from the sea, on stumpy legs big enough to make a brontosaurus look like Twiggy. With all its bulk, it wore its bones on the outside: a skeleton of catwalks, gantries, railings, pipes and girders caging the world's worst eyesore tower block. What was funny, they'd painted it in reds, yellows, oranges, as though that might go some way to prettying it up. But it just looked like some gigantic sculpture bolted together from garish Meccano and junkyard scraps.

Paolo kept the boat straight, cannoning for the beast's legs. Its nether-garments were girdles of catwalks and stairways, painted in more of that high-visibility yellow, descending to a cluster of jetties. AKA, their objective.

Four people in a small grey craft weren't much of a dent on an otherwise unspoiled sea view, but the boat kicked up frequent fountains of spray. Someone on the rig must've spotted them by now.

They'd soon find out how the residents felt about visitors.

Owain waved at Paolo. He eased up on the engine. The Zodiac dropped the pace like a worn-out jogger. The bounce gentled. Owain's bones ached, now that the constant jolt had ceased.

Kara flashed a smile, for encouragement. But her gaze searched for something in return. Owain answered with a wink and a thumbs-up. That shored up her smile and she edged forward in the boat, closer to him.

Theo stuck the binoculars to his eyes, although Owain didn't know what more he expected to see at this range. They were close enough now that they ought to be able to pick out frantic movement on the rig with the naked eye. Not that Owain and his friends were liable to incite panic.

Granted, Theo could look a bit fierce. The boat trip had whipped his dark mane into wilder shape than usual and he had a face like sun-baked clay, lined from a lifetime spent frowning. A lifetime that amounted to all of twenty-eight, but when Kara had first introduced him Owain had guessed the man's age at closer to forty. Paolo was more laid back, but a combination of youth, Italian temperament and passion about the environment turned him scary, *molto rapido*, in an argument. His slick curls and beard were matted with salt spray and right now he looked like a caveman in waterproofs. Kara, well, she was about the size of the bottles milkmen left on your doorstep, but woe betide any birds that pecked at her. Currently, she was bulked out by a navy-blue parka and her ringlets were as tangled and knotted as Paolo's beard, but since Owain's wink she'd fixed her eyes on the rig with an intensity worthy of Theo. Like a tan and tiny Amazon ready to do battle.

Still, not a group likely to strike terror in the hearts of hardy rig crews.

'Any activity?' Owain asked.

'Nothing. Yet.' Theo lowered the binoculars. His eyes might as well have been ringed with ink, they were so dark and gloomy.

'That's cause for optimism, Theo.'

Theo grunted.

'Seriously, it suggests they're not bothered by us,' Owain reasoned. 'Honestly, I'd be more worried if they rolled out the red carpet.'

'That makes no sense.'

Kara laughed and shook her head. 'He means a welcome would be suspicious. If they don't see us as a threat, it's good news.'

'We shall see.' Theo returned to peering through the binoculars.

Owain shrugged. Pollution and damage to the environment could be fought. Theo's pessimism could not.

'Time to break out the jewellery.' Owain shifted to the backpack and fished inside. He produced two pairs of handcuffs and dangled them like earrings. He handed one set to Kara, tossed another to Paolo. Then dug in the pack for two more pairs. One for Theo, which he tossed into the man's lap. The guy glanced down briefly before resuming his surveillance. Owain snapped the bracelet around his wrist and gave it a tug. Secure.

He returned to the prow and looked at the network of jetties and stairways under the rig. Getting on board; that was the first big hurdle. After that, well, they'd have to play it by ear. There was no shortage of railings to which they could chain themselves. The higher they climbed, the bigger nuisance they could make themselves.

In an ideal world, Owain would love to get somewhere to interrupt the platform's operations. But in an ideal world the platform wouldn't be operating. Time for some realism.

We'll do what we can, he told himself. *And that's all we can do.*

'Hello,' said Theo. If it was a greeting, it was the unfriendliest one Owain had ever heard. The guy tensed like a mouse sensing a nearby cat.

A chopper climbed into view from behind the platform's main tower. Quite a beast, fat-bodied with a tapering fin, it looked like an airborne whale. Owain had no expertise in such things, but growing up in Cornwall he'd seen similar machines flying Coast Guard duties. A thimble-shaped radar dome protruded from one side of its nose and it wore an orange, white and blue livery. The stripes of the South African flag, those same colours, playing host to the letters VTMB along the aircraft's tail.

Vorster-Transvaal Minerale en Brandstof. Bit of a mouthful. And one Owain wanted to spit out every time he thought the name.

'Might not be anything to do with us,' Owain suggested.

'Might be a routine flight. Ferrying crews or–'

The bird turned its nose towards them.

'Step it up!' Owain yelled.

Paolo gunned the motor. The Zodiac rode up on the water, back to skimming stone mode. Owain braced against the slamming impacts, watching the chopper and measuring the stretch of sea between them and the platform.

'Go, go, go! Come on!'

The chopper dipped, buzz-sawing the air. A flight-suited figure manned the aircraft's side door. He waved demonstrably, directing them the other way. The Zodiac ploughed stubbornly on and Owain could've sworn the guy in the chopper doorway shook his head. He withdrew inside.

The aircraft veered around aft and chased the boat's wake.

Closer, closer.

The chopper dived. The rotor blades whipped up the water and beat down on them. Wind blasted around Owain's ears and snatched at his hat. He slapped a hand to his head – after the damn thing flew off. He spotted it bobbing on the waves like some scrap of woolly flotsam. The chopper swooped past, threatening a haircut.

It raced ahead, climbed a short way and spun. Hovered there, playing goalkeeper between the rig's legs.

The helicopter dropped, narrowing the headroom.

'Get us under there!'

Paolo swung the rudder, weaving left then swerving back right. An Italian striker faking out the keeper for the penalty shot. It was a wide goal, some space to play with. Not much, but—

Kara ducked. Owain did likewise, but Theo shook him by the shoulder. He pointed up. 'More company!'

Men ran the catwalks, fanning out and lining the railings. Every one of them pressed a rifle to his shoulder.

'Holy hell!' yelled Theo. 'Paolo, back us out! Back us out!'

Gunfire cracked, echoing under the structure. Bullets punched water around the boat. Paolo fought to steer her round.

Owain hunkered down and Kara threw herself flat. Theo tossed the binoculars aside and belly-flopped in the bottom of the boat. They were all shouting and screaming and crying. And

Owain heard a whole lot of swearing – in Italian, Greek and English.

'They can't do this! They can't bloody do this!' Theo lunged for the pack, digging inside.

The gunfire dulled under the raging whine of the outboard. But bullets raked the sea either side. A string of vicious thuds travelled the side of the boat.

'What the hell!' Theo was up and kneeling, camera in hand.

'Are you out of your head?' Kara snapped. 'Get down!'

'Evidence! We need to report this!'

'Please, Theo!'

Puncture wounds erupted in the boat, silenced Kara. She stared at the ragged holes. Owain's gut knotted with panic.

But it was Theo who reeled. And toppled.

His body rocked about in the bouncing boat. His head rolled limply. The camera tumbled uselessly around, occasionally bumping into him.

Owain felt sick.

Paolo too, by the look of him. But he kept his hand on the throttle, squeezing every last drop of speed out of the motor.

Tears welled in Kara's eyes and she clasped hands over her mouth. She was visibly shaking. Owain thought he should throw an arm around her.

The boat hit a concrete wave. Something slammed the underside. Owain spun like a hard-struck cricket ball. Winded, his world flipped. Kara, Paolo, the boat – Theo; they hurtled away in a mess of directions. Owain caught fragmented glimpses until he lost sight of them all in a wild spin of sea and sky.

Then he hit the waves and the sea smacked the last air from his lungs.

His head swam while the rest of him sank in cold shadow. Some dim shape loomed at the edge of his senses. He lashed out, fending off a possible attacker. Then grabbed, in case it was trying to save him. But it was neither and it did nothing. Tall and impassive – like a column? – it merely stood in the depths. A silent monument to his passing, watching him drown.

The rush of water in his ears put paid to his hearing. And the last light faded from his vision.

*

Brigadier Alistair Lethbridge-Stewart was first off the plane, with Miss Anne Travers following him down the ramp at a distance undoubtedly intended to convey displeasure. She had expressed a good deal of it during the flight and plainly saw no reason to discontinue just because they had touched down.

What was that old pilot's saying? Any landing you could walk away from... Lethbridge-Stewart was more than happy to be walking away from this one.

Akrotiri breathed in his face like an open oven. Four powerful props spun down, fanning generous and very welcome drafts back from the Hercules' wings. Across the baking tarmac, two Land Rovers arced their way towards them. The welcoming committee.

Beyond stood the uninspiring block of white buildings that would serve as headquarters for the duration. He trusted his office would be equipped with a ceiling fan. Over on the far edge of the runway, a scattered selection of hangars sat in a sea of heat haze. Two Vulcan bombers were parked out in front, enormous V-winged birds attended by a small flock of maintenance aircrew. The aircraft were painted in the standard camouflage colours that had been introduced a few years ago.

He glanced back to where Miss Travers had stopped, maintaining a very definite space between them. Her eyes were masked by sunglasses, but he suspected there was more glare to be screened from behind those lenses than from the Cypriot sun.

Sergeant Major Samson Ware had an upbeat swagger as he led a platoon of hand-picked men of the Fifth off the aircraft, most of the soldiers laden with a file box or some item of apparatus in addition to their kit. Lethbridge-Stewart had been given assurances that any further manpower required could be drawn from the local garrison, but he hoped not to be too reliant on the Cyprus-based forces. Dependent on what their investigations turned up, clearance could present issues. In the meantime, amidst the rank and file, 2nd Lieutenant William Bishop completed his team, descending the C130's ramp, only lightly burdened by Miss Travers' personal luggage.

Alistair resisted rolling his eyes and donned his own sunglasses. The lieutenant was entitled to act the gentleman, as long as he understood he was here to do more than play skivvy to the civilian contingent.

Miss Travers huffed and fanned herself with her Greek phrase book. There was no telling how much she had learned in the six-hour flight, but after sporadic objections and quarrels she had by and large buried herself in that book and a scientific journal or two. Flicking the pages with a sharpness that Lethbridge-Stewart had imagined she had hoped would inflict paper cuts on her fellow passengers. Principally him. There was no certainty she would need much grasp of the local language, but as an alternative to some of the choicer words she had hurled in his direction, Greek would be preferable.

'Hot enough to singe a chap's moustache,' he remarked, thinking a little broken ice would be just what the doctor ordered, so to speak.

'Brigadier,' said Miss Travers, her tone simmering like a kettle about to hiss, 'I am not about to be placated by small talk about your facial hair. I'm still here under protest and you know damn well where I need to be.'

'Miss Travers, I have said I am very sorry for your father's situation—'

'Sorry won't change anything,' Anne snapped.

Lethbridge-Stewart had weathered enemy fire more easily. 'Must I remind you, Miss Travers, you were not under my command at the time and I was advised that Hamilton would brief you. It would appear, for whatever reason, he did not. You can hardly hold me responsible for that.'

'I don't,' she answered, a shade too quickly. 'But I hold you responsible for dragging me here when I need to be home.'

'We couldn't very well do without your scientific expertise.' Bishop drew up behind her and loitered on some invisible perimeter, clearly sensing he had strayed onto the scene of further drama. Lethbridge-Stewart liked to avoid soap operas himself, but it was a touch more difficult when he was one of the main players. 'Moreover, we are here now so I would recommend we set aside this dispute and make the best of it. The sooner we apply ourselves, the sooner we can be on our way home.'

Miss Travers muttered something under the dying chop of

the aircraft's propellers, words further lost amid the growl of Land Rover engines.

The two open-topped trucks, in blue RAF livery, rolled up and rocked on their suspensions while a group captain wasted no time hopping out of the lead vehicle and proffering a salute.

'Brigadier Lethbridge-Stewart. Sir.' The chap sported a moustache only a few shades browner than his tan and, at least while in the role of host, had a cheery, affable manner. He nodded, acknowledging the rest of Lethbridge-Stewart's party – apart from the rank and file, of course. 'Group Captain Winser. Welcome to Akrotiri. Glad to have you with us. Air Marshal Townsend-Jones will want to greet you in person, of course, but all in your own time. I trust you had a pleasant flight.'

'Thank you, Group Captain.' Lethbridge-Stewart did not intend to enter into that conversation. He furnished the officer with a rapid round of introductions, followed up with an invitation. 'Perhaps you'd care to brief us on any updates.'

'Sir. Gladly. Perhaps on the move? I'll send transport for your men and have a detail dispatched to assist with offloading.' Winser ushered Lethbridge-Stewart and Miss Travers to the lead Land Rover. Neither Bishop nor Samson needed to be directed to board the following car. Samson instructed the rest of the men to stay put and await their taxi, as he phrased it. He left Sergeant Spooner in charge and joined Bishop in the second car.

Lethbridge-Stewart settled in the back seat and Miss Travers climbed in beside him, doing all she could with body language to slide an invisible partition between them. Winser hopped in beside the driver and turned in his seat as the Rover roared off. He smiled courteously, as though keen to assure he meant no disrespect in referring to her in the third person. 'May I ask, in what capacity is Miss Travers here?'

'A reluctant one,' she cut in ahead of Lethbridge-Stewart. 'A deeply reluctant one.'

Lethbridge-Stewart tried not to bristle too obviously. 'Scientific, Group Captain. *Dr* Travers is our Head of Scientific Research and is cleared to hear anything pertaining to the case.'

'Glad to hear it. Great to have you aboard, Dr Travers.' She nodded curtly. To his credit, Winser was quite the diplomat. 'Intelligence is something of a misnomer until it's been analysed by educated eyes. We could certainly benefit from some expertise.'

'I hope I'll be of some use,' Miss Travers said.

She smiled, but the attack registered on Lethbridge-Stewart's radar: V-shaped, with a payload intended for him. Fortunately, Winser chose or failed to detect the strike.

'As you know, we've inherited something of our own Bermuda Triangle in the Med. Or, more accurately, the Aegean.'

Lethbridge-Stewart nodded. Ships vanishing without trace. Trawlers and the like mostly. Talk of Soviet submarines caught up in nets and dragging fishing vessels to the bottom, much local protest among Mediterranean ports and particularly the Greek island communities, fierce denials from Soviet embassies. Cause for grave international concern, but not especially any of Her Majesty's business until the *Pride of Mikonos.* One passenger ferry lost with all hands. Thirty-nine British citizens among the missing, presumed dead. A Royal Navy flotilla dispatched to assist with search and rescue operations.

And then–

'HMS *Aphrodite* is limping to port in Limossol,' Winser said.

'Any ideas as to the extent and nature of the damage?'

'Not clear as yet, sir. Hopefully she'll get patched up without too much trouble. As soon as she's arrived I'll have one of my men run you and your team down to the docks to inspect the damage for yourselves. In the meantime, the Navy sent through a report for your people. It's in a sealed folder – your eyes only – but I daresay they will have included some snaps of the hull. I expect those ought to paint a thousand words and save you some reading time. Those Navy boys can be verbose.'

Lethbridge-Stewart allowed a wry smile. He wondered if there was some hitherto unknown branch of Her Majesty's Armed Forces that wasn't versed in high-word-count paperwork.

The Land Rover pulled up alongside a plain white porch of the sort that would have looked at home fronting an ordinary roadside motel. The following vehicle tucked in close to the rear bumper.

Winser disembarked and Lethbridge-Stewart followed suit.

He paused in the shade of the porch.

'What about this South African connection?' he asked. '*Vorster Transvaal* something or other? The hydraulic fracturing operation?'

'Your man, Vine, has been feeding us additional intel. We have transcripts of every call and he's mailed occasional packages. Handwritten notes, observations, photographs, that sort of thing. Although naturally we've not delved into them ourselves. And you should know,' Winser added with a touch more gravity, 'we've not heard anything from him in a few days.'

Miss Travers flashed a frown. As though to imply this was Lethbridge-Stewart's fault too.

'He's not exactly my man,' said Lethbridge-Stewart.

It was odd, hearing Owain referred to as that – and by surname too. Made the lad sound like a full-blown special agent. A label Owain himself would have protested. If he had wanted to pursue that career track, he would no doubt be serving in a full capacity by now. But he did have a knack for involving himself. Lethbridge-Stewart hadn't seen much of Owain since they had returned from New York. Then came that call out of the blue, the lad trying to drum up Corps interest in his investigations. Lethbridge-Stewart had struggled to see the justification, but he'd put Owain in touch with Akrotiri and monitored the situation remotely as best he could. The *Aphrodite* incident had changed all that.

'More of a freelancer, really,' Lethbridge-Stewart added, for clarity.

Much more of a freelancer. At the same time, he and the lad shared a past that had forged an uncle-nephew bond. Even Sally had begun to look on the young man as her nephew, occasionally throwing Owain-related questions into idle conversation, such as: 'What's our Owain up to now?' Or other casual enquiries along similar lines. Lethbridge-Stewart could almost hear her voice, asking the exact same question right at this moment.

'We'll have to take a good look at his latest reports.'

'Of course, Brigadier,' Winser agreed. 'Right this way.'

Lethbridge-Stewart couldn't help a stab of concern for the lad's current whereabouts and whatever he might be up to his neck in now. He'd proven himself a more than capable young adventurer. The news that he had also ceased communications did not automatically spell trouble, but Lethbridge-Stewart had an uneasy feeling brought on by familiarity.

It was said to breed contempt, but it also happened to generate significant amounts of worry.

Kara shivered, without feeling the cold, even though she sat in waterlogged clothes and sea-soaked skin, wedged between two men in aircrew helmets and lifejackets.

The helicopter rotors drummed somewhere overhead and the whole aircraft rattled, shaking her bones. All the noise and vibration could have been miles away.

The open side door showed a sweeping square of ocean. A lot of empty water. The waves flickered like a lost signal on a television screen, with none of the sparkle. Lifeless but somehow in motion.

Like Theo. Theo was the only thing she really saw.

She saw blood. A spreading pool in the bottom of the Zodiac. Theo rolling about in the red.

A fresh attack of shivers dropped through her like a curtain of ice. She fought back a sob. Her stomach heaved.

She threw up on the helicopter deck, splashing the boots of the men seated opposite. They wore full combat gear and cradled rifles across their laps. Other than a snort of disgust, they didn't budge.

Until, sandwiched between them, Paolo leaned forward, stretched out a hand. His fingers didn't reach her, before his guards shoved him back into place. He shook them off, elbowed one away. Then returned to sitting in furious silence.

The door view slid from sea to painted steel. The helicopter leaned into a slow arc above the rig. Kara saw a circular pad emblazoned with a huge yellow H and the aircraft levelled, revolved in the air and began to descend.

They touched down, bumping deck.

'Out! Come on. Move it.'

Kara's heart jumped. She searched about, unable to register who'd shouted at her. Even though she was hemmed in by guards. A hand propelled her out of her seat. Her legs trembled, threatened to give way. Somehow she made it to the door and all but fell out onto the landing pad.

Paolo was pushed out beside her. He looked at her, trying to catch her eye. For some reason, she pretended not to notice, avoided his gaze. He might have muttered her name, but she couldn't be sure. All she could hear was the chopper engine droning in her ears.

Out here she was somehow more glad of the din.

Rotors beat down on them, reminding Kara of the boat all over again. Wind whipped at her eyes, stirring tears. She held onto them and tipped her head back. Looked up at the slicing rotors, almost willing them to descend.

She shook her head clear of that. She was alive. Instead of Theo. She owed it to him to stay that way, didn't she? To him and Owain. Where was Owain?

The armed soldiers stamped down on either side and one grabbed Kara by the arm, the other grabbed Paolo. Kara was tugged and shoved across the pad and down a short flight of steps. She tripped but her guard fastened his grip on her arm, hurting her to stave off the fall.

A group of men – more soldiers – and one woman waited ahead.

The blonde was the only one whose hair lashed about in the gusts from the helicopter but the rest of her was perfectly still. She had a clinical kind of beauty, bone structure that could have been manufactured by Tupperware and a look in her eye like she was a medical assistant ready to conduct Kara through to some operating theatre. For life-threatening surgery. She was dressed for business though, in a crisp beige suit. All the soldiers were kitted out in bulletproof vests, except one.

Large, powerful, he filled out his military fatigues like a body-builder but it was his gaze that made Kara feel truly small. Close-cropped blond hair, square-jawed with chiselled features, he stood over her like some self-carved statue that expected her to kneel in worship. If he imagined himself a god, then he was a cruel one.

Kara knew his face. In the magazines and industry journals, all the articles she and Owain had dug up, the photographs had shown the world a businessman. Expensive suits, greed and contempt in his forced smiles. She had already learned to hate him. Now, face to face with the man, the hate surged. But there was a lid on it, clamped down by fear.

She was scared.

'These are all you found?' His voice was a barbed and poisonous sound. The South African accent finely slicing each word.

Paolo's guard snapped to attention. 'They're it, sir.'

'I was told there were four in the boat.'

'Yes, sir. Four. One confirmed corpse. No sighting on the fourth.'

'Well, how hard did you search, soldier?'

'Extensively and thoroughly, Mr Vorster, sir.'

The man, Vorster, smiled. Not like in the pictures. It was the ugliest thing Kara had ever seen.

Kara's guard spoke up. 'We can head out for another search, sir. By the time we lifted these two, the chopper was close to bingo fuel.'

'One more sweep couldn't do any harm. There's every chance he drowned and precious little chance of him swimming to shore. Eh?' Vorster looked from Paolo to Kara – and picked on Kara. He seized her chin in a gloved hand, dug fingers and thumb into her face, tipped her head so he could search her eyes. 'Your friend? Is he a good swimmer, eh?'

Breaths escaped her in panic. Tears wanted out, but she didn't want to give him any.

'And the body?' He held Kara fixed, but addressed the guard.

'The currents should take care of it, sir. There's still time to retrieve it if necessary.'

'Let's do that, gentlemen. Pick it up and drop it somewhere else. We don't want some detective tracing currents to our doorstep. And if you happen to find some sharks to feed, so much the better. I like to be thorough.'

Theo, Kara wanted to shout. *His name is Theo*. But even trapped in her head her thoughts sounded timid.

'Yes, sir.'

Vorster cracked another smile, up close and personal.

Finally, Kara felt the cold.

CHAPTER TWO
Myth Makers

'**BRIGADIER. PHONE** call for you, sir.'

'Really?' Lethbridge Stewart halted just inside the doorway and about-faced to find himself accosted by Warrant Officer Craggs. Appointed as adjutant, kindly on loan from Winser, he hovered half-outside the room. Not even five minutes back from his meeting with the air marshal and Lethbridge-Stewart was being sidetracked again.

'From back home,' explained Craggs. 'A Corporal Wright.'

Sally. Of course.

Lethbridge-Stewart surveyed the hive of activity that was the Operations Room. More accurately, the hive was still under construction, personnel busy getting everything set up.

Anne Travers looked his way, threw her glance like a dart. She returned to sifting through a portion of the files they'd brought with them and the few packages of hand-written reports and other materials Owain had sent. She shook her head a great deal. Bishop assisted her in sorting the documentary evidence, selecting clippings and photographs for display. Miss Travers abruptly abandoned her organisation detail and armed herself with a map. Wrestling the concertina-fold open, she began pinning it to the board, appearing to take an inordinate amount of pleasure in sticking pins into things. Had the cork board bled she would likely have carried on stabbing it, perhaps with even greater determination. Lethbridge-Stewart had the unpleasant notion that she viewed the board as some sort of crude representation of military implacability for the practice of voodoo.

In that respect, Sally had thrown him a lifeline. With little of practical use he could contribute until the Operations Room was properly organised, he supposed he could spare a few minutes.

'Thank you, Craggs. Is there somewhere private I can take the call?'

'Yes, sir. It's all been set up for you. This way, sir.'

Lethbridge-Stewart followed the young man out. He couldn't fault the RAF's hospitality. As base commander, Winser had gone to every effort to make their Corps guests welcome. Air Marshal Townsend-Jones had proven a gracious enough host and Lethbridge-Stewart's courtesy visit might yet provide dividends. As CBFC, Commander British Forces Cyprus, Townsend-Jones had the *de facto* clout of a governor, and might prove a handy liaison if it came to passing official requests – or bad news – up the chain. Decisions made here might easily end up ruffling the in-trays of both the Foreign Office and MOD.

Winser had assigned and shown himself, Bishop and Miss Travers to quarters and cleared what had normally served as the station's cinema for use as an Operations Room. An old film projector and screen and stacked chairs were pushed into one corner. In place of off-duty entertainment facilities, the space had been furnished with trestle tables and display boards. And now he was being conducted to his own office.

A measure of private space was due an officer, but it was particularly welcome in light of Miss Travers' continuing mood. He supposed some additional resentment had just been thrown into the mix, courtesy of his receiving personal calls while she was denied valuable time with her father. So, a lifeline for him; something of a baited hook for Miss Travers.

Craggs held the door open and ushered him into the office. Solid sort of desk, phone, couple of extra chairs besides the one for himself, all the essentials present and correct. And a ceiling fan. Currently idle, but the sight of it was a promise of relief. More than adequate.

'Line three, sir.'

'Thank you, Craggs.'

The warrant officer ducked out, leaving Lethbridge-Stewart

to pick up the phone. For the time being, he perched himself on the edge of the desk.

'Alistair? Hello. How was the flight?'

'Long.'

'Yes, you're sounding tired.'

The line crackled while Lethbridge-Stewart considered what he could say to that.

'Alistair?'

'Sorry, but I'm not sure this is the best time.'

'Really? You must have only just arrived. I thought it would be the perfect time. Before you got caught up in work.'

He caught the sting in her voice and regretted his shortness. He'd thought the distraction would be welcome, but now he was distracted elsewhere. 'I'm sorry. I think the heat here is making all of us a touch prickly.' That, at least, was a half-truth. If the phone-cord wasn't keeping him tied to the desk, he would have wandered over and flicked the switch on the ceiling fan. 'And we're all concerned for Owain. He's gone off the radar.'

'Oh, I'm sorry. I do hope he's all right.'

Lethbridge-Stewart silently reproached himself. He needn't have told Sally that. Problems shared might well be halved, but he had the feeling that he'd only succeeded in spreading the worry and rattling himself further. An all-too transparent attempt at deflection, it was a low tactic and far from one of his proudest moments.

'He's absolutely fine, I'm sure. There's very little the world can throw at that young man that could get the better of him. Don't forget how he handled himself in New York.' In some respects, Owain was more of a soldier than he would care to admit. A fighter and a survivor, certainly. 'Was there anything else? Any news?'

'No.' The line went quiet. 'No, I just wanted to make sure you were all right. Arrived safely, settled in okay. Normal stuff.'

'Yes, of course. Everything's good.' Lethbridge-Stewart rolled his eyes at that lie. If only. 'Well, if that's all...?'

'Yes. I'll let you get back to... Take care, Alistair.'

'Oh you know me. I'll call—'

The line clicked and went dead.

Lethbridge-Stewart lowered the receiver into its cradle. That went well.

He rubbed some of the sweat from his brow and a smaller quantity of the strain from his eyes.

The door burst open, admitting Miss Travers. He stood and made pretence of listening for the knock that had been entirely absent. Whether she missed his message or wilfully ignored it, she marched to the desk and flung down a pile of document folders and a small selection of photographs.

'Really?' she said.

'Really... what?' Lethbridge-Stewart moved around to his chair and cast an eye over the photographs. He hadn't yet had the opportunity to review any of the material himself. All he saw now were some half-dozen fuzzy snapshots of vases or urns, decorative engravings turned to rough grooves by time, he presumed. For the most part they were shown laid out in the bed of some packing crate or other. One photograph – fuzziest of the lot, suggesting excessive camera shake or a hastily applied zoom – showed similar pottery changing hands between two fishermen. The men's features were indiscernible but Lethbridge-Stewart could assume their profession based on the masts and prows of trawlers that had snuck into the frame.

Underneath the pictures were a few pages of notes in Owain's scrawled hand plus a number of documents of more general reference value. What he could not see for the life of him was an issue to get Miss Travers so thoroughly steamed. He supplied a suitably apologetic look.

'Oh, come off it, Brigadier!' she snapped. She gestured at the modest gallery of images spread in disarray between them. 'This? This is what I've been dragged halfway around the world for?'

'What appears to be the problem?'

'The problem – *your* problem – appears to be a taste for myth and fantasy. All this reference material you saw fit to bring with us. Sea monsters? Nessie? The Bermuda Triangle? What possible purpose is that supposed to serve? And look at this–' She poked at the photograph of the fishermen handling the urn. 'Owain has thoughtfully provided snaps of ancient relics that he believes might be significant. Have you read his notes?'

'Not yet.'

'Theories about submerged ruins. He's quite the fiction writer.'

'Fiction?'

'Atlantis ring any bells? He actually uses the word at one point. Atlantis. In barely legible scribble, but it's there on page one.'

'Well, I can't speak for Owain's theories until I've read them for myself. And we must bear in mind he is in the region operating according to an agenda of his own. As to the files, Miss Travers, given the Corps was created to protect the UK against non-terrestrial threats, I deemed it prudent for the Corps to maintain its own reference library for all manner of paranormal phenomenon. We must try to think outside the box, after all, perhaps especially since we're required on this occasion to operate outside our usual bounds.'

'Brigadier, I'm over the moon that we're considering threats to the world at large for a change. Or at least, I would be if that were the truth of the situation. But we both know we're here for the sake of British interests.'

'Our concerns are wider than that. Ships disappearing without trace is an international matter. But yes, when a vessel of Her Majesty's Royal Navy sustains unexplained damage, we are under an obligation to prioritise. Just as we are under an obligation to conduct our operations in secret. That becomes more difficult when we go traipsing across the globe, as I'm sure you appreciate.'

'As the one who least wants to be here, I think I appreciate it more than anybody.'

Lethbridge-Stewart took that bullet without a flinch. 'You are not obliged, however, to treat any of our library information as serious theories. But I thought our investigative efforts might stand to benefit from ideas. Call them starting points, if you will. The Bermuda Triangle may have no basis in reality, Miss Travers, but very little of what we deal with does – until we are tasked with dealing with it. For all we know at this point, we could be faced with something similar.'

'Similar to what?'

'Bermuda. Sea monsters. Any of it.'

Miss Travers very nearly growled. 'Really, Brigadier, couldn't you rustle up any wild geese for me to chase?'

She turned and stormed out. Leaving such a blast of heat in her wake, it seemed, that Lethbridge-Stewart looked up in hope at the ceiling, willing the fan into motion. No such luck. He quickly searched out the wall switch and flicked it on. He was definitely going to need that if he was due any further visits from Miss Travers.

Under the cooling drafts stirred by the fan blades, he sat at his desk and leafed through the documents, then re-examined the photographs. He turned them over, wishing for better focus and finer detail. On the off-chance they might tell him something more.

Atlantis? Myth and legend. Stuff and nonsense. It couldn't be. Could it?

'What have you found, young man? What have you found?'

Anne must have blown into the operations room like a hurricane, because Bill made a show of planting both hands on a stack of papers to save them from being caught up in her whirlwind.

'Very funny,' she told him and carried on to the trestle table she had appropriated as her desk.

A handful of troops were rearranging furniture, lining up tables next to hers and unpacking and depositing her lab equipment on top. Samson supervised, a role which mostly consisted of watching, arms folded, and chipping in with the occasional, 'Easy with that,' or 'Don't go breaking anything.' Anne wondered if he felt as much a spare limb as she did. She'd no idea even if any of her apparatus would prove of use. Indeed, she had ordered some of it loaded just so she could continue with a project of her own. On company time. If she had to be carted halfway around the globe she could at least endeavour to achieve something worthwhile.

She dug into one of the boxes, checking the instruments were intact.

Bill sauntered over. 'You don't think you're being a bit hard on the Brig?'

She eyed him with mock suspicion. 'What's this? The military closing ranks?'

'Don't be silly. It's just that... Well, I understand what this looks like. Ancient Greek relics littering the Med, turning up just now, when ships happen to be disappearing. You know how... *driven* Owain can be. He probably wants to read some mystical connection into it all. I'm not saying he's anywhere on the money, but we've seen stranger things. Intelligent alien plants, for example. So even if the stuff of myth and legend strikes as too fanciful next to that, well, what if there's something alien underneath all this?'

'What? Ancient Greek spaceships? *Chariots of the Gods?*' Anne wondered if the bestseller had become essential bedtime reading for Lethbridge-Stewart.

Bill shrugged.

Anne moved along the tables, rearranging some of the equipment more to her liking. Samson's troops were handling her apparatus with care, but they had no idea how she wished things to be set up. The spot of tidying calmed her somewhat.

'All right, Bill. I'd buy that over Atlantis or any of the other wild theories. But even if there's a spacecraft or the remains of some alien civilisation under the sea, why all the relics? Vases, old pottery?'

Bill held up his hands in surrender. 'Well, there you've got me. But that's what we're here for, isn't it? Mystery. Investigation.'

'Yes. Yes, I know. But... What good am I? I'm no use here. I–' *Need to be home*, she was going to add. But, truthfully, what use was she there? 'I'm an applied physicist. We need an archaeologist.'

The soldiers retreated and filed out, basically done. Samson told them to get to their bunks and warned he'd be along for inspection later. Bill followed Anne as she continued her sorting.

'Look,' he said, 'even if this is the impossible. Some predatory sea monster. Some kind of Bermuda Triangle, relocated. Ancient Atlantis reborn. Or... whatever it might turn out to be. Even if it is the stuff of myth and legend, until we know better, we need an analytical mind on the job. A clear-headed, scientific mind that can look at all this evidence and make some kind of sense of it all. Not to mention someone who can build us a device to drive back the Greek gods if they choose to show up. I mean, sorry, but with all my training I don't expect my SLR to do much against Poseidon and his trident. So while you're feeling sorry for yourself, spare a thought for us poor soldiers. We're the ones that should feel like spare wheels.'

Anne glanced at Samson. He nodded. There was an unspoken 'Amen' written all over his face. Bill did a fair impression of a pitiful puppy dog. Anne laughed.

'Relax,' she assured the two men. 'It's highly unlikely either of you will be going up against a god. Trident-wielding or otherwise.'

Bill nodded. He winked at Samson. 'That is a relief. Although, the Ymir were near as dammit, weren't they? I mean, what was it that Leigh Brackett wrote? Witchcraft and science...?'

One of those fantasy authors Bill liked so much; he'd insisted she read some of Brackett's stuff. It was okay, but she hadn't memorised it. 'Um, something like, *witchcraft to the ignorant is simple science to the learned*, I think,' said Anne.

'That. Right. Well, any enemy sufficiently advanced looks a lot like a god to a soldier who feels sufficiently powerless. That's a William Bishop quote.'

Anne smiled. The quote needed work, but Bill's humour was a tonic. At the same time, it was impossible not to think about the men who must feel the same when pitted against powerful enemies. When weapons proved useless it surely followed that the men felt themselves even more powerless.

But Bill had hit a nail on its head. Her job was to make the unknown known. Even by the tiniest degree. Piece by piece, to boil down apparent magic to understandable science, to reduce ostensible gods to manageable foes. Something that practical men of action could go after and feel like they had a chance. Ideally equipped with something that gave them that chance.

'All right,' she said. 'I take your point. Which means I have more work to do than I thought.' She glanced over the boards, the file boxes and document envelopes. Reminded that Lethbridge-Stewart had talked in terms of starting points. Perhaps she had been too rash in ruling out Owain's Greek relics as irrelevant. Even if they didn't mean everything the lad thought, they might have some bearing on the case. 'But we're still going to need an archaeologist.'

'As luck would have it,' said a familiar voice from the doorway, 'our intrepid Agent Vine found one.'

Lethbridge-Stewart.

Bill and Samson jumped to attention. Anne turned.

'At ease,' Lethbridge-Stewart told them. He clutched several pages in his hand. Waved them almost like Chamberlain's peace-in-our-time paper. 'Tell me, Miss Travers, how closely did you read Owain's notes?'

'I... skimmed,' she admitted.

'Had you read with more attention, you might have discovered his ulterior motive. He's not serious about Atlantis, but he is serious about the possibility of recently uncovered underwater sites. The fact is, Owain was trying to build a case to convince an archaeologist to come on board and lend support for his cause.'

'His cause, sir?' Bishop asked.

'Yes, Lieutenant. His environmental protest, to be precise. Seems that Simon chap he met in New York stirred up some... feelings in him, and according to his account, these artefacts have been turning up in fishing nets. He posits a theory that this South African outfit's hydraulic fracturing operation may have disturbed sites of archaeological interest on the seabed. There has been some minor seismic activity and he's convinced of a causal link between VTMB's activities and these tremors.'

'Does he have proof?' Anne asked.

'No, I'm afraid not. Wilful conjecture at this stage, of course. Owain is tailoring the evidence, such as it is, to suit his purpose. The science, as I'm sure you will appreciate, Miss Travers, is beyond me. But the important point is his motivation. With an archaeologist fighting in his corner, he had high hopes of halting the drilling.'

'I see.'

'I must say, it does nothing to solve our mystery,' said Lethbridge-Stewart, 'but this aspect of the situation sounds a good deal more plausible, wouldn't you say?'

'It does. And Atlantis is a great headline-catcher if he's after some publicity.' Anne thought about striking out for the base canteen to see if they served humble pie. 'So who is this archaeologist? Presumably someone of note, if he hoped they might stir things up against a big conglomerate.'

Lethbridge-Stewart came over. He leafed briskly through his handful of pages and handed one to Anne. 'Here we are.'

Anne quickly scanned the page. Scant information, but there was mention of a woman with quite the reputation. 'I see, yes. Says here he contacted her, tried to enlist her. But she wanted to see actual evidence before she got involved.' On the strength of that at least, she sounded like a woman after Anne's own heart. Good for her. 'Well, if these relics are significant in any way, we could do with her expertise. And probably some actual artefacts for analysis.'

'Well, all right,' Bill declared. 'Maybe we'll have better luck recruiting her.'

'It might not be that easy,' Lethbridge-Stewart said. 'We have precious little evidence ourselves at this stage. And check out the footnote. Owain enquired about her among the locals. She has a reputation for being a little... strange.'

Anne glanced to the bottom of the page. Sure enough, strange was the word used. Scrawled there in quote marks and underlined. 'Well that ought to place her firmly in our department,' Anne said with a sweet smile.

CHAPTER THREE
Smugglers

SOPHIA MONTILLA orbited Vlychada Harbour with the patience of a planet. She loved to take a stroll there or along the beach. But today was not about a leisurely stroll, although she made it appear as leisurely as possible to any observers who cared to notice her. Today, she was a spy.

Another trawler nosed its way into the circle of piers, hunting for a berth among the gently jostling vessels. The most recent arrival was tying up, a couple of the crew handing off packing crates to be stacked on the pier by a third man.

The harbour was the enemy camp and here she was, infiltrating their base of operations, casual as you like. She looked like a tourist, in her jeans, loose white-cotton blouse and sunglasses. She had even saddled herself with her boxy old Hasselblad, hanging from her neck like a ball and chain. No film inside.

She hadn't come for pictures. She wanted something more substantial than photographic evidence.

Rumours had reached her. Troubling stories.

She turned seaward and held the camera to her eye, mimed a press of the shutter. *'Clic,'* she muttered under her breath. Had she fed it with film, the camera would have taken a beautiful shot of empty waves, billowing like a vast blue sheet being shaken free of glitter. Sun, sea and a solitary yacht idling across the middle distance. Trawlermen might laugh at the strange lady taking snaps of nothing, but only if they gave it that much thought. Fake tourism was easy.

Sophia lowered the camera and returned to her wander along the curve of pier. Closing towards her target, lazy stride by lazy stride.

The harbour was picturesque. Beautiful camera-fodder. A double ring of piers, clusters of boats butting the inner and outer walls like a lot of kittens competing for their mother at feeding time. Masts and booms duelled under the morning sun. Crews busied themselves on decks, arranging and organising buckets and crates of shining fish. The air was a riot of shouts and calls, of men and gulls. The newest-arrived trawler puttered past Sophia, frothing the harbour waters in its wake.

A young fisherman, stationed near the prow, threw her a wave and a smile. She smiled and waved back. Old enough to be his mother.

She sauntered on, pretending to be flattered. There was mathematical elegance in the construction. Two circles – simple, yes – stone walls to corral sea-going wagons. Not quite the Fibonacci sequence to be found in an Ammonite spiral or a snail shell, but still something to invite the eye inward. The sort of formation that, had it occurred naturally, would have confirmed to many the existence of God.

Sophia had been raised a good Catholic girl, but she had left God a long way behind. In her childhood, where imaginary friends belonged. And if her mother's domestic teachings, filling the week between Sundays, were to be believed, 'He' had not been all that friendly in any case. More like an imaginary strict and overbearing parent, as if she had needed an additional one of those. These days, God was only a name to be invoked when things went wrong, but Sophia was not one to give 'Him' credit for anything. She kept herself open enough to the idea, that was all, enough to put her in the mindset of ancient peoples who saw gods in everything.

Ahead, a packing crate hit stone. The captain of the boat swore, blaspheming profusely in Greek. It would have qualified as comic timing if Sophia wasn't conscious of what the crate might contain.

She hurried her step.

The trawlerman who'd dropped the burden gesticulated wildly, protesting that it wasn't his fault. A fierce quarrel erupted between boat and shore.

The harbour was a monument to humanity's ability to master and shape nature. Evolving beyond God. Of course, when you evolve to the point of adapting your environment to suit you, that was when evolution stopped. Or slowed. Which was why humankind was not so advanced as it liked to think, compared to 'primitive' cultures. There, at least, was a belief in which Sophia was firm. And here were these men proving it. The butterfingered one, still proclaiming his innocence, bent over, scraping together handfuls of fragments. He tilted the shallow packing crate and scooped them in like brushing dirt into a dustpan. His fellow crewmen laughed and mocked. The captain cursed and swore, shutting down the laughter with threats of docked pay.

Sophia's blood burned. She marched up, thinking seriously about swinging her camera like a bola and cracking a few skulls.

'What have you got there? Let me see that!'

The crew traded a lot of glances among themselves and regarded her like she was some government official come to inspect their nets or impose quotas. The captain gestured angrily and swore a great deal more than he had already. Mostly telling her it was none of her business.

'It is! It's exactly my damn business!' Sophia pushed past the clumsy one to the stacked packing crates, glanced over the pieces in the top tray, then lifted it to inspect the collection underneath. Potsherds and fragments, pieces of fired clay with few markings. The pieces were clean too, as if someone among the crew had a go at preparing them for study. But if anybody here had the faintest clue what they were doing, these samples would not be strewn so haphazardly and exposed to the air in a tray meant for packing fish on ice. 'These are treasures! What have you done?'

'Hey, hey, hey!' The crewman grabbed her arm and tugged. She set the tray down so she could shake him off. Shot him a look that, she hoped, would be like a firebrand waved in his face. He backed off.

She turned to the captain. 'You've no idea what you're doing. These things need to be in water. Sea water.'

He gave an irritated shrug. Then gestured at a bucket stationed by the few crates remaining on deck. From her vantage point on the pier, Sophia discerned a figurine as well as two clay tablets lying on a bed of silt, details and features warped by refraction and the rippling water in the bucket.

She hopped aboard. Her camera swung violently on its sling, bashed her hip, but she didn't care. She went straight for the bucket.

The captain turned volcanic, throwing out a torrent of Greek like boiling magma. '*Tréli kyria!*' He twirled a finger by the side of his head and followed up with a shooing motion. 'Crazy lady! Off my boat! Go! Leave!'

The crew stared, no longer laughing. A few moved in on her, but she warned them off with a look. If need be, she really would wield her camera as a weapon.

Closer up, she could see the figurine was of the Snake Goddess. This poor lady-god clutched only one serpent, since she appeared to have suffered a broken arm. The two clay tablets were halves of the same disc, the jagged edges of the fracture matching up perfectly, and the clay was inlaid with hieroglyphs. None of the symbols were familiar. They needed to be studied properly. Not to mention saved from these scavengers.

Sophia dug in her bag. 'Here, how much? How much do you want for them?' She'd come out without a lot of money – enough for wine and cat food – but the way she'd hurriedly stuffed the handful of notes into her purse made it appear reasonably full.

The boat captain marched up and raised a flat hand like a barrier slid across her view. 'Not for sale! You want these, you go auction like everyone!'

'Auction? What auction? This is an illegal trade.' She read in his eyes, no matter how basic his English, he knew full well what she was saying and knew even better that he was breaking laws. 'Sites need to be registered and reported. Permissions need to be obtained. What you're doing here is a crime. In more ways than one. But, most importantly to you, in a way that will get you arrested and fined.'

'So call police! Go! Call!'

The captain beckoned around to his crew, inviting them to resume their laughter. They obliged, and they were entitled to mock, feeling like they'd won. By the time she'd persuaded an officer to come take a look all that would be left to find would be a clean deck, a lot of trawlermen professing to have no idea what the crazy Spanish lady was talking about, and perhaps some fish unfit for market, but good enough for a policeman to take home for his supper.

Sophia scrunched up a fistful of drachma, then stowed her purse. She grabbed the captain's hand and slapped the money into his palm. His mouth opened to object, but his fingers closed around the cash.

'I am taking that bucket. One bucket and you keep and sell the rest.' At this point, he could either accept the payment or set his men on her and create a scene that would be of interest to the police. 'And I would like to know who is buying from you. Where and when is this auction taking place?'

'Crazy lady.' The captain shook his head. He showed his teeth and not in a grin. Sophia watched him rein in his blood pressure. Slowly. He stepped back. Waved an impatient hand at the bucket. 'Villa Caldera, Agia Irinni. No place for crazy ladies. They throw you out.'

'I will be happy to give them the chance. When?'

'Tomorrow.' He held up three fingers. 'Afternoon.'

'Thank you.' Sophia picked up her bucket. 'If you are lucky you will not see or hear from me again.'

The captain cursed profusely under his salted breath and did a great deal of unnecessary telling her to go away, all the while she was taking her leave. She heard him break into a storm of shouting at his crew as she made her way back along the curve of pier with her prize in hand.

Sophia's mind got busy arranging an agenda. She still had to buy wine and cat food, but that would have to be postponed for a second outing. These people, from trawlers to traders to whatever kind of collectors were attending these auctions, would need to be reported. Oh yes, she would put a stop to that. If genuine finds were surfacing, with more out there waiting to be found, then it would have to be handled properly. That would mean biting the bureaucratic bullet, filing for the relevant permissions and allowing her own blood to simmer while waiting for official gears to turn. First priority was to get these artefacts home.

Sophia's thoughts returned to the immediate present. Her attention drawn by two men sharing a table in front of a bar. The bar was quiet, but they were quieter, deeply engrossed in a complete lack of conversation. They wore beige suits, shirts unbuttoned at the collar, their particular blend of muscular build and similarity making the casual attire look like uniforms. Their *al fresco* beers were hardly touched, so either they'd not been there for long or they weren't thirsty. Their hands were gloved in thirty-plus-degree heat.

Their heads didn't turn as Sophia passed, but she sensed eyes tracking her behind sunglasses.

When she'd walked on a few yards, she glanced back. The clean-shaven one rose from his seat and strode towards the harbour. The other, face shadowed with bristles, dumped a tip on the table and moved to follow her.

It had been some years since she'd picked up a tail. As a teenager in the streets of Sevilla, her walks were often dogged by boys with no concept of stealth. Indeed, they'd done their utmost to get noticed, with whistles and shouts of what they'd imagined as flattery. If she ignored them long enough, she lost them eventually.

That might be her best tactic today. She wasn't about to run to try to shake off this admirer, not with her precious cargo in hand. There was a good chance the man was more interested in the bucket than her. She felt safer with it in her grip. And two could play at fake-casual.

She took her own sweet time on the three-mile stroll home. And stopped to fuss over every cat she encountered en route.

CHAPTER FOUR
Rescue

TIDES. DRAGGING him in, drawing him over an invisible horizon.

Owain dreamed of endless blue. Dark and starless blue. Drowning was like sinking into sleep. So easy. If only it wasn't so bloody cold. Why couldn't he get warm? Then he could doze off with no problem.

He jerked awake. His body slapped onto a dripping deck. The world swayed underneath him. Somewhere a large engine chugged, drumming on his ribcage and in his skull. Drenched to the bone, he shivered, every salty gust of wind blasting through him.

He wondered if he'd woken to another dream; a dream of himself as a landed fish on a trawler. He blinked, getting snapshots of daylight, boots surrounding him. No sprats or mackerel flopping around. And if he was a fish and if that was what it took to fight for life, well, he didn't have the energy.

One set of boots stamped up beside his face. A hand grabbed him at the scruff of the neck, lifted his head off the deck with the rough love a lioness reserved for picking up her cubs in her jaws. Maybe without the love.

'Not the most impressive catch. I've a mind to throw this one back.'

The voice was heavily accented. Owain's water-logged senses couldn't place it immediately, but definitely not Greek. He tried to think what other nationalities fished these waters, but gave up as his brain craved less challenging puzzles. Like, where was he exactly?

He pushed with numbed arms and rolled onto his back. Taking in the piled nets, tarpaulin-covered crates, lines and cables everywhere, oxygen tanks and other diving equipment, the large crane looming overhead like a rusty gallows. A chubby yellow submersible, with a fishbowl nose and barely enough room for two Beatles inside, parked on a platform below the crane. And the crew, arrayed in a scattered circle around him. And the one man, the speaker, leaning low over him, all but slicing him open with a surgeon's eyes.

First impressions: young. Younger than he'd sounded.

Mid-twenties, thirty at most. Prominent cheekbones, taut-leather complexion and lines that could have been age or character. Dark hair, shaved well back to expose an expansive brow, a small sort of pinched mouth, currently flexed in a wry curl — nearly a smile — that was at odds with the intensity of that deep-set gaze, not to mention the severity of that haircut.

'Here. Let's get you up.' The man proffered a gloved hand.

Owain had a feeling it would be like shaking hands with a serial killer, but he accepted the help. The man — the captain? — wedged his other hand under Owain's arm and hauled him upright. Too easily. He packed a lot of muscle in his lean frame. Owain wobbled. The deck swayed, rising and dipping as the ship cut through bumpy waves. The rolling swell made standing upright more of a challenge. But Owain suspected he would've been just as unsteady on dry land.

'Thank you,' he said, riding out a dizzy spell. Then drew a step or two away from the captain, experimenting with independence. So far, so good. The deck refused to stay level, but the swaying in his head settled a little. 'I think I'll be okay. In a bit.'

'Our fish speaks. You're welcome. Now can you walk?' The English was perfect, naturalistic, easy-going even. But the accent dominated. Throaty, spoken through a mouthful of gravel chips. *Russian?* 'Watch, gentlemen. We are about to witness evolution in action.'

The men laughed.

Owain tried a few steps. Shaky, like a cyclist freed from training wheels for the first time. But he reckoned he could manage.

Apart from rust here and there, the trawler was too ship-shape. Ropes and nets arranged too neatly, as though never used. The men looked seasoned, experienced, but not weatherworn. They dressed the part: oilskins, boots, caps, and knives in their belts that looked capable of gutting sharks. But there wasn't one salty old sea-dog among them. If any of these faces adorned a packet of fish fingers, Owain would think twice about buying that brand.

The captain motioned to the nearest crewman, a broad-shouldered giant with a flat, grey face who looked like he'd been carved from a single slab of granite. 'Fetch our guest some warm clothes and a hot drink. Soup. You like soup?'

He slapped Owain on the back and nearly sent him sprawling. Owain smiled weakly and nodded weaker still. He could probably kill for soup. As long as it was a relatively feeble foe.

The captain held an arm out, guarding against a fall, but otherwise left Owain to find his own legs and gestured astern where the assigned crewman led the way. The other men stood aside, allowing Owain through while studying him like – like what? Their attention wasn't indifferent, nor was it hostile. It was as if they'd all paid the organ grinder a rouble and now waited to see the trained monkey dance. Owain shuffled forwards like an old man in slippers on a lino floor and aimed, as directed by the captain, for the bulkhead aft of the wheelhouse.

Piggy-backed on the stern section, roosting on its own pad, there was a helicopter. Owain's view of the aircraft was partially obscured by the ship's superstructure, but he got a general impression of a drab brown colour scheme and a chubby design with all the grace and elegance of a sea cow.

An energetic wave punched the ship's side, spraying the gunwales and throwing Owain off his already poor balance. He stumbled and bumped his knee on the corner of a crate.

'Ow! Sh—!' He cut the curse short. 'Sugar,' he said instead and rubbed his knee. Then looked – a little too long – at the wooden butt of the rifle exposed where his bruised knee had brushed the tarp loose.

The captain leaned past to pull the tarp back in place. He smiled. 'Dangerous waters,' he explained.

And Owain thought, *forget guns: that smile alone would deter the sharks.*

*

Music met Rolph Vorster in the passage outside his office. Rock 'n' roll. It set his teeth on edge.

He preferred the silence. Silence which wasn't silence. The language of steel. Metallic creaks on the edge of audibility. Clanking boots on catwalks. The clang of closing bulkheads. Every movement and even the stillness ringing like a bell versed in alien music. Disordered, arrhythmic, chaotic and unpredictable. No time for man's trite compositions.

Music had no business on his rig.

He marched off in search of the offending crewman and his radio. He had more important items on his immediate agenda. Whoever was disturbing the peace would get a piece of his mind. A sharp one straight to the gut, by God.

A soldier rounded the corner, blocked his path. Vorster bunched a fist, ready to hit the man. 'Out of my way.'

The trooper stamped and saluted. 'Mr Vorster, sir. Word from the Santorini team. Auction set for fifteen hundred hours.'

The man was practised at delivering reports in short, clipped packets. He must have been in Vorster's employ for some time. Vorster vaguely recognised him, couldn't recall his name. Good news was welcome, whoever brought it. His blood simmered down, but he could still hear the damned music.

'All right. Have them prep the chopper.' He glanced at his Rolex. Tiny grey pockmarks roughened the edges of the frame. Gold wasn't immune. Some damned fools might mistake it for corrosion. Its spread was controlled, moving with infinitely more patience than the second hand. 'Departure in thirty minutes.'

'Sir.' The soldier turned to go.

'First go tell whoever that is to shut that bloody music off!'

'Sir, yes, sir.'

He ran off, hiking a swift right at the corner. Vorster retreated along the passage, free to attend to his other business. No more than four paces and he stopped to listen. No raised voices, no shouts of protest.

The rock 'n' roll died.

Vorster nodded. He closed his eyes and listened to the steel. The rig's song had bite, but it didn't jar. Some noises beat peace.

He set off again, spurred to brisk strides. A pair of soldiers pressed their backs to the wall, clearing a path, and saluted as he passed by. He trotted down the steps and made short work of the walk to the cells.

Cells. Bunk rooms really, but put a prisoner in them and it made sense to refer to them according to purpose. A door ahead and to the left swung open and Cloe Van Den Haas emerged. Either she'd read his mind or identified his footsteps. She was the picture of perfection, as ever. Every facet of her appearance precision-engineered. Whatever exertions her interrogation techniques had called for, they had left her unflustered. The woman was a diamond. She could cut glass while leaving herself unscratched.

'Mr Vorster,' she said.

He nodded to the room she'd come from. 'So what story are they telling?'

'The truth, I believe. The young man – Paolo Menozzi, Italian, obviously – relates it with a touch more belligerent attitude, but it's essentially the same. Nothing more than a small band of environmentalists out to save the planet.'

Vorster spat a laugh. He liked the way these prisoners had come ready handcuffed. 'Bloody hippy paratroopers. Vegetarian freedom fighters. What was the plan? Chain themselves to my rig, call attention to our operation?'

'That's about the size of it. The girl is Kara Loukas, Greek. She is heartily apologetic at least. Mainly wants to go home. Would also like us to search for her friend.'

'We did that already. No luck.'

Vorster hated to think of the loose end floating out there in the ocean. Even a dead one. Realistically, the fourth hippy had to be dead, his men assured him. Radar and aerial sweeps had spotted only three vessels in the vicinity. And given the timeframe, they were certain, the best a ship might have scooped out of the sea was a body. The men reported it like it was good news, but it jarred with Vorster as much as the damned pop music. Theoretically, in the climate of missing ships, they could have attacked and searched each vessel, made it look good. The Mediterranean was a nice-sized carpet to sweep evidence under. But Vorster overruled the idea as soon as he'd thought of it.

Too much that could go wrong. Too much risk of drawing more attention. So now he had to live with that loose end.

'The deceased was one Theo Panagakos, incidentally,' Miss Van Den Haas supplied. 'Greek national. The MIA is Owain Vine. British. I put through a call to the UK office to see if they can rustle up any information. He's missing, presumed dead, but I thought it would be useful to determine what level of search effort or campaign we might expect from home. Embassies only tend to properly motivate themselves if families are ringing phones off the hook, knocking a few heads and doors.'

'Bah. These hippies are loners. No respect for authority, no respect for family. I expect he left home in his teens, joined a commune. We'd be better off checking on this environmental group of theirs. See if they're a bona fide organisation or just some fly-by-night crusaders who convened in a taverna somewhere and hatched a plot to spoil my bloody day.' Miss Van Den Haas nodded, mental note made. Vorster waved a dismissive hand. 'Anyway, at this point, he's one of many bodies gone missing in the Med. They'll make a decent show of it, then they'll have to leave it. Just like us. Except we won't have to write letters to the parents.'

'That's it then? We're leaving it?'

'Chopper's needed now. There's an auction coming up.'

'Will you be attending?'

'I might, yes.' Vorster didn't care much for public appearances. Even the prospect of private auctions involved greater exposure than ideally he'd care to tolerate. On the other hand, he would prefer to see and handle any treasures before he fed these parasites any cash. Money was no object, but he objected to parting with it if the funds had to go to types he disliked. Not to mention if there was an alternative means of obtaining treasures. But there was business outside the auction that would benefit from quality face-to-face time. 'There's a woman, local resident, sticking her nose in, making a nuisance of herself. She needs a lesson in non-intervention. She might benefit from a personal visit.'

'The Montilla woman?'

'You've done your research.'

Miss Van Den Haas raised a half-smile. 'Some. I will do more digging if she proves a persistent problem.'

'Good, good. We'll have to see if she can be warned off or bought. If not... well, some digging might be involved, one way or another. An archaeologist ought to have a few skeletons in her closet, eh.'

'We'll find something.'

Vorster was none too bothered. As long as the woman merely presented a spot of competition at the auction, outbidding her would be straightforward. On the other hand, he enjoyed eliminating competition and opening up a clear field for himself. Given the Montilla woman was an archaeologist, he understood her interest. And appreciated that she would most likely be driven by passions. Not unlike the youngsters currently detained at his pleasure.

Well, fear was a breed of anti-passion.

He looked past Miss Van Den Haas to the door. Glanced to the other door on the right. Pictured the girl, especially, probably perched on her bunk, shaking. An idea coalesced around the pitiful image.

'Second thoughts, I might take a couple of guests with me. The girl wants to go home, right? Not an option, but she and her friend might enjoy a little trip. They can be my representatives at the auction.'

A couple of concerned environmentalists with financial backing, out to preserve historic treasures. It made for an amusing scenario and the Montilla woman was unlikely to interfere with a pair of kids with such noble aims.

'Is that wise, sir? They might make a run for it. Shout to anyone who'll listen.'

'Oh, I think we can make sure they stay within arm's reach.' Vorster gestured at each door. 'Which one's the girl?'

Miss Van Den Haas stood aside and nodded to the left.

'Invent a quick background for the two of them,' he instructed as he made for the door.

Miss Van Den Haas was the most honest, efficient, loyal employee in Vorster's army, but the woman was a creative genius when it came to lies. It was one reason she was so adept at seeing through them and why she always handled interviews and/or interrogations. Of course, once the questions were answered, truths divined from the deceptions, there was the matter of what to do with your hopeful applicants or your hapless prisoners. That was the part where Vorster liked to get hands-on.

'I'll have them swearing allegiance in a few minutes,' he said.

'Yes, sir.' Miss Van Den Haas walked off, boots drumming a brisk beat.

Vorster twisted the handle, pushed the door open and readied a smile for the girl. The smile inherited a trace of sincerity as he laid eyes on a scene that was an exact match for the one he'd pictured. Excellent judge of character could sometimes feel like prescience.

'How are we doing, Kara? Miss Van Den Haas took good care of you, I hope?'

The girl stared ahead and down, fixated on the legs of the chair that faced her as an alternative to looking at him.

He closed the door behind him. The satisfying clang had the note of a death knell and the girl glanced at the exit she'd just been denied. She shivered some more.

A change of clothes was piled neatly on the bunk beside her, but she sat in the same dowdy ensemble she'd worn when they'd dragged her out of the water. Shame. She could have been a very pretty girl if she'd simply make the effort. Vorster could not abide girls who wouldn't help themselves.

He sat on the chair in front of her and tugged at the fingers of his right glove. Unmasked the flesh and flexed his hand, letting the skin breathe.

The girl, Kara, stared.

She shrank back on the bunk and screamed.

A raw, wild sound that raked her throat and Vorster's ears. The walls lent its echo a metallic quality.

There was a kind of music to it. One that Rolph Vorster could enjoy.

Owain tugged down the pullover. It was a poor fit, hanging off his shoulders like a woollen poncho. But it was dry and he felt a bit more human. A weak and feeble human, but it was progress.

He took a minute, battling a bout of dizziness that was only half due to the swaying deck. The captain would be waiting for him and this was his last chance for a spot of isolation and some much-needed headspace. Adrift and floating in and out of consciousness for however long didn't count as quality alone time.

A knock on the cabin door and an impatient bark of Russian called his breather short. Owain went to the door and opened it to the imposing sight of the man who'd escorted him there and handed him the set of clothes.

'Your soup. Is ready,' he announced, like the surliest of waiters. 'This way.'

The passage barely accommodated the man's broad shoulders and Owain was obliged to follow blindly. The absence of any guards at his back showed a surprising degree of trust, but Owain had the sense that this man would catch him before he got far. Besides, where would he run? He certainly wasn't going to jump overboard.

He passed a few open cabins with a sailor or soldier stretched out on bunks, one with a pair of them playing cards over a large trunk. They eyed Owain as he walked by. In their striped shirts they could've been mime artists, with the minor addition of a beret and some greasepaint, but none of them looked the sort that liked clowning.

Owain's escort swaggered through into a cramped mess and stood aside to present a big table bolted to the deck and three loose wooden chairs. The captain occupied one of the chairs, a steaming tin mug waited in front of another. Owain headed for that one.

He sagged into the chair, drained by the short walk. Just sat for a while inhaling the soup fumes. Hot, watery, purple and swimming with beetroot chunks. *Borscht*. Of course.

It looked and smelled better than home-cooked bangers and mash.

The captain pushed a tin plate across the table. A hunk of crispy bread rolled around the plate. Owain ripped at it and dunked a piece in the soup. Shoved it in his mouth and chomped greedily away.

Heaven.

The captain watched him eat for thirty seconds or so before

growing bored of the quiet. 'So, Owain, what were you doing out there?'

Here comes the restaurant bill, thought Owain. He'd already given his name in exchange for the dry clothes. 'Drowning. What about you, Captain?'

The captain laughed. 'Captain Bugayev. You may call me Grigoriy. Behind you there, that's Oleg.' Behind Owain, the big guy shifted. Probably not a threat, but the movement unnerved Owain enough to deter him from looking over his shoulder and nodding hello. 'No need for formality. Much less for secrecy.'

'Look, I'm not a spy. I'm not James Bond. I'm grateful for the rescue. *Really* grateful,' Owain stressed and met Grigoriy's gaze with an honest, thankful look. 'But I don't know that there's anything I can tell you.'

Captain Grigoriy – as Owain decided to think of him – leaned back in his chair. He laughed. Sighed. Drummed fingers on the table. 'Okay. Well, I guess that leaves me with nothing to do but to speculate while you enjoy your soup. Until you turned up, there were only two things in these waters of particular interest to those who profess to not know very much. One; several sunken vessels which may or may not be here but, after all, they are all over the news and might attract any number of individuals wanting to assist in the humanitarian effort or perhaps claim salvage. Two, which I think is more likely for you, Owain; an offshore hydraulic fracturing platform drilling close enough to an active volcano to make some people nervous. Including myself, I have to say. And believe me, I've spent unhealthy amounts of time in proximity to munitions and high explosives. It takes a great deal to make me nervous.'

Owain believed him. He swallowed a big mouthful of soup and soggy bread. He struggled to think of a good answer. Until he'd left it too long and felt it was better to say nothing.

'I see that I am warm.' Grigoriy leaned forward, dragging his chair close to the table. 'This sea hides more than those lost vessels. I don't know to what extent you are aware of those other mysteries, Owain, but I see you are a young man, impassioned – idealistic, I would hazard, yes? – someone who cares deeply about – what? The environment. Someone who would strongly oppose the harm that platform is inflicting on the Earth, let alone what damage it might be doing to potentially the greatest historical find of our time. I understand. I am a revolutionary, myself.'

Owain had a sudden horrible feeling, like these guys had somehow opened his head while he'd been out cold on their deck. 'How long was I…?'

'Out there?' The captain shrugged. 'Difficult to say. If you were in the vicinity of the platform, taking into account the speed of the currents, perhaps nine or ten hours.'

Either they'd done their calculations before or Grigoriy was quick at maths.

'Captain, sorry, listen, I – I wasn't meaning to be rude. I'm just – well, I'm British. And you're Russian. Nationally speaking, we're not best friends.'

Oleg snorted. Owain glanced behind to see an amused smirk pasted across the big guy's face.

'Most of us are Russian, yes. But this is an oceanographic research vessel,' said Grigoriy. *Oceanographic research. Right.* 'She sails under a Greek flag. We are in international waters. We can afford to set borders and ideological differences aside. There is no need for us to be friends. But we don't have to be enemies.'

Don't we? Owain wondered. He slurped some more soup. It was too easy to imagine himself shipped off to a Siberian gulag or something. He was a British citizen, protected by Her Majesty's Government. Even if his passport was somewhere out in the Med, its ink run to splotches and pages turned to mulch, his citizenship had to count for some protection. Maybe he could afford to feel a little safer.

Safer than—

Friends.

His friends.

His mind flashed on snapshots of each of them. Kara. Paolo. Theo. It was hard to know which hit him worst: fear for their safety or hating himself for forgetting. No. Theo's picture was the worst: an image of him in the boat. That instant before he fell.

'Oh my god.' Owain clamped a hand over his mouth. Bread and beetroot surfaced as far as his throat. He tasted acid. 'Did you...? Please, tell me you...'

Grigoriy shook his head. Slow, with sorrowless eyes. 'We found no one else.' After a moment, he added, 'No other bodies, either.'

Owain stared. Was that supposed to be cause for optimism?

'The situation just got real for you, didn't it?' Grigoriy added.

'No. It was – real before. We wanted to stop their operations. Make a nuisance of ourselves, you know. So they'd have to ship us back to the mainland, hand us into the authorities. Their report on us draws a bit of attention on the news. It wasn't meant to turn out like this. Like some... commando raid.' Owain stopped for breath. 'Can't you take me... Can't we go back for them?' *You've got guns*, he was about to add. But stopped himself. Even if he knew the cards in his opponent's hand, should he play them out in the open? Was the captain his opponent, as such? *We don't have to be enemies, do we?* he wondered. 'Look, we both know I saw those weapons. In the crates. And I've seen marine research ships on the news, in the North Sea, only they call them Soviet spy vessels. So if you're some sort of actual commando outfit, isn't there some way we can go back and rescue my friends?'

Grigoriy applauded, with a single clap. 'At last. Blunt honesty. I like it, Owain. I like you. But an assault on that platform would be seriously off-mission. More off-mission than fishing you out of the drink. Although I believe we can justify catching such an unusual specimen as yourself in the interests of marine research. We might justify more, depending on what information there is to be learned from you.'

Owain nodded. He understood.

No such thing as a free lunch. Heavenly beetroot soup included.

Supplying intelligence to the Soviets might be more than frowned upon in some quarters. Uncle Alistair, for one. But it wasn't as though he'd be giving up national secrets. And what was his alternative? Not doing everything he could for his friends. That would be the greater treason.

CHAPTER FIVE
Flight Time

ANNE CLOSED the file and tossed it aside. Loch Ness and other monsters. The Selkie. Giant squid. Morgawr, the Cornish plesiosaur. And Puff the Magic Dragon, no doubt. The oceans were full of colourful and unlikely suspects. Apparently. Her father would have had a field day with the contents of the file.

In the absence of substantive evidence, she supposed they might as well refer to assorted myths, strange tales and dubious and uncorroborated eye-witness accounts for ideas, pointers to the kind of phenomena they might be faced with here.

After all, science was about positing hypotheses and seeking to prove – or disprove – them. The London Event had opened her mind to possibilities beyond her previous understanding of established science, regardless of the stories her father had told her as a girl. Subsequent events, at places like Fang Rock, Strommach, even Hull, had compounded or built on that. It was difficult sometimes to train herself to see it as an expansion of her horizons, rather than an undermining of the laws of physics.

'If you hear hoof beats,' she said, 'think horses, not zebras.'

'So, seahorses then?' offered Bill from the other side of the room.

'Giant mutant seahorses.' Anne threw her hands up. 'Why not? It's as believable as anything else. But no, I was rather thinking normal horses; the ordinary answer when it comes to vanishing ships would be weather. Or, since we've no reports of extreme meteorological conditions, submarines. But,' she added, rising from her desk, 'I promised myself to look at the facts in the light of all the possibilities. Weird, wonderful or otherwise.' She wandered over to join Bill at the display board. 'This is me, keeping an open mind.'

Bill turned to peer at her, as though searching for the window in her forehead. 'Really? Come on, Anne, we know better. It's not always the obvious answer.'

'I know. I'm just...' She sighed.

'Upset with the Brig still,' said Bill, lowering his voice so murmurs of mutiny wouldn't reach the ears of the rank and file.

'Yes. Obviously.' Bill knew her too well. 'That and every time I open my mind to the improbable and bizarre, life expects me to open it even more.'

'Nature of the job, true. Which is why we could use starting points.' He returned to his prior task: namely, sticking the map with pins like a novice acupuncturist uncertain of his nodes. In between fishing a drawing pin from a tin on the desk, he referred to a sheaf of papers in his hand.

Anne cast a quick glance over the array of pins. 'I take it those are the ship positions.'

'None of your sharpness dulled, I see. Yes, I thought we could do with a look at the big picture. Trouble is, the last known positions of too many of these vessels aren't points. They're circles. Don't let the pins fool you. These are very rough approximations. According to last radio contacts, sightings by other vessels, that sort of thing. Depending on course and speed, most could be anywhere within up to twenty miles. More in at least one case.'

'Hmm.' Anne coaxed the reports from Bill's hand. She eyed the map, noting the three coloured pins already inserted. One green, two red. 'Any significance to the colours?'

She knew the answer: Bill was a military man, so of course there was a colour code in operation.

He nodded. 'Absolutely. Red for trawlers, since they're the most common and that happens to be the colour we have most of. Green is ferries and private commercial boats, and that blue one is HMS *Aphrodite*. That one, at least, is our most accurate plot. Largely because she's not lost.'

'Merely damaged.'

What did that mean? Had the naval ship escaped lightly because she was tougher? Or had the circumstances been different? Had she simply been lucky? Too many questions, not enough hypotheses.

It was important to be wary of too open a mind. But even when faced with a collection of outlandish theories, there was value in proving a negative. The results could signpost the proper direction to take.

Without troubling herself with specifics, she could categorise all of these alleged phenomena very broadly and examine the data in light of each. And hopefully arrive at some sort of conclusion, even if that conclusion was to rule out all of the above.

'I can't even be sure we're hearing hoofbeats,' she said.

'If it's actually a question of what we're hearing, then there are those reports of seismic activity to be taken into account. Any significance there, do you suppose?'

'Could be.' Anne beelined for the file cabinets. She pulled open a drawer and started rifling.

'Try E for Earthquake, or S for Seismic,' Bill suggested.

'You just stick to your pins,' she told him. She pulled another drawer. Searched. Then another. Gave up. She moved to pounce on the stacked folders capping the nearby desk. A handful of the brigadier's men were assigned the unenviable task of filing, bustling about like uniformed clerks, but plenty of documents had yet to find a home. Most could be filed under U, for Useless.

Finally, she dug out what she was looking for. A disappointingly flimsy folder. She opened it and a single typewritten sheet almost slipped out, as though ready to fly away. She snatched it and scanned the columns of figures. She flipped it over, hoping for more on the reverse. Blank.

'I'm confused.'

Bill looked over and laughed. 'That's our job.'

'We could build a fortress from all the reports and documents here. But where are the detailed seismic reports?' She flapped her solitary page. 'Someone has thoughtfully typed up the broad essentials; epicentre, magnitude, date and time. But where's the original data? How was the activity registered? Really, of all the data that might actually tell us something, that's the stuff that goes missing?'

Bill abandoned his map and pins. He examined the page over Anne's shoulder. 'Those are the essentials though, yes? We can plot those in relation to our ship positions, can't we?'

'Yes, you can play with more pins.' Anne shot him a wry glance. 'But I'd still like to have the source documentation.'

'At a guess, if it's marine seismic activity, I'd say it originated from SOSUS.'

'SOSUS?'

'Sound Surveillance System. Array of underwater hydrophones. Meant for monitoring submarine traffic. Politically seismic activity, but it would certainly register underwater quakes.'

'Right. Well, perhaps you'd best get hold of Lethbridge-Stewart and ask him where he mislaid that data.'

'Somewhere safe, I expect,' Bill quipped. He gave her a friendly salute and headed for the door. 'I'll get on it.'

Hoofbeats, Anne thought.

Honestly, the listed magnitudes were nothing to trouble surface vessels. Or submarines, for that matter. But seismic activity was a natural phenomenon. Scientifically quantifiable. Something to go on. Moreover, a link to the hydraulic fracturing operation could be penciled in without stretching the bounds of credibility too far.

In some respects, it sounded too ordinary. Too insignificant.

But if these tremors were the hoofbeats she was listening for, had someone gone to the trouble of covering them up? And if so, why?

She approached the map. The big picture was missing a great many pieces. One in particular.

She called out to the uniformed file clerks. 'Can someone give me a map reference for that rig?'

Anne searched Bill's tin for a colour that hadn't been used yet.

The twin-propped Beagle Bassett droned like an angry dragonfly. Lethbridge-Stewart was grateful for the muffling effect of the headphones. He allowed his gaze to skim the expanse of sunlit blue below.

At some point in the future, their Hercules would undergo a refit into a fully-equipped mobile command centre, but even then it would hardly be worth relocating an entire aircraft of that size for a simple recruitment jaunt. Besides, while the rough and ready airfield on Santorini would have been well within the Hercules' take-off-and-landing capabilities, arrival in such a plane would attract undue attention.

No, this loaner would serve more than adequately. And everyone, himself included, was in civvies with the similar aim of maintaining a low profile.

With Samson and Private Atkins tucked into the row behind, the small aeroplane's slightly bulbous fuselage permitted a modest amount of spare room to spread out his work on the vacant seats beside him. At his request, Craggs had supplied type-written précis of the intelligence he had judged to be of most potential significance. There was little enough.

Lethbridge-Stewart wondered whether he needed to be taking this flight.

He could have delegated, left the task of enlisting this expert to Bishop. But, by all accounts, the archaeologist was a difficult woman and a measure of added authority might convince her of her value. Although in his experience one had to exercise care with a particular breed of specialist individuals and avoid over-inflating their sense of self-importance. In any case, the trip afforded a chance for some peace and quiet – engine noise aside – for review of the case's essentials, including contemplation of certain details for which Miss Travers was not cleared.

While she was party to the highest-level secrets that necessitated talking in code words, some matters of strictly national interest need not concern her. Air Marshal Townsend-Jones had put him in the picture and the news had made for uncomfortable listening. Whether it amounted to anything directly germane to the investigation remained to be seen. Honestly, he hoped not, so that he might be able – eventually – to file it away and forget it.

He wondered at the deceptiveness of that sheening surface stretched out beneath them. An enormous mirror that revealed little beyond the mood of the weather. Any naval man would testify to the menaces prowling its depths. While ancient mariners told tall tales of giant serpents, modern sailors had much more to fear from man-made monsters.

Submarines.

In theory, there should be few – if any – enemy boats frequenting these waters. The Soviets maintained a nominal Mediterranean fleet for wartime deployment, but *in theory*, with both Greece and Turkey onboard as NATO member states, they were a threat safely bottled up behind the Bosporus. Caged in the Black Sea.

Still, theory only counted for so much. Lethbridge-Stewart had been obliged to re-evaluate a number of theories since the London Event. It seemed unlikely that the Soviets would initiate hostilities by preying on random civilian maritime traffic. But he wondered, if the culprit behind the missing ships turned out to be a Soviet submarine, would he find that preferable to some alien or paranormal threat?

'What's our ETA?' he inquired of the pilot, a Flight Lieutenant Chapman.

The answer came back in his headset. 'Seventy-two minutes, sir.'

Lethbridge-Stewart checked his watch. They had been in the air a while already. Time really did fly.

'Sir,' put in Samson, presumably gauging the brief exchange as permission to speak. 'Anything we need to know before we land?'

Lethbridge-Stewart admired the fellow's keenness, Samson had always been the same, but the information weighing heaviest on Lethbridge-Stewart's mind was not for a RSM's ears either, irrespective of friendship. By way of substitution, he elected to feed Samson alternatives of somewhat lesser note.

'Not much. We have some credentials on Miss Montilla. Group Captain Winser was able to supply some information. Apparently she gave the RAF quite the run for their money over potential archaeological finds on the Akamas peninsula firing range. If we have to strong-arm her into coming on board, I'll leave that honour to you, Sergeant Major.'

'Very good, sir.'

'There's also this South African connection that might present some complications. Owain flagged this Vorster chap as a suspect. While I appreciate Owain may have his ulterior motives for pointing fingers at Vorster and his company, well, we ought to be on our guard. Just in case.'

'You think Owain might have stirred up some trouble?'

'It's possible.' Altogether too possible. 'Opposing the company's hydraulic fracturing operations is bound to have drawn some attention. And if there is any substance to these concerns about damage to archaeological sites it may be that VTMB takes a vested interest in our activities. Particularly with a woman with some academic clout to call their operations into question.'

'What do we know about Vorster? And VTMB?'

'*Vorster Transvaal Minerale en Brandstof.* That's minerals and fuels to you and me.' Lethbridge-Stewart flicked through the notes at his side. 'Rolph Vorster was born in Pretoria. Son of a wealthy mining magnate. Self-made multi-millionaire on top of the family inheritance. Not much of a playboy though. Travels the world on business a great deal but doesn't appear to enjoy his wealth the way some in his position would. Maintains his own private security force at all his company's facilities. There are reports of two separate catastrophes at his mines in the Transvaal. High loss of life according to various sources, but surprisingly little information to be had on either incident.'

'Some mess swept under the carpet?'

'Possibly, Samson, possibly.'

Probably, appended Lethbridge-Stewart to himself. But he wasn't in the mood for judging a man for harbouring unsavoury secrets. Not when his government was guilty of similar.

'Will we be needing the firearms, sir?'

'I should hope not.'

Lethbridge-Stewart had brought his own service pistol and ordered the men issued with sidearms and stowed two rifles in the aircraft purely as an added precaution. Air Marshal Townsend-Jones had notified the Greek government of the presence of their team in the region. Ostensibly as part of a NATO-led investigation relating to the missing ships. A vague half-truth cover story designed to fit the situation without inviting too many probing questions.

'Sidearms only. We'll leave the rifles in the aircraft,' Lethbridge-Stewart told Samson and Private Atkins. 'No need to turn up on the woman's doorstep and frighten her off. And Vorster has a lot of friends in high places who are keen to see this hydraulic fracturing operation bear fruit. So if we do manage to upset any other interested parties we'll have to tread lightly and handle them as diplomatically as possible. Let's just see about recruiting our expert and try not to ruffle any feathers, shall we?'

'Yes, sir,' the two said in unison.

Lethbridge-Stewart settled back, returning to his reports and his thoughts. He reached for Owain's scant notes on Sophia Montilla.

In truth, he had little idea what to expect but surely this archaeological expert couldn't be any more difficult than other scientific consultants he'd had to work with in the past.

Bill returned, empty-handed. 'No luck,' he said. 'Sorry. The Brig may have taken the intel with him, but meanwhile we'll have to make do with—' He stopped beside Anne, stalled by the sight of the map. She said nothing, knowing what was coming next. 'You went ahead and finished my masterpiece without me?'

'Worse, I took all the pins out and started again. I hope you don't mind.'

Bill rolled his eyes, but combined it with a smile. 'What? My work isn't up to scratch.'

'Oh no, it'd pass muster in any pin-sticking contest, I'm sure. Its only... Before we examined the big picture, I wanted to build it.' She wagged the pair of compasses that she'd grabbed from one of the desks earlier. 'And I thought if we couldn't narrow down the disappearances to a single point, we may as well see the circles.'

Bill eyed her handiwork. It wasn't a work of art. In fact, if anything it looked a bit of a mess. Clusters of pencilled rings with different coloured pins piercing their centres. Times and dates scribbled in tiny lettering within the circles. Along with annotations for spikes of seismic activity where any coincided anywhere vaguely close to a given circle or timeframe.

'Care to explain your workings?'

'How are you on chess puzzles?' Anne returned.

'I know one end of the board from another, but I'm pretty confident you'd thrash me.'

'Father used to set me puzzles. One principal piece on the board – the Queen, say – pawns arranged in different patterns. The object was to find the shortest route – the fewest moves – to take all the pawns. The trick, which I cottoned onto very quickly, by the way, was to locate the last one in the sequence – the one standing out on its own – with only one possible path connecting to any other pawns. Then track back from there.'

Bill nodded, with what might have been pretend comprehension. Bless him. 'You think some alien menace is playing chess with our ships?'

Anne gave him a disapproving-teacher look. 'No, but I thought the method might be useful for identifying patterns if there are any to be found.' She jabbed the head of the blue pin. 'So I started with HMS *Aphrodite* here, since she is our latest known incident. Thirty-six degrees eight minutes north, twenty-four degrees twenty-six minutes east. Approximately eighteen hours ago. And worked back from there, one lost ship at a time.'

'Right. At least no circle necessary for her,' said Bill. He seemed almost proud to note his precious green pin right back where he'd placed it previously. 'And, uh, what's this right here?' He pointed to the white pin planted apart in a western patch of the Sea of Crete.

'That would be the VTMB platform. I wanted to see how that factors in to any potential pattern – if at all.'

'And?'

'And,' said Anne, 'we can rule out marine predators. Mythical or machine.'

'We can?'

'Yes.' Anne riffled through the pages, almost fast enough to create a flickerbook animation of figures and data. She indicated two distinct circles with a large expanse of blue between them. 'Two of these boats vanished perhaps two hours apart. But look, nearly a hundred miles between them. Even Krakens have their speed limits.'

'What about more than one creature?'

'There'd have to be an entire school to explain some of these times and positions. Or a very active mating pair at the very least.'

'All right, so…?' Bill prompted. 'Can we eliminate that possibility altogether?'

'Well, one thing strikes,' said Anne. And she replayed her plotting process as she surveyed the pins and circles, trying to visualise something moving beneath the blue while all those vessels traversed the surface. 'If we do have some sort of supercharged sea monsters at work, then the species hunts in the shallower waters. Look. Only one of these incidents

occurred in waters of a depth greater than two hundred metres.'
The chart's bathymetric scale only gave a very broad idea of Aegean topography. Different shades of blue, light to dark, indicating ranges of depths. Anne tapped the blue pin.

'*Aphrodite*,' Bill said. 'And she escaped with hull damage.'

'Right. And what size beast do you imagine could swallow a passenger ferry? Let alone take on a Leander class frigate?'

'Something big.'

'And therefore something that ought to prefer the depths.'

Wherever the local waters were darkest on the map, the areas were conspicuously clear of incident. According to the chart, depths ran to perhaps five to six thousand feet. Perfect hunting ground for submarines or sea monsters.

Bill searched the map for further inspiration. 'So does this tell us anything? Do you see a pattern?'

Anne stood back, scanning the board. She shook her head. 'I admit I'm a little wary of patterns. We tend to look for them in everything. See them when they're not there, because the human mind prefers order. Canals on Mars, faces in toast, all that sort of thing. But spirals exist in nature. Snail shells, for example. And a spiral... A very *rough* spiral is what I'm seeing here. The thing is, it could be something natural. But it could be a sign of some intelligence at work.'

'*The* Intelligence?' Bill asked, with a smirk.

Anne wasn't impressed. 'I hope not. But look. The *Aphrodite* sustained damage here. And we know that incident is the most recent, but these three earliest ones occurred within thirty miles of one another.'

'Right.' Bill glanced quickly from pin to pin. Anne could tell he was doing some maths as he did so. 'There are still a couple of casualties nearer what you'd call the centre. But most of the later ones are further apart.'

'Exactly. Whatever is at work here, it's expanding its influence.'

Anne thought of the Web and its malign spread through the London Underground system. That had behaved like a noose, encircling and steadily closing around their base of operations in Goodge Street. This enemy could well be expanding outwards.

'Our real difficulty here,' she said, 'is we have two distinct effects coinciding. Two systems overlapping, if you like.'

'Okay,' said Bill, staying with her. 'Let's hear it.'

'We have heaven knows how many vessels routinely traversing the Aegean on a daily basis. Some of which – the trawlers and pleasure craft and such – we have no data for. But the ferries adhere to established routes. Those shipping lanes are one system. The other is whatever is interfering with them. And that is a complete unknown.'

'But we can draw one of those systems, right?' Bill hunted out a pencil and ruler. 'Ferries don't likely travel in exactly straight lines, but for the sake of simplicity let's say they do. *Queen of the Cyclades*. What route was she operating?'

Anne thumbed through her clutch of report sheets. 'Pireas to Heraklion.'

Bill ruled an arrow-straight line from departure port to destination. Anne flicked to different pages and supplied him with the other three ferry routes.

'Pireas to Santorini. Kalamata to Rhodes. And, Kithira to Naxos.'

Three more pencil lines crossed the seas, dissecting some of Anne's circles. It was an over-simplification, but a potentially telling one. Every line transected an area approximate to the centre of her ostensible 'spiral'.

Bill tapped the area with a fingertip. 'This right here could be the heart of the trouble. We've no exact course data for the trawlers and private craft, but what if they all crossed this stretch of water? What if we are dealing with something that spreads, like the Web that surrounded Bledoe?'

'An underwater web then...'

'Not the *Web* necessarily. But some force with an area effect that, once ships come into contact with it, drags everything down to a watery grave.'

'Maybe.' Too much guesswork. Too many stabs in the dark. Her gaze latched onto one thing, however. The white pin.

Stationed to one side of their hypothetical underwater web. Distant enough to look like an innocent bystander. Close enough to observe.

Not unlike a morbid spectator loitering ringside at a traffic accident.

CHAPTER SIX
Visitation

SOPHIA WAS being watched.

Feline necks craned, lending a lot of cats' eyes a better view of her activity from several vantage points around the edge of the garden.

Tabbies, gingers, blacks, black-and-whites, ginger-and-whites, white-and-grey-with-brown-patch-above-nose, and tortoiseshells. Her cat family, patchwork tigers, observing her with wary interest as she scooped spoonfuls of jellied meat into the row of saucers along the poolside. Timid mercenaries, every one of them. Stationed atop the fence, two on neighbouring rooftops, one on the garden chair, another on the table, three risen from sunbathing on her patio to perform little anticipatory dances, circling each other as they awaited that come-and-get-it signal: a final ching-ching-ching on the last saucer.

Athena hauled herself from under the caper bush, heavy with the after-effects of a lengthy siesta – and more besides. Pregnant.

Sophia chimed the saucer. Standing, she wagged the spoon reprovingly at the mother-to-be. 'Either you are going to have to mend your ways, or something will have to be done about you, my girl.'

A lot of feline ears perked up. Most of the cats scattered. One or two of the braver ones paused to stare towards the house – and then bolted. Sophia tutted. Timid mercenaries; they would be back.

But for now...

Her thoughts shot straight to her two shadows on the journey home. She had lost them eventually. That, or they had tired of the very poor sport.

She returned inside, taking her time, wary as one of her cats.

She left the patio door open, thinking about escape routes. Ridiculous. But she had a feeling that maybe she hadn't taken her two followers seriously enough.

Somebody rapped their fist on her front door. Impatient, insistent. Presumably a second knock. The first being what had startled the cats.

Sophia stopped by the hall cupboard to arm herself with the broom. The hall was narrow and would only accommodate one attacker at a time. It wouldn't allow for a decent swing of a broom, but she would be able to thrust it like a blunt spear or deliver a swift uppercut to a masculine chin.

Another knock.

Okay, impatient or no, these people were polite. Attackers might've barged her door down by now. That was the silver lining.

Sophia relaxed her grip on the broom. She approached the door and eased it open.

'Madam Montilla?'

The group at her porch were not the same as her followers from Vlychada. But the men had a similar demeanour. That way of filling out their suits to make them resemble uniforms. Military. And their front man's moustache was one of the most regimented examples of facial hair Sophia had ever seen. More clipped than his very British accent.

'*Señora* Montilla, yes.'

'Brigadier Alistair Lethbridge-Stewart.' He gestured to his colleagues, a West Indian with a hint of Caucasian and a rather flattened boxer's nose, plus a pasty-faced and freckled redheaded lad. 'This is Sergeant Major Ware. And Private Atkins.' Underlings, then, rather than colleagues. 'There is a matter of some urgency we would like to discuss with you. May we come in?'

'Hmm,' said Sophia.

She supposed she must appear like she was standing guard, with her broom in hand. This brigadier eyed her oddly, as though she were one of his soldiers on parade and had done a sloppy job of presenting arms.

'That depends,' she said eventually.

'Depends?'

Sophia nodded. 'On whether or not you have anything to do with the men who were shadowing me this morning. I don't believe so, but still I would like to hear assurances, and then I will be able to make up my own mind, won't I?'

Brigadier Lethbridge-Stewart looked to his companions, but found no verbal support from that quarter. 'Madam, I can assure you that if you have been the subject of any surveillance it has nothing to do with us. In fact, if it will put you better at ease I can have one of my men stationed outside to keep an eye out for unwelcome observers.'

'Thank you. Yes, I think that is an excellent idea.'

It would mean fewer military bodies cluttering her house.

'Atkins,' the brigadier addressed his junior underling. 'Guard the door. Samson, recce the rear of the property.'

'Sir.' The sergeant major scanned the street. Sophia read his thinking: Fira's alleys were almost as narrow as her hall, unfit for watchers interested in her house. 'Clear out here. If you don't mind, *Señora*, but how's the view out back?'

'Scenic,' she answered. And stepped back. 'Perhaps you'd best come through to the garden. As long as you promise to stand quietly and don't frighten the cats.'

Brigadier Lethbridge-Stewart eye-rolled, then did his best to disguise it when he saw she'd noticed. 'Just as the lady says, Samson. Recce the rear of the property. And inform me if you spot anything suspicious.'

'Yes, sir.'

'In which case,' Sophia said, 'please come in. You will have to excuse the state of the place. I have been doing some cleaning.' She nudged the door wide and left it as an invitation. She led the way through the hall, stowing the broom away en route. Listened to her visitors brushing the soles of their shoes on her mat.

She could tell this brigadier wanted something. Mercenary, like her cats. Not nearly as timid. But civil.

It couldn't do any harm, she decided, to hear him out.

'Who have we got here now?'

Hollis fine-tuned the focus on his binoculars. Beside him, Fyler assembled the rifle.

A short minute after the subject had disappeared indoors, a few of the mangy cats had returned to investigate the food bowls. They'd scattered again as some kaffer stepped into the yard. The man patrolled the poolside, scanning the neighbouring rooftops.

He looked their way and Hollis slapped a hand over the binocular lenses. He waited for the newcomer to start searching in another direction. Then unmasked the lenses and went back to observing.

Hollis assessed the figure for tell-tale details, anything to provide clues as to his identity and what he was doing there. He paced and searched, paced and searched, head up and alert like an alpha male springbok guarding the herd. Guarding. The thought prompted close scrutiny of the man's belt: occasionally, as the figure turned, the jacket flapped and revealed a glimpse of holster. The subject's social caller packed a sidearm.

'What, she's gone and hired muscle now?' Fyler flipped the bipod on the rifle and flattened next to him. He put his eye to the scope.

'Not locally, that's for sure,' Hollis said.

'Moves like military.'

Hollis nodded. He'd thought exactly the same. 'Military or ex-military. Either way, he's playing sentry.' Which meant she was meeting with someone else inside. Probably this guy's superior. 'She's not had time to call anyone in. So unless she sent for help before today, they've come to pay her a visit.'

'Pass me the silencer.'

'We need to know what we're dealing with here.'

'Sure,' Fyler said. 'So get down there and cover the front entrance.'

'That's a call for the boss to make. We should check in first.'

'Damnit, can't we just make a judgment call of our own for once?'

'Why so antsy?'

Fyler broke off from squinting into his scope. 'Because I hate having another man's voice in my head.' He had a point. A thirty-second conference on the radio would have been a different matter. 'He'll want the artefacts; you know he will.'

'Sure. He'll thank us,' Hollis concurred. '*If* things don't go pear-shaped.'

Fyler scoffed. 'One woman and a visitor or two? Go knock on the front door. Assess the numbers. Draw them out. Then we can make a judgment call.' Fyler curled his finger around the rifle trigger, practicing the shot. 'Send some running out the back if you can.'

*

'Smoke?' Sophia Montilla thrust a cigarette at Lethbridge-Stewart. It caught him so off-guard she might as well have been trying to prod him with a tiny spear.

She was a handsome woman. Classic movie-star looks really, easy to imagine she'd once graced the silver screen. In her forties or possibly fifties, she had either conquered or embraced age in such a way that the world would be hard-pressed to pinpoint her years. A woman, Lethbridge-Stewart mused, who would prove impossible to date.

'No, thank you,' he said.

She shrugged, tapped the cigarette on the packet and popped it between her lips. Her slender fingers fished a silver lighter from her pocket. She lit up and inhaled.

Lethbridge-Stewart manoeuvred clear in case she had a mind to blow smoke in his face. He pretended to peruse some of the woman's ornaments adorning the shelves in front of him. He supposed some of them might be authentic antiquities, but there were a number of what looked to his inexpert eye like cheap souvenirs. Including a lot of cats.

The ceiling was low, giving the impression of a small house, but open-plan, and the ground floor appeared to range through several rooms. Terra cotta tiling, white walls, no paintings hanging anywhere but a fair few tribal masks and even archaic weaponry of various cultures. All the neatness of the shelves was counterbalanced by points of unruliness here and there: ash tray and untidily stacked magazines on the coffee table, a desk against one wall cluttered with note books and text books, a camera and, of all things, a red plastic bucket.

It was there she headed, tossing her cigarette pack onto the coffee table in passing. She fetched the bucket and carried it through into the kitchen.

Lethbridge-Stewart followed.

'Madam,' he began.

'*Señora*. Please.' She lowered the bucket into the sink and pulled a pair of rubber gloves from a drawer, as though ready to do the washing-up.

'*Señora*. Permit me to come straight to the point. We are in need of your expertise and would welcome your assistance. If it's a question of remuneration, then Her Majesty's Government will be happy to—'

'A question of...?' She laughed. Setting her cigarette to rest on another ashtray, she plucked a toothbrush from the open drawer and reached into the bucket. 'If I were motivated by money, I would never have chosen archaeology as a career.' She fished out a clay crescent, water dripping from one broken edge. She worked the toothbrush bristles with a light touch into the engraved symbols. 'No, Brigadier. Although I won't say no to fair pay. You know, researches need funding. And I have to keep myself in tea for unexpected guests. But what I would need most are assurances. Guarantees. Promises. Which I am afraid to say are frequently more fragile than anything I dig up. They would not last thousands of years in the dirt. Most barely survive a day out of someone's mouth.'

Lethbridge-Stewart was beginning to think he should have brought Miss Travers along to negotiate this recruitment, female to female.

'What kind of guarantees? Your safety will be—'

'Please. I will take care of my own safety, thank you. The artefacts, Brigadier. Those will be my paramount concern. I do not wish to invest my time and attention studying artefacts only to see them trampled under some military boot – figuratively speaking, you understand. Or crated and shipped off to be stored in the vaults of the British Museum, for that matter.'

Lethbridge-Stewart braced himself for a lecture on the Elgin marbles. The woman was Spanish, but he suspected her attachment to historical artefacts had precious little to do with nationality. It appeared she had said her piece, allowing him his turn as she scrutinised the piece of clay.

'Any artefacts you can authenticate will be your responsibility. I can't claim any familiarity with the legalities relating to your field, *Señora*, so I'll be obliged to leave that to you, in any case.' He assumed the Greek government would lay claim to any relics found in their waters. As to anything discovered in international waters, well, he supposed maritime salvage laws might apply. However, there were exigencies he couldn't go into at this stage, not until he had this woman sign the Official Secrets Act. 'It's my duty to warn you, however, that should you uncover any… abnormalities, then those finds may be subject to other regulations.'

'Abnormalities?'

'Anomalies of... any description.'

'That's remarkably vague. So vague it has to be hiding something very definite.'

'Given the military involvement, you can assume there are interests at stake beyond the purely historical.'

'I see. Not political, but... something else.' She narrowed her eyes. It was easy to picture the thoughts flaring in their depths.

'I am aware you were approached by a young man, Owain Vine—'

'Oh, you know Owain. Yes, he and his friends and their theories of Atlantis. Is that anything to do with the anomalies you'd be looking for?'

'Well, Owain's imagination may have run away with him.'

'Not without some clever strategising,' *Señora* Montilla remarked. She lowered the clay piece back into the water. And wagged her toothbrush. 'He was onto something. A smart sales pitch. People, they want to believe in Atlantis. We do the detective work, but people want the myth. Here on Santorini, we're standing on the volcano that even noted archaeologists believed might have been the historical basis for that myth. For hungry imaginations, it does not matter whether that is proved or disproved. I do not believe in fairytales. What matters to me, Brigadier, is whether there is a site out there being damaged by industry. And if there is, I will fight to preserve it with all my heart. But that young man – your Owain – wanted a big story. The biggest possible ammunition for his crusade. I admired his passion and his flair for invention. I should have seen past that and looked into this further, sooner.'

'Be that as it may, *Señora*, it is my job to consider every angle. As you say, myths may have some roots in reality. But I'm afraid I can't furnish you with any more detail until I know whether or not you are on board.'

'I must say, Brigadier, you are not doing a great job of recruitment.'

'I'm not?' He was not entirely surprised.

'But I can see you are bound by all manner of secrecy. And you are trying to be honest.' *Señora* Montilla retrieved her cigarette and puffed on it, managing to hold it quite adroitly between the fingers of her rubber glove. 'As honest as you are able at this point. You are making me feel almost sorry for you.'

'I am?' That was a surprise.

'I am not easily flattered or fooled. You need an expert and you came to me because – why? – because I am local. I am the expedient choice. This suggests some urgency and I have to agree, the situation is urgent. Trawlermen are plundering the site. Looting, in essence. Soon we will have treasure hunters all over the Aegean. For this, I will help. In return for whatever protection you can afford... Not me, but this site. This discovery.'

'Thank you, *Señora*.'

'I hope – I trust – that I will not be later made to regret my involvement.'

'We will do our best.'

'And will I be able to publish my findings?'

'That,' said Lethbridge-Stewart slowly, 'remains to be seen.'

And that, again, was as much honesty as he could grant. *Señora* Sophia Montilla appeared to appreciate it, with a wry smile.

She was on board.

'Welcome to the team.' Lethbridge-Stewart extended a hand.

The lady rubbed her rubber glove on her jeans before accepting.

Samson patrolled the poolside. There was no sign of any cats, just the saucers of dinner laid out for them.

He'd caught that glint though. Sunshine on glass over on a neighbourhood rooftop. And it had blinked out as soon as he'd looked hard at it.

Just like magic.

Yeah. Right.

He sauntered around the yard, pretended to search the hedge. His attention provoked some rustles, probable evidence of a feline presence. He drifted by, back around the pool and towards the patio window. Directed his eyes towards that rooftop again, without turning his head.

Sure enough. There was the reflection. Winking at him.

It gave him an uneasy feeling. An old, familiar feeling from past days in Cyprus. Something he'd managed to not think about even when he'd stepped down off the aircraft on Akrotiri's tarmac.

Something told him it wasn't a friendly wink.

CHAPTER SEVEN
Fury from the Deep

A BLARING klaxon jolted Owain off his bunk. Shouts and a clanging stampede filled the corridor outside the cabin.

He was at the door in an instant, ear to the metal. More shouts and the heavy hammer of boots passed by, loud enough to punish him for eavesdropping. Amid all the noisy Russian, the boots were the only part Owain understood.

There was some sort of panic on. For a moment, he imagined some NATO jet taking exception to Soviets engaged in oceanographic research in these waters. But he couldn't fathom how Grigoriy and his team might have been discovered. Besides, surely he would've heard the jet screaming overhead by now.

He rushed to the porthole, but there was only open sky, open water. The ship had been stationary for too long. Idling in the same position, just like Owain.

The alarm continued, but Owain relaxed. Any inbound strike aircraft would be under orders to make warning passes while the pilot issued official ultimatums. There was nothing scary about a fly-by. It would be like an Air Day at Culdrose, with menaces.

He returned to the door. In time to hear another stampede fading past. Finally, the klaxon shut off.

Owain eased the door open and poked his head out. A lot of urgent exchanges hailed from up top, dulled by the intervening deck. Otherwise the corridor was quiet – and empty.

He stepped out, straining to listen. Even knowing what he heard would tell him as little as the porthole.

Technically, he was under orders to stay in his cabin. But his mind was nowhere near as idle as the rest of him. Sleep wouldn't come and on top of all the thoughts thrashing about in his head he had to contend with the discomfort of being confined in someone else's quarters. There was nothing to do in borrowed space. Just stretching out in the bunk had felt like trespass. There were a few personal effects around the cabin, none of which he dared touch. He did pick up a scruffy paperback and flick through, but it was all in dense Cyrillic script and even if it had been in English he suspected it would have hurt his brain without the mercy of sending him to sleep.

He'd felt pretty bold picking up that book. How much braver would he have to feel to take a proper nose around?

Surely, they were beyond the point where the captain might have him shot. So the worst he could expect was a severe ticking off and a force-march back to the cabin, to be kept there under lock and guard.

It wasn't a pretty prospect. But as deterrents went it wasn't up there with firing squad. Besides, *quid pro quo*. Grigoriy had promised him some assistance in return for what he knew. Owain had supplied the *quo*, as far as he understood it, and thus far all he'd received was solitary confinement while the ship remained on station conducting its mysterious and euphemistic research. An unguided tour was one way of collecting on that *quid* he was owed.

Owain took a breath to still his heart. Then picked a direction and walked stealthily, while trying not to look like he was creeping about. He rehearsed excuses: 'Sorry, mate, I was looking for the loo. Or ship's head, whatever you call it. Got lost.' In his mind, they sounded totally plausible but none met with any success when he pictured Oleg's stony expression. Worse still, when they came up against his mental image of Grigoriy.

Distanced, the shout and clamour up on deck sounded like a far-off football match in a steel stadium.

Owain peered through open and half-open doors along the corridor, breathing a sigh as he found the quarters deserted. Then moved quickly on, in search of richer pickings.

There was no sense poking around in other cabins. If he was going to get caught intruding, it should be somewhere serious. Somewhere he stood to learn something worthwhile.

He arrived at a door emblazoned with stencilled letters.

Cyrillic, of course. But they looked forbidding. An engineering light was strung above the door, the red-tinted bulb currently inert. But red equalled *Stop* or *Danger* in any language, didn't it? Anyway, it was signal enough for Owain.

He tested the door lever. It turned easily and the door swung inward with an oil-starved squeak.

Owain slipped into the room. A dark room.

Trays, chemical baths, jars, all the usual equipment for a dedicated photographer. Mounted on a side-bench, a bulky printer of some sort. And potential intelligence gold: large sheets of printouts spread over two counter-tops plus rows of photographs hanging like starched laundry on a number of washing lines.

The printouts were kind of spotty, like the works of a pointillist with a brush several sizes too large and a palette of mostly browns. Marked out in grids, the images showed pits and depressions and ridges and rises. They could have been maps of the Moon, but they weren't nearly so cratered. In some the terrain was dotted with more regular structures.

The outlines were vague, broken by the patchy image resolution, but Owain could make out what resembled discarded piles of giant bricks and maybe disc-shaped platforms or mesas.

He moved on to the strings of photos.

He reached up and pinched the corner of one picture between finger and thumb, tugging it downward for a closer look without plucking it from the line. It showed a grooved trunk of stone. Truncated, rooted in sand and bathed in blue shadow. A Greek column?

Owain scanned along the row, picture after picture. Then moved onto another string, finding more of the same. Grigoriy's 'research team' had amassed quite the gallery.

Other photos of columns, sometimes groups of two or three, as well as pictures of rough stone blocks half-submerged in sand and or nestled among coral and rock formations, dark square openings in their sides. Houses?

A strange cold crept through Owain. Like an outbreak of goosebumps in his heart and stomach.

An image lashed out from the back of his mind. A towering column in blue gloom. Him, sinking in shadow.

Shouts, boots and a hell of a lot of bustle snapped Owain

back to the present. His heart clenched like a fist in his chest. He stared at the door, expecting it to burst open and unleash an angry Grigoriy on him.

The commotion carried on by. Doors clanked. More boots stamped about. Words were traded like bullets in a firefight. Bootsteps tramped past on their way back up top.

Time to return to his cell.

Owain tugged the door open. The coast was clear.

He pulled the door quietly closed and trotted back towards his cabin.

And almost made it.

Bootsteps crashed and banged down the stairs and men clogged the corridor. Oleg led two stretcher parties, more men behind. The stretcher-bearers were a frightening sight, bulked out and rendered inhuman under gas masks and rubber coveralls. The patients laid out between them were clad in wetsuits. Divers, then. But what was with the protective gear for the men carrying them? Wasn't that the sort of kit reserved for chemical or gas attacks? And if there'd been some sort of leak or contamination, why wasn't everybody suited up? What about him? Was he breathing poison air?

Owain ducked into the doorway. Not quick enough.

'Out the way!' Oleg barked. And shoved Owain aside.

Owain watched the grim procession pass. Captain Grigoriy broke off issuing orders long enough to glance in on Owain. It wasn't a happy glance.

'What happened?' Owain blurted.

But Grigoriy ignored him and marched on by. Followed by a close parade of anxious faces.

Owain shut his door and sat on the bunk. Grigoriy would be coming back at some point, with questions. About what Owain was doing outside his cabin and what he might have seen.

His thoughts churned, trying to come up with answers better than his stupid toilet and getting-lost excuses.

Nothing surfaced.

Except a waking nightmare of recurring images: the gas masks, Grigoriy's look and, worst of all, the faces of those men on the stretchers.

The knock came sooner than expected. In fact, Owain hadn't expected a knock.

Despite the civil gesture, the door burst open before he had a chance to tell his visitor to enter. Oleg just blocked the entrance, signalling with a curt beckoning gesture.

'Come. Now.'

Owain rose like a condemned man from the bunk and followed. Aside from the wall that was Oleg's back, he caught glimpses of a lot of grave faces in the cabins they passed. They walked by the dark room, the Cyrillic lettering now serving up an extra helping of accusation and guilt. He wondered if there was a gallows awaiting him at the end of the passage.

The reality was worse. Oleg hung a right turn and ushered Owain into a scene that hit him like a kick to the stomach.

It was a sick bay. In disarray. Cold electronic beeps counted time erratically. Four men in chemical warfare suits bustled around one of a pair of tables. A body lay untended on the furthest table. Stretched out and abandoned, it seemed, on a plastic sheet. Past all the shifting and jostling figures, Owain glimpsed horrible grey lesions covering the man's torso and arms. A gas-masked and hazard-suited attendant drew the flaps of the plastic sheet up over the corpse, effectively wrapping it. Out of sight, but far from out of Owain's mind.

Nobody else paid the corpse any heed. All attention and the glare of an overhead light was on the patient in the foreground. The man, stripped of his wetsuit, was besieged by frantic activity, rapid-fire bursts of Russian flying everywhere, every word muffled by the gas masks.

A handful of silent onlookers lined the walls. Chief among them, Grigoriy, his arms folded, head bowed, gaze fixed like he was at the funeral and vowing vengeance.

The beeps expired into a single endless monotone.

One of the rubber-suited medics grabbed paddles from the trolley behind him. Someone called out a command. Everyone stepped back. The medic fired the defibrillators. The patient jerked, his torso arching. Owain felt the shock as the body thumped back flat on the table. Another barked command. Another point-blank shot with the paddles pressed to the man's chest. Another violent jerk. Another thump of the body hitting the table. Then another. Same sequence. Same result.

The medic held the defibrillator paddles, raised, halfway to surrender. He turned his masked face to Grigoriy.

The medic set the paddles down on the trolley and muttered something.

Owain missed them. Then he realised, had he paid close attention he might have learned a few words of Russian.

Time of death.

Grigoriy spun and kicked a cabinet, splintering the door. Trays of surgical equipment and jars clattered and jangled on the counter and Grigoriy punished them by sweeping them onto the floor. The metallic crash and shattering glass drowned out the prolonged beep.

In the aftermath of the din, someone flicked the machine off.

Grigoriy shot to Owain's side and seized him by the neck.

'Ow! Hey– What–!'

Grigoriy propelled Owain in a stranglehold. Medics parted, opening a path to the table. Grigoriy pushed Owain's head down like he was shoving a dog's nose in a mess of its own making.

Owain was face to face with a dead stranger. Unrecognisable, probably, even if it had been someone he knew. What he'd thought of as lesions on the other man had spread over this man's face like a mask. A stone mask. All that was left was a crude sculpture of features with the texture of granite.

'Did you know about this?' Grigoriy hissed. 'Did you know?'

Owain shook. His face hovered perilously close to the scabrous grey that used to be a man's skin. 'No, I... What? Know about what?' He squirmed and fought to recoil, but he couldn't budge an inch in Grigoriy's grip. 'This... Condition? Infection? What is it? I've never seen anything like it. Is this what you've dragged up off the seabed? With your oceanographic research? Because if it is, then maybe that's what's attacking all these vanishing ships! Maybe this is what's happened to their crews! But I'm telling you, I think it has something to do with Vorster and his rig! This is something they've dug up, I'd bet on it! I bet they know!'

The moment protracted like that terminal bleep.

Until Grigoriy yanked him away from the table and released

him. The captain stared furiously, breathing hard. The anger still burned, but Owain had a sense he wasn't the target any more.

Grigoriy stormed out.

Oleg pushed Owain to follow.

He walked in Grigoriy's wake, with Oleg lending him the occasional nudge. They caught up with Grigoriy up on deck. He leaned on the port bulwark, peering out to sea.

A sizeable patch of deck to starboard lay in a mess. Far from shipshape. Discarded diving masks and oxygen tanks were a minor part of the story. The biggest was the ragged gaping hole — maybe six foot in diameter — that had been cut, with no sign of the missing deck section anywhere. One man, clad in the same protective gear favoured by the medics, was on his knees and examining the area around the hole, scouring every square inch up close like he'd lost an engagement ring. He was armed with an oxyacetylene torch, so Owain had to assume he'd been the one who'd carved up the deck. The cutter's fuel tanks were stationed upright on a trolley and occasionally he'd reach to pull it with him as he moved on with his search.

Nearby, a rumpled tarp had been spread like an oily and hastily thrown picnic blanket. No food or basket on it, just a couple of oddly misshapen rocks smack in the centre of the tarpaulin. Owain frowned, hankering for a closer look but he dared not wander over. He had a feeling like he was on an invisible leash held by Oleg. One wrong step and he could imagine himself being yanked back into place.

A hundred questions went begging. Mostly just the one: *What the hell happened?* But Owain clamped his mouth shut. As much as he wanted answers, he didn't want to repeat the mistake of speaking out of turn. Not now. Especially not now.

The torch guy stood and peeled off his gas mask. He reported something in Russian, prompting Grigoriy to turn. He nodded, answered and waved the engineer away. Tugging his hood down, the engineer marched off but left his torch in position.

'Go on.' Grigoriy gestured at the exhibits on the tarp. 'Take a look.'

Owain moved slowly. He was grateful that he was not having his face shoved into things, but something made him as wary as if there was another pair of corpses laid out in front of him.

He crouched at the edge of the tarpaulin.

One of the 'rocks' turned out to be a stone or clay figure. A female torso with raised hands mounted on a cylindrical base. Not unlike the one he'd photographed in the hands of a trawlerman on Santorini. The other 'rock' was... something else. Some sort of granite block with crudely carved handles.

'What is that?'

'That was an underwater camera.'

Owain blinked. Yes, he could just about recognise it now. The low plateau on its upper surface must have been the lens mounting. But it was like some relic that had been lifted from the seabed after centuries of collecting barnacles. Its outline was distorted, its surfaces turned to rough-hewn and pitted stone.

'How did it get...' *Get what?* Owain thought. The right words failed to suggest themselves. 'Like that?'

Grigoriy loomed beside him. 'One of our divers picked up that statuette. He became contaminated. As did his comrade, as did the camera. And as did the deck when the camera came into contact with it. Their wetsuits were unaffected and as you can see the tarpaulin appears to prevent the spread of the contamination.'

'Contamination? What kind of contamination could do that? And... I mean, are we safe?'

'Have you turned to stone yet?'

'Only inside.'

'Well then. As long as we don't get too near, I believe yes, we are safe. I had the men break out the NBC suits as a precaution.'

'NBC?'

'Nuclear Biological Chemical.'

'Right.' Owain swallowed. 'Sounds like a wise move, if you ask me.'

Grigoriy nodded. 'Back in the sick bay—'

'No, no. Don't... don't worry about it. You were upset, I get that.'

'Back in the sick bay,' Grigoriy resumed, 'you were making your case for a rescue mission. For your friends. I understand that. And if I had evidence that VTMB were behind this, I would order an assault right now.'

'Listen, they shot at us. Me and my environmental protestor

friends. I'd say that's pretty strong evidence they have something to hide. And this... This could be what they're hiding.'

'It could be. Their hydraulic fracturing could easily be a cover. And what about you, Owain? Your environmental protest; isn't that like our oceanographic research?'

Owain had to laugh at that. Not out loud, but the man had a point. Everybody had a cover. 'To some extent, yes, okay. I was aiming to learn something. Any useful details I could pass on to my other friends. Maybe attract some publicity, expose something of whatever they're up to. But the environmental protest was genuine. Because I happen to care about that sort of thing. And I care about my friends. Getting on that rig, well, yes, I'd want you to save them. But you'd stand to learn something, maybe shut them down. I know that's what my people would do.'

'Once they have gathered sufficient evidence, yes, I'm certain they would.'

'And don't you have enough evidence?' Owain didn't want to spell out the fact that two men had died. 'Not just what we've seen now. But...Well, you know I had a look in your photography room. You've found ruins on the seabed, haven't you? Just like I suspected. And even if VTMB are running a legit operation, that's the sort of thing that could seriously mess up their works.'

'So, what? You believe they contaminate these waters; these ruins?'

Owain grimaced. That didn't add up. Not even to him, not even for a man like Rolph Vorster.

'Besides,' Grigoriy said, 'even if these people of yours would act on your say-so, I will not.'

Owain was aware of Oleg behind him, across the deck. But something emboldened him. 'Why not? Who would ever know? I mean, those guys shot at us. They murdered one of us. And they did it right out in the open because, take a look around, nobody's watching. There aren't even any seabirds for witnesses. Well, that works for everybody. Seriously, what's to stop you going in there and doing whatever the hell you like to them?'

'Is it rescue or revenge you're after?'

'That depends, doesn't it?' Owain said, feeling ashamed of

himself as the words spilled out of his mouth. 'On whether or not my friends are still alive.'

Grigoriy chewed that over. Owain could almost hear teeth or thoughts grinding. 'It makes no difference, in any case,' declared Grigoriy eventually. 'They are a corporate concern. Your passions are a laudable trait. In an angry young revolutionary. You should take up terrorism.'

'Okay, okay. I'm being stupid.' Owain didn't need Grigoriy to point that out, but his words stung and Owain knew why.

'You are reacting. My preference is to act.'

'So act. Please. Listen, my people will be here already. Investigating. They could stand to know what we know. And they might be able to tell us a few things in the bargain.' When did Owain and the Russians get to be 'we' and 'us'? *When they fished me out of the drink*, Owain answered himself. 'RAF Akrotiri, Cyprus is where I've been reporting to. They'll be based there. I know you're not meant to co-operate but can't you meet and exchange information? Unofficially.'

'How do you propose we do that?'

'Contact them. Call them up on the radio.'

'Unofficial does not include logged radio calls to a Royal Air Force base.'

'I could make the call.'

'Not from my ship.'

'So, telephone then. Put me ashore and let me arrange some sort of meeting.'

'Really? And where would you like to be delivered?'

Only one place sprang to mind. 'Santorini. There's a contact there. Not really a contact. Someone I was trying to recruit to the cause. She's an expert – archaeologist. She may even be able to tell us something about these contaminated relics or whatever they are.'

Owain watched Grigoriy chew more thoughts. 'Very well, Mr Vine. You have secured yourself transport.' He waved to Oleg. 'Relay to the helm. Set a course for Santorini.' He walked to the ragged wound cut in his deck. And stared into the steel and shadows with a promise of payback.

CHAPTER EIGHT
Chase

SEÑORA MONTILLA fished another item out of her bucket. A figurine, which she turned around in the kitchen window light.

'This is the Snake Goddess, Brigadier. Examples of her kind have turned up at other archaeological sites – principally Crete – and she is a rather ubiquitous deity replicated in many of the local souvenir shops.'

The sculptor had invested the statuette with a great level of detail, from a jewelled tiara down to a long skirt comprised of individual squares, bare breasts above an embroidered bodice. The Goddess clutched a snake in one raised hand and she appeared to have sustained an injury, namely one broken arm. *Señora* Montilla set at the Goddess with careful strokes of her toothbrush.

'And can you attest to this one's authenticity?' Lethbridge-Stewart asked. 'Or is this some sort of replica or forgery?'

'Oh, I believe she is genuine. If other pieces of her quality are showing up here on Santorini, I should have listened to your friend, Owain. I tried to explain to him the bureaucratic difficulties of obtaining permissions and so on. But had I known at the time there were others who were not so bothered about official channels, well, I could have saved more like her.'

'And the breakage? That's unimportant?' Lethbridge-Stewart could tell by the way *Señora* Montilla pointed her toothbrush at him that he'd said the wrong thing.

'Unimportant? No, it's criminal. I've every reason to believe both she and the disc came out of the water intact and it is only because they have been handled by imbecilic amateurs – pah! not even that – fishermen! – that you see them in this state! It's my fault. I should have begun my own investigations before. Put a stop to this.'

'Could they not have suffered the damage lying on the seabed?'

Señora Montilla returned to her tender brushstrokes. 'These items are too clean. I believe they were once well cared for.' She might have been discussing children. 'There is a possibility someone is seeding sites with treasures. You know, just as unscrupulous cowboys seeded gold claims with shotguns loaded with nuggets. Or however they used to do it. It's been a long time since I watched a western. But I'm sure I saw Audey Murphy or Gary Cooper or someone do just that.' Lethbridge-Stewart considered it unlikely, as those gentlemen tended to play the good guys. Still, he took her point. 'And people can be just as underhanded when it comes to historical treasures. Which reminds me...'

'Yes...?'

'We need to attend the auction.'

'The auction?'

Señora Montilla lowered her Goddess back into the bucket with the gentleness of a mother giving her infant a bath. 'Yes, the auction.'

Before she could say more, Samson burst in from the back room. 'Excuse the interruption, sir – *Señora* – but we have company. Watchers on one of the neighbouring rooftops. I hope I only saw flare off a pair of binoculars, but...'

Lethbridge-Stewart understood that look in Samson's eyes. 'Good idea, Samson. Go, find out what kind of people we're dealing with.'

'I can tell you that,' supplied *Señora* Montilla. 'If they're the same as the ones who followed me from Vlychada. Big, muscle-headed, and their idea of summer-wear involves suits, sunglasses and leather gloves. Also, they like beer but don't drink it.'

'Really, *Señora*, you will have to tell us more about these men.' Lethbridge-Stewart glanced at Samson, who waited with the eagerness of a pointer itching to go after a downed guinea fowl. 'In the first place, did you happen to notice whether these shadowers of yours were armed?'

'Not that I noticed.'

Lethbridge-Stewart considered for a moment. He nodded to Samson. 'Might be useful to get a look at our competition. Get close enough to work out who they are, but not close enough for a fight, understand?'

'Sir,' Samson said with a sly smile. 'I'll do my best.'

'And take Atkins with you.'

'Yes, sir.'

Samson carried on through. Lethbridge-Stewart listened. The front door opened and shut. If nothing else, one way of driving off spies was to let them know they'd been spotted. Even if Samson learned nothing, he could hope the mysterious watchers received the message they weren't wanted here.

Atkins felt like a lemon. Out on this lady's front step, on display for the tourists and natives passing by. To be fair, most paid him no mind. But a few looked at him like he was some kind of local feature. Maybe he should have been out there in a red coat and bearskin hat.

He sat on the step in an effort to look more casual. Colourful human traffic streamed by, paying him a bit less notice, chattering away and pointing out this or that. He quietly thanked them for their disregard.

Not two minutes later there was some guy among the steady to and fro. Not a tourist, or a local. He looked like a catalogue model without the camera-ready smiles. The sight of him had Atkins back on his feet. He clenched a fist, thinking about rapping discreetly on the door, alert the brigadier and the lady of the house.

Suddenly there was no need: the door opened and Sergeant Major Ware almost knocked Atkins off the step.

The suspect – because that was the only way to think of the guy – halted in his tracks. Swung around, ever so casual, and strolled back the way he'd come.

'Sergeant Major!' Atkins piped.

'I see him!' Ware pointed across the street and nudged Atkins in the direction of a side lane. 'Try and get ahead of him. Cut him off.'

Ware hopped off the step and hurried after the suspect.

Atkins sucked in a deep breath and ran for all he was worth.

*

'All right, *Señora*,' Lethbridge-Stewart said, 'I think, especially in light of the fact we appear to have drawn some attention, it might be time to pack a few things and fly back to Cyprus. We have a hired Land Rover parked on the outskirts of town.' Few streets in Fira were conducive to vehicles larger than motorcycles or scooters. 'I'll be happy to introduce you to our head of scientific research and you two can work together in—'

'I'm sure that will be very nice, Brigadier. Sooner or later. But I'm not sure you appreciate everything that needs to be done here.'

'Ah, yes, this auction. Am I to take it those items in your bucket are insufficient for research purposes?'

Señora Montilla pulled off her rubber gloves and went to the freezer. She reached in and retrieved a tub of ice cream. Vanilla. 'They might be a start. But yes, I am going to need more. A good deal more.'

Returning to the sink, she set the tub down, lifted out the bucket. She removed the lid from the tub and dumped the ice cream, wholesale, into the sink.

'Well, perhaps if you'd care to run the list by me, I will see what I can arrange,' Lethbridge-Stewart said.

'Perfect, yes, that will work for me.' *Señora* Montilla rummaged in the drawer for a spoon to scrape out the remnants, before proceeding to wash it out. 'This should suffice as a container. We can dispatch these artefacts to your scientist. Actually, I should like to keep the disc. The hieroglyphs make no sense to me and some further study might change that. Your scientist can have the Snake Goddess. But she must be kept in this same water—' she tapped the bucket '—and handled with gloves at all times. I will write some instructions. There, that is another item on the list. My photographs should be developed by now; I shall attach them along with some notes.'

She shut off the tap and inspected the tub's interior. Replacing her gloves, she set to work carefully transferring the figurine from the bucket and decanting some of the water.

'Number one, I am going to need a boat. And two, diving equipment.'

'I, ah, daresay those can be hired,' said Lethbridge-Stewart. 'You intend to go searching for more artefacts?'

'These examples are wonderful. As I told you, almost too

fine. But they lack context. Tell me, does your laboratory have equipment for radiocarbon dating?'

'I'm not sure.' Lethbridge-Stewart doubted it.

'Well, no matter. Because we have nothing you can radiocarbon date. We need other materials found at the same site. Wood, charcoal.'

'Won't wood have rotted?'

'If we find any, that too will need to be preserved in the same water. Besides, I want to see the condition of a site that can turn up treasures in such exceptional condition. Just in the remote case they have not been planted.' She finished up at the sink and sealed the lid on the tub. 'Item two, I have already said, we need to attend that auction.'

'Ah yes. What's the significance of this auction?'

'These treasures are being brought ashore and sold to a dealer who then auctions them to the highest bidder at private sales.'

'Private, I imagine, might be a key word there. One which could present difficulties.'

'Nonsense. They will let us in. I have a reputation and they would not bar an impassioned buyer. Especially one backed by funds of the British Government.'

'Well, probably best we don't advertise that. And obtaining these artefacts is absolutely necessary, is it?'

'Absolutely. For my research and to keep them out of the grubby hands of illegal traffickers.'

'*Señora*, my job is not to police—'

'These people are looters. The army shoots looters.'

'In times of martial law, yes, very likely. But I hardly think—'

'Brigadier, how invested are you in obtaining your answers? Hmm? I must ask because you don't appear very committed. Of course I am not asking you to shoot anyone. I am only asking you to accompany me to attend a local event. And loosen the government purse strings enough to ensure these treasures find their way to the right home. Believe me, if the other items auctioned are of remotely similar quality then their value is immeasurable. Much more so to those of us who know what we're handling and those of us who stand to learn from them. If it's a question of Bank of England funds, I am sure the Greek Government will reimburse you for items of such historical and cultural significance.' She flashed him a taunting gaze. 'Now, what do you say?'

What *could* he say?

*

Samson enjoyed a brisk walk, even in the heat. Got the adrenalin pumping and sharpened the senses. Easier to keep his target in his sights.

Added to which, the man in the suit stood out like a sore thumb. And made no real attempts to evade, seeming to enjoy leading Samson on the chase.

The man worked his way against the general flow of pedestrians, forging upriver like a salmon. Samson kept pace, following the same sort of steps like a good dance student. Difference was, the target brushed and bruised a few shoulders and didn't bat an eyelid. While Samson dodged out of folks' way and threw them an occasional 'excuse me' or 'pardon'.

Despite the civil approach, Samson was gaining yard by yard.

His man looked back above a babbling stream of heads and seemed to make the same deduction. He ramped up to a jog.

Samson side-stepped a couple of old women in black, apologised for a near-collision, and hugged the right of the street as he ran.

The target barged on through the middle lane. He shoved people aside. Grabbed one, then another and shoved them into others. Playing a rough game of dominoes. More than a few ended up face-down on the cobbles, jamming up the rest of the traffic in the narrow street.

Samson stuck to one side, hurdling doorsteps.

The target broke left, squeezed down a lane. Samson weaved his way across, dodging bodies and hopping over one of the fallen. The tourist looked red around the cheeks and mortally offended, otherwise unhurt. Samson sprinted along the alley. He vaulted a bin chucked in his path, then a trashed window box, a lot of spilled earth and flowers. Then burst out of the alley into a motor-scooter whining and bumping its way up the cobbled street. He steadied himself and saved the rider from a crash – just about. Thankful for his stuntman training, he searched up and down the hill for his target.

Spotted him diving down another lane. Raced after him.

No obstacle course left for him this time, but the alley was tight as hell and his shoulders clipped the walls.

He charged out into the next street, searched left and right.

First thing he saw: Atkins on the ground, curled up and clutching his gut.

Samson ran up, scanning past the downed private. For all its narrowness, like a picturesque trench, this looked like a main thoroughfare. A lot of bodies moving this way and that and clustered at café menus or the windows of souvenir shops.

Thankfully, Atkins was still moving. And groaning a lot. Samson stooped to pick him up. All the while, he scanned the street, taking stock of the milling people. None of them looked likely to topple a soldier of Her Majesty's Armed Forces.

'Blighter fetched me a right one, Sergeant Major,' Atkins complained, through pained breaths. 'Punched like he had a horseshoe in his glove.'

'Which way'd he go?'

Atkins gestured woozily up the street.

There, loitering at an alley corner, the big guy in a suit. The target even waved, showing off the gloves the *Señora* had described. He turned and disappeared down an alleyway. Giving Atkins a quick pat, Samson rushed on.

At the corner all he found was an alley with barely a trickle of pedestrians. A number of them stood still, as though recovering their breath from the heat. More likely from a muscle-bound thug ploughing rudely past. Samson picked out the complaining tone in a variety of languages.

'Sergeant Major?' called Atkins. 'Perhaps we'd best let this one go.'

Probably the right call, but it left a bad taste. Samson strolled back to the wobbly-looking Atkins. If these blokes were willing to take a crack at a soldier in broad daylight, then maybe it wasn't wise to go at them unprepared. Besides, whoever they were, they'd got what they were after. A good look at their opposition.

Samson assisted Atkins down the street, through *Señora* Montilla's front door and into her living room and a comfy chair. All the time hoping for another bout in the ring.

Vorster turned in the co-pilot's seat and looked back at his passengers. Sandwiched between soldiers in the rear section of the chopper, the two youngsters stared ahead, somehow avoiding eye contact despite the fact that they were seated opposite one another. Quite the feat.

Vorster tapped his headset mic. 'Horger. Can we fit our guests with headsets, please?'

'Right away, sir.'

Neither moved as Horger issued each with a pair of headphones. An accessory to help cut down on any extraneous noise. And hopefully leave them free to meditate on their condition.

Vorster continued to watch them.

The Italian was a bottle of pent-up aggression. Another half-hour of sustained vibration from the chopper engine might shake him up fit to explode. The girl was merely withdrawn. No man is an island, but it was a simple enough matter to isolate oneself even in a crowded room. Or under close guard in the back of a helicopter. Any prisoners might have adopted the same introverted silence, but Vorster recognised the symptoms. They were experiencing what he liked to think of as the incubation period. Not for the infection, no. But for the subjects. The individual retreated into itself, the personality withdrawing into some internal cocoon. And there would be no telling what nature of person – if any – would emerge. It was interesting to observe, especially in these two. The majority of his soldiers responded the same, leading to a reliable commonality in the results. Military training pared down the individualism, shaped the men into templates to some extent. These two revolutionaries reintroduced a degree of uncertainty into the experiment. At this stage, the only outward measurable effects were continued fear from the girl, belligerence and defiance from the boy, no different to the assessments Miss Van Den Haas had delivered post-interrogation. No different to what Vorster had witnessed for himself when he had paid each of them a visit. Curious, how their respective emotional states at the time of infection had seemed to lock into place. Set in stone.

He hoped not. Actual permanence of their current state would render them both useless. And that would necessitate disposal.

He turned back to gauge flight progress. The dials put them level at three hundred feet, with a lot of open water scrolling by below. A craft or two dotted the surface within his field of view. Islands were painted as indistinct smears, like daubs of watercolour on the horizon.

Probably sufficiently safe from potential witnesses to allow for dumping unwanted cargo. But there was already that question mark over one missing body. He didn't want any further loose ends floating about. No, if it came to disposal they would have to resort to more thorough methods. For now, there was still time for these two to turn into promising recruits.

All they required was a little inspiration. Something to coax them out of their shells. He would treat them to a pep talk.

Mr Vorster, sir.

The words were a thought, not his own. They didn't have a voice as such, but his mind gave them one. Hollis.

What is it? he sent back. And hoped his voice was as irritating as the interruption.

British Intelligence has operatives on the scene. They're talking to the Montilla woman. Likelihood is she'll want them to attend the auction. Bid against us or show some official red card and sequester the lot.

Damn. All right, so the interruption was unwelcome, but necessary.

He sieved through a rush of images. Someone else's stuttering slide-show projected on his memory, now slotted in alongside his own. *A flurry of push and shove through flocks of bleating pedestrians. Over-the-shoulder-glances at some sweating kaffer in pursuit. A fleeting contact with a freckle-faced youth, terminated with a punch to the gut. Other flashes:* Señora *Montilla, viewed through binoculars, feeding cats. The same kaffer reconnoitring the area from the poolside.* Hollis' assessment was probably on the money.

You felt the need to stir the nest? They know someone is watching them.

They've no way of knowing who, sir. There's no connection that can be traced back to you.

They have other backup on the scene?

Not as far as we can tell.

As far as you can tell? Well, they would have to come by air. So go as far as the airfield and check what planes are in residence.

Yes, Mr Vorster.

Then go wait for me at the mansion. If they are a small team, then they should be no more than a mosquito in our ears. Still, I fancy a change of plans is called for.

What's the play, sir?

CHAPTER NINE
Sea Devils

LUCY SAMUELS heard her children scream. She smiled.

She looked up from her book and searched the water's edge. It was busy, lots of tanned and pale bathers and paddlers competing for their slice of this sparkling band of blue, making the most of the unusual mid-November sun. But she could make out Chrissy and Felicity running up the beach with the foamy wash nipping at their heels. As the wave reached its limit, they whirled and danced and laughed, daring the sea to try harder. Then dashed back to splash in the shallows again.

She raised an arm, supplementing the shade provided by the brim of her sunhat. Watched them play a while.

Such a blessing to see them getting along so... well, swimmingly. Back in the hotel room or in the restaurant every evening they'd lurched from one squabble to the next, driving her spare. Chrissy was constantly teasing his little sister, but out here on the beach the two had found a common enemy in the sea. Kicking about in it and taunting when it gave chase.

Well, good. Their cries and screams were a kind of peace, as long as they were followed by laughter.

Lucy adjusted the tilt of her sunhat, then flattened a rebellious page of her Mills & Boon and returned to her reading.

The romantic clinch between hero and heroine was ruined by a loud snore from the deckchair beside her. She rolled her eyes and glanced at her husband. Vince had dozed off, the newspaper like a collapsed tent over his head, hairy chest and beer belly browning in the sun, limbs hanging over the sides of the chair. Not a holiday picture she wanted to take home and show off to her friends.

She laughed. Then laughed some more as she read on and the novel's next paragraph waxed lyrically about the hero's muscular torso. And went on to present hot and sweaty as something appealing and desirable. She had to hand it to the writer for that. Quite the gift.

Even so, she fancied a break from the escapism. Crimping the corner of the page, she set the book down in the sand and reached for the Thermos. Poured herself some of the iced orange juice she'd brought as an alternative to the beers Vince had packed into the cooler. One of them had to keep a clear head to play parent. That much was the same each year, wherever they ended up: yes, it was their family holiday, but Vince was always more on holiday than her.

Never mind. She wasn't going to say anything. The kids weren't the only ones who needed a break from bickering.

Peace was worth a lightly bitten tongue.

Lucy sipped her juice. She tipped her head back and closed her eyes. Drew her knees up and rested with the cup cradled in her lap. With a little focus, she filtered out the rest of the beach sounds and listened to the shushing sea and her children's screams. Screams which broke apart in giggles like the wave breaking as it rode up the sands.

Beautiful.

Vince snorted like a pig. Lucy stifled a laugh and ended up snorting herself.

Her kids screamed again.

She smiled, waiting for the giggles.

The giggles never came. The screams spread.

Lucy sat up. The whole beach was screaming. People ran from the water.

She jumped out of the deckchair, knocked her cup flying. Searched for Chrissy and Felicity. She couldn't see them, couldn't pick them out from the scattering mob.

'Oh my god, oh my god! Vince! The kids!'

She didn't wait. She raced for the water.

The only one running that way, she sprinted against a tide of people. Searching and searching, knots in her gut, head in a spin. As the crowd rushed past, it thinned. She was alone in open beach and...

There! Chrissy and Felicity running to meet her. Chrissy tugged Felicity along, pulling her arm so hard she was crying. She stumbled but Chrissy didn't let go, hauling his sister after him.

Lucy somehow closed the last few yards between them before her legs gave out. She dropped to her knees, wrapped her children in a huge embrace. Sobbed her heart out as she checked them over.

'Oh my god, what is it? Are you okay? Are you both okay?'

They screeched and wailed. Something about something in the water.

Lucy hugged them close, fighting to calm them. Vince trotted up and knelt beside them, laying a big arm across Lucy's shoulder.

'What is it? What the hell's going on?'

Lucy peered past her crying, trembling children to the shoreline.

The sea had emptied of people. But bodies, dark shapes, wallowed and writhed in the lapping shallows.

'What is that? Sharks?'

Sharks? No fins sliced the waves.

Lucy found the will to stand. Rising, shaking, she shepherded her kids around behind her and backed up the beach. Vince scooped up Felicity. All around the beach was a riot of noise and motion, families clustering together, some rescuing a few belongings amid the stampede.

Lucy held onto Chrissy and retreated slowly.

The things in the water crawled. Heads broke the surface. Limbs reached and plunged and pulled bodies through the washing shallows. Like sluggish swimmers. Except swimmers would have stood to wade ashore.

Lucy quickened her pace. Vince hastened alongside her. He passed, kicking up clouds of sand. He made for the deckchairs, dipping, with Felicity in one arm, to gather their stuff – flask, book, towels, even the paper – and chuck it all into their bags.

'What are you doing?' she yelled at him, catching up. 'Leave it! Forget all that!'

She looked back to the sea.

The shapes emerged as figures, the dregs of a wave swilling about. They dug hands in the damp sand and dragged themselves forward on their fronts as though weighted with fatigue. With a painful lethargy they rose to hands and knees. Human in shape alone.

Their heads lifted. Lucy saw no eyes in the faces, only shadowy pits, depressions under their brows like gouged stone. But it seemed like they looked at her and through her.

Lucy pressed Chrissy close and spun and ran. He screeched and sobbed into her hair and held on tight. His wails were drawn out and pained, the same sounds over and over. On the third or fourth repeat, she made out the words.

'It touched me, Mummy! It touched me!'

For her baby's sake, Lucy trapped a scream in her throat. Forced herself to make soothing noises into his hair. Behind her, the stone heads turned and scanned with hollow gazes watching the fleeing crowds. Like a pack of predators picking their choice of prey from the herd. One by one they raised themselves to stand. Until ten or twelve granite statues of men lined the shore. Weed or rags of tattered fabric – something – hung from their crude-carved forms.

Beyond, in the water, more shapes crawled their way towards the beach.

'Everything set?'

Vorster wandered to the window and inspected the row of BMWs parked in the grounds. A couple of the men were out there stowing large plastic containers in the back seats. Breakages weren't going to be a factor, but even so he wanted one man sitting guard on each box. Hell, he should have had them nest on them like mother hens.

He turned. The rest of the team were taking up space in his lounge. Cleaning and maintaining weapons or standing over the sideboard, going over the sketched layout of the villa.

Only two figures were conspicuous in their inactivity.

Miss Loukas and Mr Menozzi, seated together – and yet far apart – on the couch. A study in motionlessness. As withdrawn as on the flight and on the ride over from the airfield.

Vorster had seen the RAF plane for himself, sitting with its nose towards the terminal building. A six or seven-seater, just as Hollis and Fyler had reported. The pilot had been there, kicking his heels in the hall as Vorster's party had passed through. The British Intelligence team would be notified, but the plane's size confirmed a small group of operatives.

Mosquitoes, just as he'd hoped.

'Our two virgins strike me as a touch nervous.' Vorster glanced at his watch. 'Maybe we have time for that pep talk. Everybody shut up.'

Hollis made a cutthroat gesture at the others. They quit what they were doing and sat or stood perfectly still.

Vorster sauntered to the coffee table and stationed himself in front of his two star guests. They looked distant, several kinds of elsewhere just now, but they would see him sooner or later.

'Will,' he advised them. 'Willpower is the key.'

Willpower is the key.

The voice reached for Kara across a vast rift. Like when she'd been on the helicopter that had carried them here, with the engine drilling into her brain, its noise muffled by headphones which had rested like a lead weight on her head. All sound, all noise, had come from afar, and now Vorster's poisonous voice seemed to slither forth from the same place. Far away.

But not so distant as emotion. Her thoughts mined for veins of feeling within her, but if they were there at all they were buried in some pit. Lost.

Assertion of self.

Kara turned her head left and saw Paolo. He seemed to float around the edge of her vision, even when she tried to look directly at him.

It was like battling through some wall of amnesia. But no, there was no trouble remembering. Recognition was automatic. But there was no sense of the person that came hand in hand with the memory. She could no longer *see* Paolo.

She wanted to cry for her loss. She wanted to scream, to wake herself from the nightmare. She wanted Paolo to reach over and grab her and shake her back to life.

She leaned towards him, seized by the impulse to shake him. But her head swam. And when she looked down at her knees she hadn't budged. She'd only bent at the waist, leaned less than an inch closer. And left herself feeling even further away.

She saw the men positioned around the room, she saw the guns. They didn't scare her. They made no impression. They were less than background.

Forget others and what they mean. This has nothing to do with anything outside of you. This is all about you.

Theo. Kara pictured Theo. Saw him die again. And felt nothing.

It all comes down to who you are. You feel isolated. Use that. Who are you in isolation? Who are you without all those ties and connections that tether you to this world?

Owain. Kara pictured Owain.

There was only a portrait and numbness. Many portraits, images of him she'd caught in different lights that she'd filed away without thinking. She'd been sweet on him. She knew that. Not that he would ever be sweet on her in return. She knew that too; had seen the signs. He'd been kind and gentlemanly. She recalled his kindnesses, the smiles, the laughs, the energy and passion with which he'd enthused over the briefly shared touches, the moments of deep quiet when he'd sat nearby, mulling over a beer, not a word to say but somehow at his most alive. When she'd watched him one stolen glance at a time and would have paid a small fortune to hear one of his thoughts. All of that, every strand, every fragment of what had drawn her to him was there, recorded in her mind. But the memories were recited back at her like a string of facts. Just as with Paolo, there was no sense of person. There was no sense of Owain.

Up to this point, your lives might have been comprised of any number of people. They might have contributed to your manufacture. But even if you allowed them to shape you, none of that matters. They no longer have any part to play in who you are. You're alone and they can't help you.

Kara glanced down at her sleeve. Her hand shot to her cuff. Her fingers fiddled with the button.

Her arm itched. She imagined an army of ants crawling up and down her skin, nipping at her cells and carrying them away like crumbs. Her fingers snatched away from the button and curled, set to scratch.

Forget fighting. The trick for both of you will be to know that you can surrender and emerge on the other side.

Kara remembered Vorster's grip. A clamp of granite around her wrist. Her arm trapped, unable to move. Her heart much the same, squeezed by fear. Her screams filling the cabin.

She tried to dredge up a scream now. But her throat was deadened. And she knew that even if she found a scream it would be a distant noise. Like the helicopter engine, like Vorster's instruction.

You can allow this to shape you. Or you can shape it to your will.

Kara couldn't even feel afraid any more. She wished she could.

It seeps into you, through you. Takes root in your bones. The marrow. It's excellent at mastering structure, but not mechanisms so much. Even simple ones. Joints, for example, it can find those tricky. If you don't take control, guide it, it will run its course, eat you away. Those joints will break down and leave you crawling in the dirt. But that's nothing to the complexities of the nervous system. Trust me; it won't manage to navigate that without your help. You won't be able to stop the change. Don't waste concentration trying. All you can do – for yourselves – is make sure you're still resident once the conversion has run its course.

Kara nodded. She didn't want to, but she understood.

Somewhere on the edge of her world Paolo nodded too.

'Good.' Vorster clapped. 'Now, take a couple of minutes, then I want you to go with Hollis here and get yourselves dressed. There's something I want you to do for me and it's important you look the part.'

Hollis approached, leaned in for a murmur. 'Are you sure they're ready for this, boss? They're just kids.'

He sounded a bit sour at having drawn wardrobe duties. Serves him right for pulling that stunt at the archaeologist's house.

'We're all children at some point,' Vorster said. 'Then we learn to walk on our own two feet. All too soon we're exercising our own initiative, not even looking to our parents for permission or approval.' He served that to Hollis with a barbed smile. 'This is how they learn. They'll do the job, or they won't. And if they don't, then you get to put them down.'

Hollis brightened a little at that prospect.

Vorster patted the man on his arm. 'Don't say I never give you anything.'

CHAPTER TEN
A Battle of Wits

FIRST STOP, the airfield.

They found Flight Lieutenant Chapman ready and waiting inside the very basic and ramshackle terminal building, and to the chap's credit he didn't bat an eyelid as *Señora* Montilla handed over the ice cream tub. She laid her notes and photographs atop the lid.

Lethbridge-Stewart had told her that she could wait in the car, but she insisted on delivering the relics herself.

'Try to avoid any turbulence or aerobatics,' she told Chapman.

'I'm sure I'll find some way to secure the package on board, Madam.'

'*Señora*.'

'Just see to it the contents reach Miss Travers safely, would you, Flight Lieutenant?' said Lethbridge-Stewart.

'Yes, sir.' Chapman half-turned to go, then stopped. 'Sir, I think you ought to know, a VTMB chopper arrived a while ago.' The possible significance was not lost on Lethbridge-Stewart. 'The bird's still out there on the apron. Quite the cavalcade turned up to collect the men on board. Can't say I cared for the looks some of them gave me as they came through.'

'Thank you, Flight Lieutenant. Safe flight.'

'Sir.'

Troubled, but keeping his thoughts to himself, Lethbridge-Stewart walked with *Señora* Montilla back to the car.

Bad memories.

Owain struggled to shake them off as he sat in the inflatable and waited out the boat ride to shore. This time he wasn't up front playing observer and much of his view was obscured by the broad backs of soldiers – or *oceanographic researchers* – including Grigoriy and his faithful sidekick, Oleg. Owain was grateful for being dropped off but he could've wished the boat wasn't so similar to the Zodiac. The outboard growled and nobody said a word. Which left Owain alone in his own head.

Along with those memories.

Kara, Paolo. Theo. All came to haunt him again, just like the face of his dead twin, Lewis, often did. He couldn't lose more people.

He told himself they weren't ghosts. They were alive and on that rig. Had to be.

Grigoriy's attention was fixed ahead. The captain – like all his men – was dressed like an average, everyday fisherman: oilskin jacket, chunky pullover, thick enough to hide the pistol he'd stuck in his belt. Crazy, thought Owain, how he'd ended up with this lot. Sure they were just a bunch of guys at the end of the day – and enough of them had been friendly, hospitable even – but he couldn't get past the sense that they were also hardened killers. On the one hand, he couldn't help wishing he'd had them with him on the Zodiac. On the other, they were another reason he was going to be glad to get out of this boat.

A blue-hulled liner walled off any view to port and did a good job of dwarfing him. Until the launch passed the ship's bow and opened up a full view across the caldera. Centrepiece to the ring of islands was a pair of sprawling rocky mounds. Heavily pitted, gouged and scarred, the nearest resembled a heap of coal and ash with a giant bite taken out of its side. That, more than anything, was a major reminder that they were inside a volcano. A premium choice of base for villains, if not for all the sea water.

Forward, past Grigoriy, the world showed Owain a swaying, bouncing panorama of high cliffs, glimpsed between several shoulders. A town nested all along the clifftop. Picturesque white houses, like decorative barnacles clinging to the island's coast in one expansive cluster. Bright blue domes and golden-crossed church towers dotted the colony of white here and there.

The boat slipped in towards wooden jetties, finding a berth among a few ferries and passenger launches belonging to the liners in the bay. Their arrival drew a little attention from other crews and bystanders, as well as the tourists sipping drinks at sun-shaded tables fronting the waterside cafes.

Grigoriy hopped onto the jetty. As did Oleg, who quickly looped a rope around an available post. And another of the men who reached back and helped Owain out. Owain thanked the guy, but got no reply. Taciturn lot, many of these Russians. As though a simple 'you're welcome' might contravene some official secrets act.

'Okay, thanks for the lift. What will you do? Wait here while I–'

'Lead the way,' Grigoriy ordered. 'I'm coming with you.'

He shared a string of Russian with Oleg then turned, ready to follow Owain. Except Owain hadn't started leading yet.

'You, ah, want to catch a ride? It's a bit of a climb.'

'Pah. It's not exactly Everest.'

Owain was sure Grigoriy did assault courses in his sleep, but even so he wondered if the captain knew what he was letting himself in for. The trek had taken its toll on Owain the first and only time he'd made it. A steep, zigzagging donkey path in skin-roasting heat. And Kara refused to ride a donkey, not wanting to burden one of the animals even with her negligible weight.

It wasn't quite so baking today, but he didn't fancy it, especially on legs still wobbly from too long off dry land. Still, he kept his reluctance to himself and headed up from the harbour.

This time of day a few donkeys were already plying the route, guided by their handlers as they bore sun-hatted tourists up the hill. Owain and Grigoriy wove easily enough between them. A lot of straw and dung lay trampled between the cobbles. The stones were hard on the soles of Owain's feet and his thigh muscles started their complaints before they were a third of the way up. Annoyingly, Grigoriy appeared unbothered.

Owain barely had breath to speak by the time they crested the final step and emerged in the warrens of Fira's streets. The closely huddled buildings afforded some shade at least and Owain flapped a hand in front of his face to help the cooling off.

He led Grigoriy past a bakery with a window display that was a treasure trove of sugary treats. Dismissing his sudden hunger pangs, he took the next left into a short alleyway almost blocked by bins and someone's parked motor scooter. Breaking out into the next narrow street, he singled out one of the houses a short way down the terrace. White and flat-roofed like any other, but Owain remembered it.

'That's the place.'

Broad daylight, so there were no lights to indicate whether anyone was home. Owain glanced warily at Grigoriy as he approached the front step.

'Wait. You're not planning anything nasty, are you?' Owain asked.

'Nasty? Like?'

'I don't know. We're only here to ask her some questions about archaeology. Use her phone.'

'I understand that. What do you take me for?'

Owain shrugged. 'Sorry.'

He knocked on the door.

Nothing. After a while, a man's voice piped up. 'Who is it?'

'Seems she already has visitors,' Grigoriy muttered.

Owain spoke to the door. 'Owain Vine. I was here before. A friend of *Señora* Montilla.' The *Señora* would probably have said that was overstating the case. 'Sort of,' he added. 'We need to speak with her.'

Another pause. Then the rattle of a door handle and Owain was greeted by the sight of a lad not much older than him. Cropped ginger hair, an unfortunate set of freckles that made him look fresh out of school, but after registering Owain his eyes latched onto Grigoriy with a measure of suspicion.

'Vine, is it? The brigadier's nephew? Who's this?'

'He's...' Owain plucked a lie out of those that sprang to mind. 'He's a concerned environmentalist, like me. We wanted to see the *Señora*, consult with her on something. And you would be?'

'Atkins. Private Atkins.'

'Right. So is my uncle about?'

If Uncle Alistair was here in person, that could make arranging a useful meeting a heck of a lot more straightforward. They couldn't be that lucky, surely.

'He is,' said Atkins slowly. 'Some villa, not far, I don't think.

They're auctioning relics. I'm on house-sitting duties. Her Majesty wants me to feed the cats, can you believe?'

'Excuse me? Her Majesty?'

'*Señora* Whatsherface.' Oh yeah, Owain recalled she had a thing for cats. Putting food out for strays in her yard while he and Kara and Paolo had tried to talk to her. 'Thing is, I'd say you could wait here. But I'm not sure I should let you in.' A puzzled frown played over his face. 'And I don't think the brigadier would thank me for calling him on the radio. They're supposed to be under cover.'

'It's all right. Don't trouble yourself, soldier,' said Grigoriy. His English had lost all but the faintest trace of accent. 'We'll attend the auction ourselves. Where is the auction? The address?'

'Agia Irinni. Some villa. Can't remember exactly.'

'We'll find it. Thank you.'

'Hold up, I'm not sure you should–'

Grigoriy had turned and was already headed down the street. Owain nodded to the soldier by way of apology and hurried after the captain. 'We will? Find it, I mean?'

'Sure. Fira is not a big place. Agia Irinni is one street and it will be the villa with the most cars parked out front.'

After a fifteen-minute drive, Lethbridge-Stewart pulled in and parked the car behind six others queued on the driveway. The premium spaces, around an ornamental fountain, were already taken. The villa's front entrance lay under an over-elaborate portico with ionic columns, a doubtless expensive architectural feature that nonetheless resembled a cheap Parthenon. It waited a short walk away, through a garden of clipped shrubbery and the occasional bit of classical statuary.

Señora Montilla strode ahead, leaving him feeling rather like a chauffeur or some other servant. A guard in a shiny grey suit stopped them by the small circle of cars ringing the fountain. Lethbridge-Stewart handed him the car keys.

The guard scowled, apparently displeased to be appointed as valet. 'Name?'

'Sophia Montilla. Plus guest.'

The man tilted his head like an owl that had heard some small prey rustling in the bushes. 'I'm not sure…'

'Not sure I have an invitation? Oh, I don't. But I'm here with a guest and lots of money and a profound and heartfelt interest in archaeology. How many of the people on your invitation list can make that claim, hmm?'

'Madam...'

'*Señora.*'

The opportunity to observe someone else getting the *Señora* treatment was something of a treat. Still, Lethbridge-Stewart wondered how far, realistically, such bluster might get them.

Another guard sauntered over. He loitered several paces off, hands on hips as though casually interested, but plainly primed to intervene if trouble developed. Lethbridge-Stewart noticed the brown straps of a shoulder holster under the fellow's jacket.

'*Señora,*' the first guard corrected himself.

She cut him off simply by pointing a loaded finger. 'I tell you what, why don't you go clear this up with your boss. If he has lived on Santorini any length of time and has any interest in historical treasures he will know who I am. Actual acquaintance seems unlikely, but by reputation at least.' She glanced up at sunny skies and inhaled the lightly toasted air. 'It's a beautiful day, but my gentleman friend is perspiring and I'm willing to bet it's cooler inside. We'll wait in there.'

She strode past the guard and Lethbridge-Stewart threw him an almost apologetic look as he followed her. The man scowled, left holding the car keys. He tossed the keys to his colleague, appointing him valet, and chased *Señora* Montilla and Lethbridge-Stewart into a hall of white walls and beige ceramic tile.

He caught up and waved them to a halt. 'Search,' he informed them. 'I must insist.'

Lethbridge-Stewart sighed and lifted his arms. The guard attended to a brisk pat down. Finished with Lethbridge-Stewart, he moved to face *Señora* Montilla. She met his look, inviting a staring contest.

'Please, *Señora*. Your bag at least.'

She slipped her shoulder bag off, handed it over. He popped the clasp and hurriedly sifted through the contents. He returned the bag and appeared slightly pained as *Señora* Montilla snapped it closed.

'Left. Through there,' he gestured. 'You may wait with the other guests for now, but do not be surprised when I return to escort you out.'

He veered down the passage to the right.

Señora Montilla flashed a half-smile. 'More hostility than hospitality, wouldn't you say?'

'I can't say I altogether blame him,' Lethbridge-Stewart allowed. 'But nicely done, all the same.'

'A great part of my career was built on not taking no for an answer.'

They ducked under a low arch, down a single step into a spacious semi-circle of lounge. The room was fronted on one side by an arc of patio window looking out onto a veranda. Beyond the balcony lay the perfect panorama: sunlit bay, a trio of anchored liners dotted about the caldera and the other islands curving around the backdrop, screened through a concave lens of haze. A small boat blazed a thin white trail across the sparkling blue between the liners.

Tables had been set out on the veranda, arrayed with objects currently veiled in cloths. Presumably the items for today's sale. Despite the presence of other guests, the view remained largely unobstructed.

Around a room of more white walls and beige tile, a dozen or so people were sparsely distributed, primarily in pairs. One man sat alone on the couch, sipping at a tumbler of Scotch, and a single group of three – two women, one man – clustered before an abstract and garish painting, conversing in murmurs while casting furtive but rather obvious glances everywhere. For a party, there appeared to be very little mingling going on.

The only individuals circulating were two waiters, one with several champagne flutes on a silver tray, the other with a platter of *hors d'ouvres* balanced on one hand. They flitted from group to group like bees pollinating flowers.

'Honestly. And I thought academic circles were bad,' *Señora* Montilla remarked.

'I beg your pardon?'

'Look at these women. All dolled up in jewellery just so they can adorn some man's arm.'

Lethbridge-Stewart noticed a lot of jewellery – on the men and the women. He also observed a profusion of low necklines and overcooked tans, as well as expensive suits and rather aloof gazes.

'I see. Well, perhaps feminism hasn't been embraced by the criminal fraternity or the art world – or whatever sector of society these people represent – but please, can we save emancipation of these women until after our business is concluded?'

'You would say that. How is the military on gender equality these days?'

Lethbridge-Stewart scrutinised *Señora* Montilla until, eventually, her very serious expression folded into a smile. Assuming they encountered no graver dangers, he was sure her sense of humour would be the death of him.

The waiter bearing nibbles swanned by and *Señora* Montilla liberated a petite snack from the selection and popped it in her mouth.

Lethbridge-Stewart looked around for the guard, expecting him to reappear and make good on his promise to show them the exit. So far, no sign.

'Assuming we are permitted to stay, the fact that nobody is mingling should work in our favour,' he noted. 'I suggest we maintain our distance – like everybody else – keep a low profile and just get on with the business of bidding whenever this auction decides to start.'

'Right. Agreed.' *Señora* Montilla clicked her fingers. '*Garçon.*'

The champagne waiter answered her summons and she helped herself to a flute from his tray. While she took a swig and swilled it around like a wine-taster, the chap presented the tray to Lethbridge-Stewart.

'No, thank you.'

Señora Montilla swallowed, then made a face. 'I don't blame you,' she said. 'Cheap stuff.'

Lethbridge-Stewart slow-blinked to cover a roll of the eyes. At least she had refrained from spitting into the glass, he supposed.

'May I fetch you some alternative? Mr Stathopoulos keeps a well-stocked bar and an excellent wine cellar,' the waiter said.

'No, thank you,' said Lethbridge-Stewart again.

Señora Montilla replanted her glass on the tray. 'Scotch.

On the rocks.'

The lone man on the sofa appeared to be savouring his drink, so there was some chance the Scotch would meet the *Señora's* standards. The waiter bowed his head and scuttled away.

'Is the drink absolutely necessary?'

'You might be on duty, Brigadier. I'm not. Besides, it will help calm the nerves.'

'You? Nervous? *Señora*, if I'm ever granted the opportunity to meet you when you're fearless, remind me to come armed.'

'Like some of the household staff here?'

So, she had glimpsed the shoulder holsters under the jackets too. Lethbridge-Stewart nodded. *Señora* Montilla opened her mouth to answer but clammed up under a smile as the waiter returned with her drink. She accepted it graciously and gave the glass a swirl, jingling the ice cubes until the waiter had wandered out of earshot.

'I guess my two followers rattled me more than I would like to admit,' she confessed. 'There was something professional – soldierly – about them. The guards here are probably from a sloppier outfit. But I don't doubt this lot would turn just as nasty if they choose to take exception to a couple of unwelcome guests.'

'Yes, well, that chap we managed to offend has been gone a while. I think we might interpret that as an encouraging sign.'

'Maybe.'

'Quite. Well, let's keep our wits about us, shall we?'

Señora Montilla raised her glass. 'I'll drink to that.' She knocked it back.

The guard – their guard – came through the arch, but he flicked them a sour glance. *Señora* Montilla tilted her glass towards him, a toast he ignored. Another man swaggered in after him, spreading his arms and a beaming grin almost as wide. Generally making a big entrance.

'Ladies, gentlemen, welcome, welcome.'

The host, Lethbridge-Stewart concluded.

Dark hair with salted sideburns, a moustache with considerable volume, pale suit and a black shirt open to expose an expanse of swarthy chest. Two young women followed close behind like maidservants in attendance. They wore their hair up and were robed in fine gowns not unlike togas.

He bowed. 'Allow me to introduce myself. I am Vadik Stathopoulos. We are here to conduct business, of course, but do not let that detract from your comfort in any way. Please, make yourselves at home. Eat, drink, and we shall get to the sale in due course.' He clapped his hands, apparently happy with his little speech. 'I believe we only await one more guest.'

Done with the spotlight for the time being, he donned an unsavoury expression and swaggered breezily in their direction, blowing straight at them like one of those ill winds spoken of in proverbs.

Lethbridge-Stewart braced for trouble. The man smiled, showing too many perfect teeth. The guard lurked behind his boss, with the two attendant girlfriends.

'Sophia Montilla.' The host spread the words like the butter that wouldn't melt in his mouth. He proffered a hand.

'See, I told your man you would have heard of me.'

'The whole island knows of you, *Señora*.'

At least he addressed her right first time, Lethbridge-Stewart thought. He really was too smooth.

'And who is your gentleman friend?'

'He's with the authorities.'

Had Lethbridge-Stewart been drinking, he imagined he would have sprayed his beverage everywhere. As it was, their host's smile died instantly. But in the ensuing – and deathly – quiet, it slowly re-emerged. He laughed and wagged a finger.

'You joke. I will allow you that much, *Señora*, but it is a dangerous game. I am not in the best of spirits. You see, a little bird told me – no, I believe it was actually a fisherman from Vlychada – that you acquired a number of items ahead of today's auction.'

'Yes, I like to buy at the harbourside. That way I get the pick of the day's catch and I can be sure the goods are as fresh as possible.'

Lethbridge-Stewart kept an eye on the guard.

'But by doing this you cut out the middle man,' Stathopoulos argued. He laid a hand on his chest, in a pitiful show of inviting sympathy. 'And I am the middle man. By all rights, I should have you and your "authority" friend thrown out.'

'How will that look?'

'You are right, *Señora*. Appearances are important. So, I will tell you what I will do. As a sign that I bear no grudges, I will allow you to attend and bid to your heart's content. But you must understand I am a man of business, any of your winning bids I will mark up by ten percent. Consider it the price of admission.'

'Smug, but fair.'

Stathopoulos fumed like a matador outplayed by the bull. His hand shot up, actually set to slap *Señora* Montilla. She stood and maintained her smile like a dare. In other circumstances, she might have stuck out her tongue.

A second guard nudged in between the girlfriends and muttered in the host's ear. Lethbridge-Stewart, despite being so near, managed to catch few words. And they were, as the saying went, all Greek to him.

Stathopoulos turned and clapped loudly, back to playing the showman for the benefit of his audience. 'Aha!'

Two further guests appeared in the arch. A young man, Latin complexion, smooth waves of dark hair, accompanied by a petite young girl with soft-tanned features and a head of brown ringlets. They were dressed in suitable finery – blue gown and pearls for the girl, tux for the gentleman. They surveyed the room without a smile, not even for their grinning over-friendly host. Something else, possibly their youth, made them look out of place in this gathering.

Señora Montilla twitched oddly. She sipped at what was left of her drink. Which was mostly slow-melting ice.

'Welcome! Welcome. Everyone is here. We can soon begin!' The host, with his entourage in tow, moved to greet the newcomers.

'Something wrong?' Lethbridge-Stewart asked *Señora* Montilla.

She gave a facial shrug. 'No. No. Unexpected, that's all. I've met those two before. They're friends of your friend.'

'My friend?'

'The young man. Owain. I have no idea why this auction would interest them.'

Indeed, Lethbridge-Stewart thought. *Neither do I.*

CHAPTER ELEVEN
Massacre

'HELLO,' SAMSON murmured. 'Who've we got here?'
A quartet of BMWs pulled up at the villa's gate, parked in a neat row. There was too much sun on the windscreens. From his position along the street there was no clear shot of the figures inside.

Until now, only the one car – a sleek Mercedes – had slipped in behind Alistair's car. Now that – along with the other guest vehicles – was effectively blocked in. The couple who'd stepped out of the Merc – kids, pretty much, from what Samson had been able to make out between the railings that topped the villa's garden wall – weren't going to be happy when it came to leaving time.

Something about the BMWs smelled bad. Turned his scalp prickly.

Nobody emerged. They did nothing.

Just sat there, asking for a ticket.

'You're certain it's them?'

Lethbridge-Stewart eyed the two youngsters circumnavigating the room. Where intervening people permitted, they adhered to the edges like a pair of spiders hugging the skirting board. Behaviour that might have been attributed to nervousness, but they weren't sizing up the other guests with stolen glances the way shy types might when confronted with a room full of strangers. They paid the other guests no heed, orbiting within their own private world. The girl wore elegant gloves that reached to the elbow, quite in keeping with her gown, but the fact that the boy also wore gloves struck as odd.

'Of course I'm certain,' said *Señora* Montilla. 'I only met them the once, but it was a matter of days ago. Kara and Paolo. Kara Loukas. I forget the Italian boy's surname.'

Lethbridge-Stewart recalled the names from Owain's notes. He wondered how closely associated they were with the lad's activities and how recently they might have last seen him.

'Hmm. I should go talk to them. See if I can get an update on Owain's whereabouts.'

'Good idea. I'll handle the auction side of things, shall I?'

'Well, I trust you know what you're shopping for.' A faintly wicked glint in the *Señora*'s eye gave Lethbridge-Stewart pause. 'Although do try not to spend the entire gold reserve of Her Majesty's Government, won't you?'

'I will do my best to bid conservatively. You may rely upon me.' She plonked her glass on the tray of a passing waiter, not seeming to care that it was in fact the half-empty platter of *hors d'oeuvres*. 'At the same time, it is fair to warn you I do not intend to allow a single one of these historic artefacts into the paws of these scavengers.'

Lethbridge-Stewart cleared his throat. He had not helped himself to the refreshments provided, but felt like a diner expecting to be hit with an exorbitant bill.

'Please, just... exercise discretion.'

Señora Montilla smiled. It was bright and not encouraging.

Lethbridge-Stewart eased away and navigated an intercept course, strolling at a pace designed to head off the two youngsters near the veranda window.

Movement.

BMW doors swung open. Samson tensed.

Men climbed out either side. All of them on the heavy-set side, two from each vehicle. One man from each pair reached in the back of their respective cars and fetched out a box. Some kind of plastic storage container. Drivers and maybe other passengers remained inside. Hard to tell. Bulges, nothing to do with muscle, bulked out every man's jacket.

They pulled on balaclavas.

'Oh, hell no.'

Lethbridge-Stewart interposed himself between the youngsters and the veranda. They regarded him like a wall suddenly erected in their way. He frowned but did his best not to let their stares unnerve him. He thrust out a hand. 'How d' you do? Miss Loukas. Kara... and Paolo, isn't it?'

Neither noticed the dangling handshake.

No, Lethbridge-Stewart thought. *Definitely something not right with these two*. The hairs on the back of his neck stood to attention. Memories of the possessed walking over various graves, so to speak. Subjects of the Intelligence – poor Arnold, for example – returned to mind. And yet that man had appeared so normal while under that malign influence. These two, well, they sort of hung in place like puppets awaiting the pull of strings.

What could they be doing here? Chasing up leads in Owain's crusade? If so, where was Owain?

'Please, please. Clear the way.'

Stathopoulos swept in, motioning everyone aside. Lethbridge-Stewart backed up, but the youngsters remained fixed in place.

'Please, please,' repeated Stathopoulos. He beckoned two guards up, one either side of him. 'I will open up the veranda and viewing can commence. I am sure every one of you will find something to your—'

The tiny girl turned and reached up. She clamped a gloved hand around the host's throat and snapped his neck. The boy, Paolo, grabbed for Lethbridge-Stewart.

Move.

Vorster. In his head like a talking migraine.

Hollis obeyed, leading his party through the gateway and slipping the weapon from its sling.

The guard out front turned his head, clocked the balaclava, the gun, the whole group marching up his driveway. He dipped a hand inside his jacket – and died in that pose, with a hole in his forehead. Gun to the shoulder, Hollis swung the weapon to meet a second guard rushing around from the far end of the line of cars. Popped a whispered bullet in the man's skull. He dropped on the patch of lawn near the front path.

Hollis waved his party onward. Fyler and Horger muscled up and booted in the front door.

'Knock knock,' Fyler said.

They barged in, sweeping left and right with suppressor-fattened barrels. He followed and waved in the men carrying boxes.

'Hold here. We'll clear the place.'

He left them waiting in the hall. So far, so clockwork. Hollis hoped it kept ticking that way. He could do without more commands from the boss giving him headaches.

Samson drew his pistol. Hesitated, wondering what play to make.

A man stepped out of the lead BMW, whipped out a submachinegun. A nasty-looking piece of artillery with a silencer. It helped Samson make up his mind.

He dashed to the wall. Strafing bullets chased him across the road. He squeezed off a token return shot. The gunman hunkered down by the BMW's wheel arch, fired a wild burst. Samson grabbed the railings, hauled himself up and over. He dropped into the villa's garden.

Guns. Damn, he knew they should have brought the serious guns. A sidearm wasn't going to cut it against SMGs.

In the face of superior firepower, improvise.

Ducking, he scrambled from cover to cover, used the bushes. Trouble was, at least one of the bad guys knew he was there.

Lethbridge-Stewart back-peddled out of the Italian boy's reach.

The guests screamed and pressed themselves to the walls or ran as Stathopoulos flopped to the tiles, dead. The host's guards moved on the girl. The lone drinker dived from his place on the sofa and belly-flopped on the glass coffee table.

One guard laid a hand on Kara's shoulder, the other pulled a pistol. A gunshot cracked loud. Somewhere outside.

Lethbridge-Stewart had no more time to think about that. Paolo lunged at him. He tried to dodge, but the Italian shifted course and ploughed hard into him. Shoved him over, smashing into the window. Lethbridge-Stewart flew through a shower of glass and landed smack on his back on the veranda. The boy sailed down on top of him.

Lethbridge-Stewart rolled aside and kicked away.

Across the room, amid a tide of guests rushing for the archway, *Señora* Montilla froze, looking his way.

Lethbridge-Stewart waved at her. 'Go! Get out of here!'

*

A lot of milling, panicked people made the room feel really crowded. The petite Greek girl knocked a handgun from a guard's grip and jabbed another guard in the stomach, doubling him over. She grabbed the man and threw him away, sent him reeling into a sideboard.

Sophia thought about running for the gun. And about whether she'd know what to do with it. She saw the brigadier mouthing from the veranda, failed to read his lips, but the signal was clear.

She spun and raced for the arch. And ran up against a traffic jam, a dense knot of people jostling and shoving to get out.

Suddenly they reversed.

Sophia skipped aside to avoid getting trampled. The press of people retreated, falling over each other. She flattened herself against the wall. Someone pushed up against her. A waiter, empty platter clasped to his chest while he crossed himself and prayed. A mess of *hors d'ouvres* spattered the tiles around his shoes.

A man in a balaclava advanced through the archway. He raised a big ugly gun and aimed at the retreating pack of guests.

They whimpered and screamed and pleaded.

He shot one of the women in the head.

Lethbridge-Stewart scooted back, knocked the leg of a table. Paolo came at him again. Back against the parapet, Lethbridge-Stewart pushed himself to stand. Threw up his arm to fend off a chopping blow.

The Italian latched onto the arm, hand closed in an iron grip. Lethbridge-Stewart wrestled the lad, but the grip tightened. The boy had the strength of a Yeti packed into a medium frame. He barely grimaced with the effort, while Lethbridge-Stewart winced at the pressure threatening to break his arm.

'Sorry about this,' he said.

And punched the lad on the chin. His head jerked back and Lethbridge-Stewart drove his shoulder into the lad's chest. Shoved him into a stagger, back and back until he slammed into the house wall. Winded, he lost his grip.

Lethbridge-Stewart shook free, glanced in at the lounge. Where the girl stamped on the hand of a guard as he reached to retrieve his dropped gun.

In the space of that glance, Paolo recovered. He grasped at

Lethbridge-Stewart's collar.

Lethbridge-Stewart ducked to the left.

And pitched over the parapet.

Sophia tried to swallow a scream. It lodged in her throat.

She snatched the platter from the waiter and smashed it down on the back of the gunman's balaclava. Then gave him a push towards the terrified guests. Some of the quicker-thinkers made a grab for the man.

She wished she could stay and help them. Instead she ducked under the archway and ran from the room.

Yells and screams resounded from other rooms, upstairs and down. She sneaked swiftly up the corridor. Peeked around the corner. Three men stood guard in the hall, arms laden with plastic boxes. Even if they didn't just drop their payloads and switch to weapons, Sophia didn't rate her chances against them.

She slid back to the nearest door. Listened.

A man sobbed, begging in Greek. A vicious noise, half-hiss half-spit shut him up. Weighty footsteps headed her way.

Sophia bolted for the room opposite. Slipped inside. Found herself in a pink-tiled bathroom. At least she'd die somewhere pretty, she guessed. She pushed the door closed, maybe not soon enough.

She pressed her head to the door. Tensed. Listened.

Her heartbeat hammered in her ear, threatening to give her away.

Hollis elbowed a group of assailants away. Most squealed and shrieked at his slightest movement. He flipped his SMG around and clubbed a face or two with the butt.

'To me!' he yelled. 'Get in here!'

Boots pounded tiles. Comrades came running down the hallway.

One civilian stumbled away, hands cupped over a busted nose. Blood spattered the front of his posh shirt. Hollis straightened up and snarled, driving the herd back further. He turned the gun around and showed them the barrel.

Past them, other guests cowered in different corners. While the pint-sized princess, Kara, knocked a guard senseless.

No witnesses.

Vorster in his head again. Stabbing syllables. Hollis didn't need telling twice.

This whole thing had turned messy real fast. Time to tidy up.

Samson scurried from bush to bush. Feeling like a rabbit on the hunt for foxes.

He darted from cover to huddle beside a statue. Popped his head around the marble legs of some goddess. Peered past the cars to the villa doorway. Coast clear. The door was open and he made out figures in the hall. But they turned and traipsed out of sight. Nothing coming out. For now.

Staying low, he ran for the vehicles parked around the fountain. Crept around the bumper of a sleek black limo, into the ring.

Great. Now he felt like a cowboy, holed up behind a circle of wagons.

Lethbridge-Stewart clung to rocks, his feet feeling for purchase.

Finding a toehold, he climbed. Sidling carefully left as he worked his way up. Perhaps his own height and a half above, rugged cliff met the low garden wall.

He kept one eye on the parapet, expecting young Paolo to look over it at any second. So far, not a sign. Frantic screams and cries erupted over and over from within the villa. They cut off, one by one. Sometimes, he heard the vicious bite of a silenced shot, punctuating the cries. Most times, he did not and there was one less voice amid the panic.

It was a slaughter.

With no railings on the cliffside, the garden wall presented a minor hurdle. Lethbridge-Stewart pulled himself up and over.

He landed in a crouch on open lawn. He moved towards the parked cars. Stopped at the sight of a body sprawled on the grass. Ten yards away. The dead man's hand was tucked inside his jacket.

Lethbridge-Stewart sprinted for the corpse.

Sophia listened to diminishing screams. Dying to a few sobs.

Then nothing.

'*Madre de Dios, madre de Dios.*'

Neither God nor his mother had anything to do with this, but she needed a mantra to rein in her breathing. She remembered that poor waiter, crossing himself.

She half-collapsed against the door. It clicked shut and she tensed and listened all over again.

Nothing. She'd heard a group of attackers stamping by. None returned to investigate a simple latch-click. The villa fell silent. For some reason that seemed to mean the terrorists were busy.

She was safe. For now.

She searched the bathroom. No window. Wonderful. She was also trapped.

Hollis' boots crunched on broken glass. He took a quick tour around the veranda, poked his head and gun over the parapet. No sign of the moustached guy he'd seen disappear over the side.

'Gone,' he declared.

Behind him, three of the men set their boxes down and whipped the covers off the table, unveiling the sale display. Looked to have been a couple of breakages, but that didn't matter. They got to work, picking up the pieces and whole items and stowing them in the boxes.

Hollis wandered back into the lounge.

The place was littered with stiffs and a lot of blood on the tiles. Some broken glassware and the like, but hardly a stray bullet hole. The two young recruits were stationed to one side like a pair of standing corpses. From their gazes, they looked miles away.

Hollis shook his head. Those kids weren't cut out for this business.

He toed the corpse of a waiter. He stepped over the body, walked on crockery shards.

That reminded him. 'There's another one somewhere,' he told Fyler. 'She got me one on the head with a damn plate.'

Fyler laughed. 'Oh, poor you. Did she hurt you, mate?'

'Shut it. Go look for her. I'm pretty sure it was a her.' He'd glimpsed long dark hair at the periphery of his vision. 'And the rest of you, get all this stuff packed and out to the cars. And keep your eyes open. Somebody outside got a few shots off. We might have police company any minute.'

Fyler sighed, moved off slow. The kids cut unexpectedly past him, walking out through the arch into the hallway.

'Hey, you two. Wait up.' Hollis looked at Fyler. 'What the hell?'

Fyler shrugged. The boss working his puppets maybe?

Hollis hoped those two got headaches like him.

Lethbridge-Stewart flicked the safety on the borrowed automatic. Then skirted around for a better view of the villa's entrance. He slipped between two parked cars for a spot of cover and searched the open doorway for signs of movement.

'Sir!' hissed someone behind him.

Samson. Sidearm at the ready.

'Sam. Am I glad to see you! Were those your shots I heard?'

'My work, Al. But all without result.'

'No shame in that. We're outgunned, that's for certain.'

'Do we go for an assault?'

'We're not Butch Cassidy and the Sundance Kid, Sergeant Major. But we have to do what we can for the civilians. Perhaps we could scout for other entrances, try to flank the—'

Shadows stirred in the hallway. Figures emerged.

It was the Italian lad and the Greek girl. They walked the path as though on rails. Lethbridge-Stewart edged back, putting more car between him and the entrance. Allowing them to wander by.

A punch was one thing. Superhuman strength or no, he wasn't about to shoot two youngsters in cold blood.

Sophia waited in her pink prison.

A pair of footsteps passed her door. Including heels, tapping the tiles. They were soon followed by heavier steps, in boots. More came after. A whole group of them tramping down the hall.

'Should I search every room for this woman?' South African voice, a lazy sort of drawl.

'Forget it, I'll do it myself. Get after those two and get them into one of the BMWs. We'll leave the car they came in.'

'On it.'

The footsteps wandered away. Quiet. The door handle turned. Sophia slid the bolt home. Then cursed herself for doing so. *Estúpido!*

Hollis heard the bolt. He smiled.

'Come on out of there.'

Silence. Of course.

He stepped back and sprayed up and down, left and right.

Stupid! Idiota!

Sophia bruised herself diving in the bathtub. She threw her arms over her head while bullets chewed the bathroom door to shreds.

Wood exploded in splinters. Tiles shattered and fell from the wall, the basin and toilet bowl cracked. Impacts smashed the mirror to hell and bottles burst apart, splattering their perfumed contents everywhere.

Sophia cursed herself again.

The remains of the door bashed inward.

The Italian lad and the Greek girl were halfway down the driveway when the rest of the group started to emerge. One man ran out and rushed down the path to catch up with them. Others filed out, three bearing boxes.

'Now,' Lethbridge-Stewart said.

He popped up and fired over the bonnet of the car. Samson did likewise, cracking off two rounds.

A box-carrier flinched, clipped in the leg. He limped to one of the porch columns. Two gunmen ducked back inside the doorway and let loose from there. The whispered spits of suppressed fire were quickly drowned out under the thunderous hammering into the car's side.

Samson kept his head down and fired blind. Lethbridge-Stewart couldn't afford to be so free with his rounds. The guard hadn't been carrying a spare magazine.

More fire rattled in from their left. From the gunman who'd gone after the youngsters.

Lethbridge-Stewart popped up and aimed that way. But grimaced.The guard retreated towards the gateway, both youngsters at his back.

Lethbridge-Stewart ducked back down. The gunman opened up on where his head had been.

'Damnit, what now?'

Hollis listened to the gun battle going on outside. He swore and hauled the woman out of the bath. She struggled and wriggled, but he had a fistful of her hair. Better than a leash.

He tugged her out and along to the entrance hall.

Two of his mates knelt either side of the door, firing bursts into the car right out front. A pistol showed above the car's hood, answered back with three shots in a wide spread.

'Get to the cars,' he ordered. 'Now!'

He hooked an arm around the woman's throat, pulled her nice and close. Pinned the SMG barrel to the side of her head. He had to kick her legs to get her moving, but he walked out the door, wearing her as armour.

'Take another shot! Come on! I dare you!'

Lethbridge-Stewart had seen all he needed to see, framed too vividly by the glassless windows of the car.

Señora Montilla wasn't panicking. But she had that look on her face, like a tightrope walker, fearful her next step might mean death.

As soon as the man had appeared with her as hostage, the rest of the gunmen were up and on the move. Easy targets, although enough of them had weapons trained this way. No question, he and Samson could put paid to two or three of them. No question either, however, this gunman would carry through on his implicit threat. If anything, the man had sounded like he genuinely wanted them to try.

Lethbridge-Stewart let his mind race. Chasing very few options.

Beside him, Samson waited.

Behind him, footsteps beat a hurried withdrawal down the driveway. Time was running out.

Lethbridge-Stewart risked a peek over the vehicle. Most of the enemy were out beyond the gate. One man and his hostage were last to leave. The SMG was lowered from the *Señora's* head and levelled this way. Perhaps half a head and one shoulder was all that was exposed of the target.

'Sam, do you think you could you take the shot?'

Samson took a swift look. 'Dicey, Alistair.'

Even if he could, there was every probability another gunman would gun the *Señora* down. And there was an equal chance this fellow, once in the clear, would murder her anyway.

Lethbridge-Stewart craned for another recce. The gunman backed through the gateway. He put his weapon back on *Señora* Montilla's head. One way or another, time was up.

CHAPTER TWELVE
The Unwilling Warriors

GRIGORIY WALKED up on the man's right and put a round through the side of his skull.

He caught the woman as she fell free and shoved her aside through the gateway. Dropped to his knee and fired, popping the back tyres of the rear vehicle. Another gunman – the one he'd watched bundling the girl and boy into the BMW – sprang from the passenger side and raised an SMG.

Grigoriy shot him twice. Chest. Head. He keeled over on the other side of the passenger door. He stuck his Makarov in his belt. Scooped up the SMG near his knee, rose and strode to the car. The lead vehicle drove off, the second peeled away from the curb. The third started off as Grigoriy reached the driver's side window of the fourth. He fired a three-round burst into the man at the wheel. Then swung the weapon to cover the back of the third vehicle.

All three other BMWs accelerated away down the street. Grigoriy watched them until they were out of sight.

Then he pulled open the car's door. The girl and boy looked out at him. Stared, as though in shock. 'Out,' he beckoned. 'It's all clear now.'

Owain ran up. He'd been smart enough to stay on the sidelines. Grigoriy gestured inside the vehicle. 'There you are. Two friends, rescued. You're welcome.'

'Oh my – wow – you just—' The lad leaned to look inside. 'Kara! Paolo! I can't believe… Are you okay?'

The pair paid their friend as much heed as they'd paid Grigoriy. He left them to it and walked back towards the gateway where two men were checking on the freed hostage and regarding him with due caution.

The man with the moustache had British officer etched into every inch of him. This had to be Owain's brigadier uncle.

Grigoriy chucked the borrowed SMG to the pavement. Introductions were in order.

Close by, *Señora* Montilla shook herself free of all the attention.

'I'm all right, I'm all right,' she insisted. Although she was clearly rattled, understandably, and she dabbed at drops of blood on her cheek. Then made a face and appeared not to know where to wipe her hand.

Lethbridge-Stewart watched the man approach. He was all intensity about the eyes, but perfect calm in every nerve. Something about him had Samson immediately on the alert.

'I suppose we owe you our thanks, Mr...?'

'Captain. Save the gratitude. How is the lady?'

Was that...? Lethbridge-Stewart was sure he'd detected a trace of Russian accent. Suddenly, he was as on his guard as Samson. Still, past the man he spied Owain at the BMW. Bending to speak to the vehicle's occupants. A friend of a friend, then?

'I'm... all right,' said *Señora* Montilla. 'Thank you.' She mouthed something like 'yuck' at her palm.

The Russian dug in his pocket and handed her a handkerchief. 'Better someone else's than yours.'

She regarded the handkerchief like a foreign object. Then accepted it gratefully and wiped her face.

'Might I ask what brought you to our aid so precipitately?' Lethbridge-Stewart enquired.

The captain directed a thumb aft, returning Lethbridge-Stewart's attention to the BMW. 'The boy. Owain. Listen. Police will be here soon. I'll leave them to you. With the lady's permission I will wait at her house and we will speak then.'

Grilling this captain would have to wait in any case, as Lethbridge-Stewart was acutely conscious that the two youngsters ought to be detained and questioned thoroughly.

'Is it okay?' asked *Señora* Montilla. Lethbridge-Stewart realised she was seeking his permission. 'I'd rather not wait around here if it's all the same.'

'No, I quite understand. Strict procedure would demand witnesses remain on the scene. But I think we can exercise a measure of discretion under the circumstances. Don't you, Sergeant Major?'

The Italian boy and Greek girl turned their heads slowly, as though surveying their surroundings for the first time. Owain appeared to be pleading with them and getting nowhere.

'Yes, sir,' Samson agreed. 'Do you want me to escort the *Señora*?'

'That won't be necessary,' said the captain.

Señora Montilla glanced at him. 'I'm sure I'll be okay. I don't need anyone to hold my hand. But someone watching my back for a while couldn't do any harm.'

'Very well,' Lethbridge-Stewart agreed, not best happy about it. But he would need Samson's support when the police showed up.

Owain, plainly frustrated, walked around the car to his friends.

'Atkins should be here any minute, sir,' Samson supplied.

'Hmm? Right. Good. The more the merrier, as it were.' Although merry was far from the word. The enigmatic captain turned to go. 'One moment, Captain.' Lethbridge-Stewart nodded towards the BMW and the dead gunmen littering the street and pavement. 'Have you any idea who these people are?'

'None. You're welcome.'

Over by the car, Owain was much too close to the youngsters for Lethbridge-Stewart's comfort.

'Owain! Come away from there!'

Owain half-glanced this way. He looked to his two friends, but they turned their backs on him. With a sag of his shoulders, he jogged over.

'Uncle Alistair. It's been a while.'

'It has indeed. How have you been keeping?'

The small talk disguised a multitude of unspoken words. Owain shrugged, smiled, and seemed to consider a thousand different answers. 'This is Captain Grigoriy... Sorry, I mean Captain *Bugayev*. He really needs to talk to you. And trust me, you need to talk to him.'

'Is that so?'

'It is. Really.'

'And what can you tell me about your two friends there?'

Owain shook his head. He half closed his eyes, as though

shutting down some pain. 'I don't know. They won't talk to me. Can't even look at me. I bet it's something Vorster's done to them.'

'Rolph Vorster? Why do you say that?'

Owain's mouth was half open, answer on the way, but his attention strayed up the street. Lethbridge-Stewart looked and Miss Loukas and Paolo were on the move. The couple walked away.

'Hey! Kara! Paolo!'

Neither head turned at Owain's shout. He scooted after them.

'Owain!' Lethbridge-Stewart called. With as much result as Owain had garnered from his friends.

Captain Bugayev spun and strode after Owain. 'I will bring him to heel and meet you at the *Señora's* house.'

'Sergeant Major Ware, go with him.'

'Sir.'

Samson joined the hunt.

'And detain those two youngsters if you can, but approach with caution!' Lethbridge-Stewart watched them go. He sighed, his earlier relief all undone.

This was cruel. Torture. To find them and not find them. To see them wander away and leave him. Owain had spent too long fearing they were lost.

'Kara? Kara!' She kept on walking. Maybe even stepped up her pace. 'Paolo!'

Paolo gave him nothing either. He and Kara walked silently off down the street, for all the world like a couple taking the evening air, albeit too calm. In a trance, like a couple of sleepwalking tourists, only leaving a taxi behind them and not a bloody crime scene.

Owain hurried after them.

'Owain! Wait up!' someone called out. It sounded like Samson.

'They're my friends!' he hollered back and raced on.

The pair walked on, side by side.

Owain caught up easily enough at the first corner. If they heard his footsteps they showed no sign. He eased to a trot and darted around in front of them. They walked on, prepared to walk through him.

He backed up and pushed out a hand, flat against Paolo's chest. That stopped him.

Kara continued on her way, brushing past Owain's right elbow. 'Hey, hey! Kara!'

He grasped her arm. She halted. Turned her head and stared with empty eyes.

'Oh no, no no. Kara!' He glanced at Paolo, still stationary. He wore the same blank stare, like waking death. Inevitably, Owain's mind churned with memories of the Intelligence. Possession of some kind. What else could turn two friends so full of life into zombies?

Kara's lips peeled back, baring teeth like some cornered animal. She tried to snatch her arm free. Owain's grip tightened reflexively. Her long-sleeved glove rode down her slender arm. Revealing an expanse of smooth skin that gave way to something like grey sandpaper. Rough and scaled; a sight that turned Owain's stomach cold.

Owain let go, and backed into somebody.

He spun to face Paolo. The young Italian's face was fixed in a snarl. He pulled off a glove and clenched a stone fist. Then threw a punch at Owain.

Owain sent up a guarding hand. The fist smacked his palm. Something grazed the skin. He felt the sharp bite like an insect sting. Then he felt a shove; Kara pushing him into the wall.

Winded and dizzy, Owain watched Kara and Paolo walk on. The street revolved, buildings and cobbles turning over and over as though in a washing machine.

Owain looked down at his grazed palm. Where he expected to see a cut, he found a scab. Grey and hard as rock.

Skin turned to stone.

Owain collapsed and his world turned over and over, crushing him under its wheels.

'Step on it!'

Vorster fumed, fit to steam the insides of his Mercedes. Memories ran riot through his head, ransacking and vandalising his practised calm. The airfield was the shortest of rides away, but the damned chauffeur couldn't get him there quick enough.

The memories belonged to his men, some now dead. Jump zooms and whip pans on the villa, the fatuous dealer and his mown-down guests, swarms of bullets, the British agents shooting from behind cars, screams and chaos, blood and tacky décor and broken glass. The relived images were an assault in themselves. On him.

And then there was that damned Spanish woman. And that last sudden cut to black. No mug shot of the culprit. Just the hard knowledge of a bullet like a hole-punch to the skull.

Vorster closed his eyes and emptied his mind of the garbage. In the deeper space within, he sought out Miss Van Den Haas. Found her at his side as sharply and efficiently as if he had summoned her into his office.

Who the hell was that?

There's no way of telling, sir. Miss Van Den Haas and her unfaltering calm was often a spot of oil on troubled waters. But right now it was as grating as rock 'n' roll music. He wanted anger to match his own. *At best we would have a description to go on – if any of the men caught sight of the attacker – and I do not recall seeing anything. Even then it would be nothing we could use as a starting point in a search.*

So, she had been monitoring the operation from her safe remove out at the rig. A faint jolt alerted Vorster to the car braking. The chauffeur announced their arrival and Vorster hopped out without a word.

He strode towards the waiting chopper attended by three BMWs. The car engines were running and the helicopter's rotors were winding up. The men loaded the boxes onto the aircraft and climbed aboard. At least they had secured the goods. Only the drivers remained at their wheels.

Vorster rapped on the window of the lead car. 'Get these bloody vehicles out of here. Ditch them, torch them! And not all in one place!'

The vehicles peeled away in different directions.

Vorster clambered in and installed himself in the co-pilot's seat. He grabbed a pair of headphones and rammed them on, shutting out everybody but Miss Van Den Haas.

If someone else – anyone – comes busting in on my operations I want to know who those people are.

Can we be sure they were there to disrupt your operations? she wondered.

What other motivation could they have but to mess with my day?

And armed, no less. Ready for a shooting match.

These auctions have attracted attention from a number of parties, countered Miss Van Den Haas. *The finds have drawn treasure hunters from various quarters. Many have filed for diving permissions, but many – probably more – might not bother with permissions. Other less scrupulous parties may leave the discovery and retrieval to either of those groups and acquire their treasures by alternative means. Whether by going through dealers like the late Mr Stathopoulos or by force.*

You think it was an attempt to rob Stathopoulos? Vorster asked.

It's possible. Or you, if they had any notion that you would have representatives in attendance. I am not sure Mr Stathopoulos had much of a reputation, but perhaps these individuals are unfamiliar with yours.

Oh, if I find who they are – I will give them a lesson in my reputation and more besides. They'll pay with blood.

Miss Van Den Haas fell quiet, but remained a lingering presence in the midst of his thoughts. A brief glance around revealed the chopper was airborne, leaving the Santorini shores behind.

What of the two youngsters? she enquired.

Vorster sent out a few tendril thoughts. They touched space like empty pockets.

Them? Gone. They're lost. Not enlistment material, it turns out. Like the few artefacts that slipped through his fingers, he would have to write them off. They had done their part. *Miss Van Den Haas, I want you to call every contact. Intelligence circles, corporate, political. Everything. You find out what other players are active in the region – and you dig up everything you can on this British Intelligence outfit – and you bring me names. People I can hurt.*

I can do that, but it will–

Do it.

Santorini's caldera slipped by below and they flew on over open sea. Clear blue all the way to the rig. Homeward bound.

And what of the minor detail of our fallen heroes?

Heroes. Vorster laughed. He did enjoy her sense of humour. Hollis and Fyler. The dead. They could be written off too.

Not a concern. The remains will take care of themselves. Eventually.

CHAPTER THIRTEEN
Hand of Fira

ANNE LAID the phone to rest. She rubbed her eyes dry. Stupid. What had she been thinking? What did she expect?

Nothing much had changed at home. That was the good news. But ten minutes of conversation with Charlie Redfern's assurances, and a well-meant account of progress as he worked with her father on his memoirs, proved unexpectedly wearing. In the pauses, she ended up berating herself again for her absence. Her own fault for insisting on making a personal call of her own. Work was her escape. It was what helped her forget for whole minutes at a time. She should have stuck at it. Here she was, doing her bit to save the world. Why was it so hard to let one small corner of the world take care of itself?

Because it wasn't small.

Some answers came easily. She breathed deep, composed herself. Bill. She'd go and find Bill. He was an anchor of sanity.

She left Lethbridge-Stewart's office, she was fairly sure, exactly as she'd found it.

Outside the door, she ran into traffic: soldiers filing past in something a hurry, rifles and kit bags over their shoulders.

'Scuse me, Miss,' said one as he side-stepped to avoid a collision.

She waited out the jam. Then walked along to the operations room.

Bill looked her way. He'd just deposited an ice cream tub on her desk and set some papers down beside it.

'Anne. Everything all right? Delivery from the Brig, courtesy of Chapman's courier service. I was about to send out a search party for you.'

'I'm flattered, Bill, but I'm not sure I need an escort for trips to the lady's room.' She set a stray hair in place, possibly an imagined one. She hoped her eyes didn't betray her smile with signs of recent tears. She strode over for a closer examination of the package. She hadn't met Chapman so was reasonably sure he hadn't bought her ice cream. 'What's going on?'

'We're shipping out. Orders from the Brig. We'll leave you a section of the platoon to back you up. Assist you with… Whatever you need assistance with.'

Anne glanced over the tub: vanilla, Greek brand. The papers were a few photos paper-clipped to a sheaf of hand-penned notes. 'I get to order them about, do I?'

'You have my full permission. If any man doesn't jump to it, you give me his name, rank and serial number.'

'So… Really, what's going on?' she reiterated. A quick thumb through the photos revealed shots of a one-armed priestess figurine, brandishing a snake. Not something that ought to tie her to Akrotiri while Bill got to fly off to other pastures. 'Why does Lethbridge-Stewart need all the manpower? And why doesn't he need me?'

'He and Samson ran into some opposition. Armed opposition. Sounds a bit of a mess, to be honest. None of our people hurt, but it's pretty serious. Not a place for—'

'Women?'

'Scientists,' Bill stressed. And she knew he'd never intended to complete his sentence any other way. 'Besides, Group Captain Winser has just notified me that HMS *Aphrodite* was spotted three hours from port. No word from on board though. She must have lost communications. You need to be our first eyes on her. Let us know what's what.'

More on her plate. The first page of notes were headed, *Handle only with gloves, keep out of water for only short periods at a time.* In a heavier hand and underlined several times. Well, thought Anne, that lent the subject some extra weight. Maybe enough to justify her remaining tethered to her lab.

'We'll stay in touch,' said Bill. 'Keep you updated. And the Brig will want reports on your lab results asap.'

'I'll provide what I can when I can. When you say

"armed opposition"...?'

'Gunmen. Terrorists. Nothing alien or robotic, I'm afraid.'

Bill's efforts to make light of it were transparent. Anne decided to play along though, fighting down her own sudden unease.

'You'd rather they were?'

'Not really. There's just something especially... ugly about this lot. Current reasoning is they're connected to VTMB. Vorster's private army.'

'So Owain was onto something?'

'Maybe. They appear to have an interest. An interest they're prepared to kill for.'

Anne's unease refused to lie down. 'Be careful, Bill.'

'Trust me.'

Anne trusted him on many things. Being careful was not necessarily one of them.

'Wheels up in fifteen minutes. I'd best get going.'

'And I'd best crack on with some studies. Safe trip.'

She smiled and watched him out the door. Then turned and popped the lid on the ice cream container.

The contents were far from vanilla.

A rather decorous female figure, drowned in a small quantity of water. And rather more impressive than the photographs suggested. Bare-breasted, with both arms raised and holding a snake in each hand. The figure's frilled skirt and headdress were especially well-detailed and she imagined the original glaze had invested the figure with vibrant colours.

Wait a minute.

She looked back at the notes. Then double-checked the photographs, tugging them from their paper-clip anchor.

The goddess was supposed to have a broken arm.

Samson worked with Captain Bugayev to wrestle Owain through Sophia's narrow hallway and laid him out on her living room couch. Between this and poor Atkins earlier, her humble abode had been turning into quite the field hospital.

Although one look at Owain convinced him the young man was going to need more than tea and sympathy. Sooner rather than later.

The *Señora* appeared from the kitchen. She took one look at

Owain and stared about a hundred questions apiece at Samson and Bugayev. 'What's wrong with him? What can I do?'

'Nothing,' said Bugayev. Either with a big helping of traditional Russian pessimism or sounding very sure of himself. He squatted beside the couch, examining the patient.

Samson reached for his radio. 'I've got to inform the brigadier.'

'Go ahead. What will you report?'

Samson paused, thumb on transmit. 'That Owain's out cold. That those two freaky kids have gone walkabout.' He hadn't thought beyond that. 'Why? D'you know something? Anything helpful you could tell us?'

Bugayev turned to Sophia. 'Have you gloves? Plastic? Rubber?'

'*Si*. I do, as it happens.'

She ducked back into the kitchen. Samson waited on Bugayev to say more, but apparently he'd placed all conversation on hold.

Samson had no idea what to make of this guy. He'd shown up at the villa and dug them out of a bad situation. But what was the response when you found out the enemy of your enemy was *the* enemy? Okay, he was playing the ally now – a long way short of actually friendly – but the Soviets were the number one bad guys on the current world Top Ten.

Sophia returned and handed Bugayev a pair of marigolds. He slipped them on, the incongruity making not even a dent on him. Hand him a bottle of Fairy and Samson wasn't sure even then he'd see the joke. Bugayev held Owain's arm by the wrist and flipped the lad's hand over.

'Take a look.'

Samson moved in for a close-up. In the lad's palm was a shard of stone. Flat like a flint, but rough-textured. More like a sliver of concrete. They'd looked Owain over in the street. How come he'd missed that? Either Bugayev had a quick set of eyes or he knew what to look for. Maybe a bit of both.

'What is that?' Samson asked.

'First of all, did you make any direct contact with him? His skin?'

Samson ran through the events in his mind. Picking Owain off the cobbles, hoisting him over his shoulders. Fireman's lift. Carrying him down the road. 'Don't think so. No, only our clothes made contact. Pretty sure.'

'Lucky for you, I'm pretty sure too, Sergeant Major. And I'd keep it that way.'

'What is it? Was it something those kids gave him? Was he holding it when we caught up to him?'

'Look again.'

Samson leaned in closer, peering intently at the lump of stone. It didn't just lie in the hand. It was embedded, as though half-buried in the flesh. Like an outgrowth, a granite melanoma. Very much a part of Owain's hand. 'Holy... What do you know about this, Captain?'

'Approximately nothing. But it killed two of my men and... affected the deck of my ship.' Rising, Bugayev pulled off the washing-up gloves and handed them back to the *Señora*, like a surgeon to an attendant nurse. 'It's the reason I came to you. Mr Vine was persuaded that your team would be equipped to provide answers. What I don't understand is why it isn't eating him up.'

'Eating him up? Excuse me?'

'I have no other words to describe it. This thing, it was virulent. Spread like wildfire. Like rot, but faster. Much faster. And the flesh does not decay. It becomes what you see here. It becomes stone.'

Samson half-lifted the radio. It didn't quite make it to his mouth on the first go.

'So tell that to your brigadier,' Bugayev advised.

'Yeah, that's what I'm doing right now.'

Only question was, how?

'How is he now, Mayhem Two? Over.'

Lethbridge-Stewart's concern for Owain vied with his acute awareness of how long he'd been on the radio already. Ideally, he needed to be conducting the two police officers on a guided tour of the crime scene. They were inside the hall now; he could hear them questioning Atkins.

'Still out cold, sir. Our *comrade* is confident it's not urgent. Reckons there's something in Nephew holding the infection at bay. Or slowing it anyway. Over.'

'All right. Thank you, Mayhem Two. Backup is en route from Akrotiri. I'll be there as soon as I can.' Captain Bugayev had seen Owain this far, there was no reason to doubt him on the matter of the lad's safety now. On other scores, that remained to be seen. 'In fact, if Nephew is in good care, I could use you up at the villa. Head on up here. Over and out.'

He closed the channel and returned the radio to his belt. In the absence of longer-range communications, he'd had to use the late Mr Stathopoulos' phone to put a call through to Akrotiri. Bishop should be in the air and on his way with two squads by now.

In the meantime, there was no escaping the bloody mess created by the attackers.

Before Samson's call, Lethbridge-Stewart had wanted badly to be back at *Señora* Montilla's house, interrogating Captain Bugayev. First a terrorist assault on a criminal auction, and the *Señora* had sworn to a South African accent among the attackers, and now Russians. If there were any alien intelligences at work behind all this, they had best join the lengthening queue. And now he had checking up on Owain to add to his growing agenda.

The two police officers, hopelessly late to the scene, had so far only surveyed the house and grounds in dismay as Lethbridge-Stewart walked and talked them through it, with Atkins following along like the stray member of Bo Peep's flock.

The two officers had done their best to take matters in their stride, but once they'd seen the carnage in the lounge they gave up all pretence.

Now, wandering back out in the garden, they rejoined Lethbridge-Stewart, muttering the occasional snatch of Greek to one another, but mostly inspecting the perforated cars with nothing to say. Plainly horrified and out of their depth.

Lethbridge-Stewart sympathised. This was well beyond the bounds of a local police force. Nevertheless, he was conscious of not wishing to tread on jurisdictional toes. He let them go through their official motions, ready to supply answers whenever they had more questions. Atkins looked glum, a young chap who, in the face of inquiries about an incident he had not been in any position to witness, had clearly run out of don't-knows.

Finally, one of the officers returned from a ponderous circuit of the lawn and the two murdered guards from Stathopoulos' staff and nodded, inviting Lethbridge-Stewart's attention with a pained expression.

'We will need to contact the mainland. A coroner's team. Detectives. We don't have the manpower.'

'I appreciate that—'

'You have this under control? Weapons should be secured. The scene needs to be processed. The dead...' The officer gestured, one hand spinning as a visual et cetera. 'You understand. Too much for us.'

'I'm afraid I understand only too well. As the situation stands, I've limited resources on site myself. What you see is what I have. Plus, another man who should be with us any minute.' This really was it until the Hercules brought reinforcements. At least Miss Travers should be cracking on with her scientific researches by now and they might learn more in due course. 'However, I've called in more men and they should be arriving–' he checked his watch '–within a little over an hour. We should have this scene locked down in no time and I'm confident we'll manage until your mainland personnel get here.'

The officers conferred in Greek once more.

'As long,' added Lethbridge-Stewart, 'as we're not trespassing on anyone's territory. We're more than happy to help, but we're not here to upset any apple carts.'

'Apple carts?'

'Apologies. I mean to say, if there are any issues of jurisdiction, we are here with your government's full authorisation and—'

'Yes, yes.' One officer nodded and his comrade copied him. 'NATO investigation. Missing ships. We had word from high.' He managed a smile. Then gestured around the scene. 'And now perhaps you find criminals behind all this.'

'Yes, well, it remains to be discovered whether there is any direct connection between this assault and the missing ships, but we can't rule it out.'

Out of the corner of his eye, Lethbridge-Stewart spied Samson marching up the driveway. 'Ah, Sergeant Major Ware. Here's my other man now.'

The two officers acknowledged Samson. Then one drew nearer Lethbridge-Stewart, almost conspiratorially. 'Uh huh,' he said. 'So will you have soldiers to spare?'

'Spare?' Lethbridge-Stewart raised an eyebrow. 'What for?'

The officer indicated his colleague. 'We are on a call to an incident on the north coast.'

Lethbridge-Stewart caught Samson's eye briefly. 'What kind of incident?'

'Some kind of attack. Not like this. No guns. Just men. Coming ashore on the beach. A lot of panic. Many calls. But one – one call came via the British Embassy. A British family in trouble. They called the police first but we are stretched, you see.'

'I see.' Lethbridge-Stewart frowned. He didn't like the sound of this one jot.

An attack on a beach... Here at the villa, these men had a clear objective: the artefacts up for auction. Could this all be disparate effects stemming from one situation?

'Well, you can count on us,' he decided. The officers had done their best to be co-operative and a measure of support was small price to pay in return. As good a man as Atkins was, he lacked the seniority for playing liaison to local law enforcement. 'I'll lend you Sergeant Major Ware until our full team turns up.' He gave the nod to Samson. 'Sergeant Major, go with the officers, assist with their investigation.' He lowered his voice a notch. 'Assess the situation as best you can, try to see if it has any bearing on our case.'

'Sir. And if not?'

'Make your apologies and get back here on the double.'

Samson saluted and accompanied the Greek officers off-site.

Lethbridge-Stewart examined his watch again. He still wasn't free to leave this blasted place until his men showed up. In that respect, promotion offered no rewards. Sooner or later, you ended up chained to a post like a good guard dog.

'Well, Atkins, it looks like it's just you and me for the moment.'

'Yes, sir.'

Just Atkins, himself, and a great many deceased.

CHAPTER FOURTEEN
Santorini Experiment

***START WITH** the basics*, Anne reasoned.

For their meagre handful of pages, Sophia Montilla's notes were comprehensive. They and the photographs described and illustrated an engraved disc, broken, with some indecipherable script, explaining that the archaeologist had held onto those pieces in hopes of furthering her understanding. Anne had found all sorts of instructions for handling the Goddess, but nothing forbidding the extraction of a sample from the artefact. Out of respect for a fellow scientist's field, however, she resolved to keep the sample tiny.

Kitting herself out with a pair of surgical gloves, liberated from the base sick bay, Anne lifted the Goddess from her watery grave in the ice cream tub. With the careful application of a Stanley knife, she scraped a minute fragment from the hem of the figurine's skirt. Then lowered the Goddess back in the tub.

And almost dropped her knife as she transferred the sample from knife blade to slide. Somehow, she steadied her hand and completed the transfer even as she observed the corrosion eating up the steel blade.

It wasn't oxidation. Although the texturing wasn't unlike rust, the discolouration was grey. More akin to stone.

She frowned and set the knife down on the bench. Where the blade continued to succumb to minuscule pitting and scarring.

'Wonderful. I'm going to have to put you under the microscope as well now.' She reached for her tweezers and lifted the coverslip over the slide.

Stopped.

The small glass rectangle was rapidly going the same way as her Stanley blade.

What on earth?

She made a quick decision. She dropped the plastic coverslip over the specimen and tapped it down, then swiftly tweezered it into the microscope stage. Eye to the lens, she focused in haste, and watched the corrosion – for want of a better name – spread across the slide. And retreated from the bench as it ate its way down into the instrument. Devouring the microscope.

And suddenly she had a better name for it.

Plague.

Anne raided the base canteen and returned to her laboratory in the operations room.

Luckily, the plague had left the wooden benchtop intact. Of course, luck had nothing to do with it, but she was determined to find out what had actually stopped the specimen short of eating all the furniture.

In truth, it hadn't eaten anything. Her microscope stood where she had left it – or something more like a monument to her microscope. A disfigured effigy of the instrument.

On a smaller scale, her Stanley blade was also a stone replica of itself. For all she knew that extended to the part of the blade encased in the handle, but she hadn't attempted to dismantle the thing yet. She could assume, for now, that the plague had as much appetite for plastic as it had demonstrated for wood. And she preferred to leave both items well alone.

She cleared another surface, one bench along from her poor microscope, and set to work.

Test one. Duration of contact.

She touched the tine of a fork to the figurine's skirt. And snatched it away immediately, despite knowing what to expect. The briefest of contacts. And yet the process was under way.

She laid the fork down on a plastic tray and picked up another. Touched that to the Goddess and held it in place for the count of three. The 'rot' began just as instantly but its spread accelerated. It was halfway up the handle by the time she had reached three.

Test two. Quantity of substance present.

Anne fished the figurine from her bath and touched the figurine's skirt to the corned-beef can. Again, the decay set in immediately, texturing the can's surface like stone. More rapidly.

Anne teased off the label and dangled that in her tweezers. The paper remained untainted and the Fray Bentos logo bright and colourful as ever.

She wondered then about the contents.

Well, there would be no getting at that with a can opener. And the key was practically fused to the lid, just another stone moulding on a stone block.

She mounted another quick expedition to the canteen and returned moments later with a second tin of corned beef, this one ready-opened.

Setting it on the bench, she repeated her experiment.

She recoiled, alarmed, as she watched the stone plague spread into the fatty beef. Just like the can, the meat retained its basic shape and form – in this case a block – but it was remade in stone. Like some artist's rendition from a lump of granite.

The process occurred in slow-motion, compared to its race through metals. As a coincidental side-effect it was more horrible to observe.

Anne flexed her fingers inside the surgical gloves. Grateful for the protection, but suddenly aware of the thinness of the plastic skin.

'All right, so you don't care for polymers and other synthetics. But you have a definite taste for organics. Even dead meats.'

She peered at the diseased materials and ex-instruments and tools on her bench. Plague or not, it was impossible not to think of this thing as her foe.

'What are you?' she asked it.

There was something eerie about an empty beach. The deserted stretch of shore might have seemed spookier at night, but Samson knew the place ought to have been crawling with tourists. It reminded him of his brief visit to John o Groats last month, although the weather had been much worse then.

Weather like today. A spot like this, on Santorini?

Maybe it had crawled with something.

Sunbathers and swimmers had recorded their panic in the sand. The large mess of footprints, coupled with the abandoned deckchairs and lilos, towels, bags, buckets and spades and what not, suggested a stampede. This was more than litter. Samson half-expected to see beach balls rolling across the scene like garish tumbleweeds.

'What do you make of it, Sergeant?' asked the officer who was standing over him as he crouched to examine some of the prints. The other policeman poked around one of the deckchairs and had a rummage in one of the abandoned beach bags.

'Well, I'm no Charlie Barlow, but it looks like somebody dragged their feet across here. Several somebodies.' He indicated where rucked furrows traversed and ploughed over the marks of general trampling. Of course, the waterline had taken care of any signs of where anybody had emerged.

As far as Samson could tell, there wasn't anything more to be learned here.

He stood and took a last look up and down the beach. And weighed what Lethbridge-Stewart had said. On the one hand, he wasn't sure if he'd seen anything to justify more Corps time. And he'd rather be chasing down those terrorists from the Villa. But something – maybe just that eeriness – tempted him to stick at it a while longer.

'And what did the witnesses tell you?' he asked the officer.

'We have not yet spoken to any witnesses.'

'No, I realise that. When they called you. What did they say in the calls?'

'Attackers. Multiple attackers. Coming ashore. Frightening everybody. Terrorising.'

'Right.' Samson had heard much the same account on the car ride over. A few choice phrases cherry-picked from too many reports. He couldn't blame the officer. Hard to imagine what it was like, some local constabulary suddenly swamped with calls from terrified beachgoers, probably all stumbling and stammering through their own versions of events. 'And how many?'

'Some said twenty, some said fifty.'

'But what did they do? These attackers? What did they do to scare everybody so much?'

The officer puffed and shrugged. 'They babbled, you understand. The witnesses. Nonsense.'

'Nonsense. What specific nonsense would that be?'

'A lot of the callers mentioned *ándres tis pétras*.' He grimaced, as though reluctant to offer the translation. 'Stone men.'

That sounded like something that warranted more digging. 'Let's go talk to some of these witnesses.'

Lethbridge-Stewart was glad to have been pre-briefed on Owain's condition. It seemed that whenever Owain got caught up in Lethbridge-Stewart's world he ended up paying for it; mind controlled on more than one occasion, a sprained ankle, and now this... On return to *Señora* Montilla's house, Lethbridge-Stewart was prepared for the worst.

This time, at least, the lad appeared to be on the far side of peaceful. Completely out of it, like many a teenager after a hard night on the town, albeit more tidily arranged on the *Señora's* sofa.

Still, appearances did nothing to temper Lethbridge-Stewart concerns over the nature of the foreign matter embedded in the lad's hand. Captain Bugayev had been more than adamant about avoiding direct contact. Lethbridge-Stewart sensed the Soviet had not been fully forthcoming on the account of what had happened to his own men, but he had told enough to underline the seriousness of Owain's situation.

'Well, is there some treatment we can...?'

'Treatment?' Bugayev said. 'Believe me, we tried everything we could. In the end, we had to zip my men into plastic body bags.'

Señora Montilla hovered nearby, dragging on a calming cigarette. She lowered her head. She had evidently heard something of the story before. She said nothing. There was nothing much that could be said. Lethbridge-Stewart had lost men under his command. He was not about to lose Owain, however.

'Perhaps with hospital facilities?' he asked.

'Perhaps. But I doubt you will want to admit a major contagion to the kind of simple rustic hospital you'll find on this island.' The Russian had an answer for everything. And never an encouraging one. A bleak worldview, possibly, but one made all the more frustrating because the fellow was right.

'No, quite,' Lethbridge-Stewart said. 'Well, now that I have reinforcements on station, the villa is secure. And I have a plane on standby at the airfield. We'll have him shipped back to Akrotiri. Right away. Which, I'm afraid, Captain, may mean we have to keep our discussion short.'

'The boy's need might not be so urgent as you feel. He looks fine.'

'Hardly fine.'

'It's all relative. The spread is... Actually the spread isn't happening. The *Señora* will tell you. It's the same size as when your sergeant major turned over the boy's hand.'

Señora Montilla nodded. 'It's true.'

'You're certain?'

'Exactly the same.' She nodded again. 'No change. Of course, I'm not sure I would take that as a cue to relax.'

'I had my men don full protective gear,' Bugayev cut in. 'Call it over-caution. But when you do get to deliver him to your base hospital, I definitely would instruct them not touch the patient without gloves.'

Lethbridge-Stewart surveyed the room, searching for better news among the tribal masks and cat ornaments. There wasn't even any of the usual sparkle to be found in the *Señora's* gaze.

Assuming Owain's condition was stable, it was clear it would serve to know everything Bugayev knew. There were other steps he could take for the patient's sake in the interim.

He got on the radio to Bishop up at the villa. 'Have Corporal Mullins sent down to us. Atkins can show him the way.' He closed out the call and explained to Bugayev. 'Our combat medic. You won't object to some additional company?'

'If privacy is needed, we can step outside.' Bugayev moved to the table and kicked out a chair for himself. Sat. 'Here will do for now.'

Lethbridge-Stewart pulled out a chair and seated himself opposite. 'All right, Captain. Let's talk.'

Samson's next stop was Blue Dolphin Holiday Villas. A terraced row of modern chalets, their architecture designed to emulate the quainter aspects of traditional Santorini houses, they overlooked the beach.

If the witnesses were home, they'd have a beautiful view of

where their alleged nightmare had taken place.

Since they were British and they'd called the embassy and had been waiting hours already, Samson figured it best to start with the Samuels family. The last thing the Brig would want was some citizens kicking up a diplomatic stink. That could end up with a lot of bureaucratic spanners thrown in the investigation works. And all manner of other agencies poking their noses into what might be strictly Corps business.

Samson trotted down the stepped path that linked the chalets. 'We want number six, right?'

Both policemen nodded and waved him ahead. For having a foreigner policing on their patch, they were pretty gracious about him taking the lead.

The curtains in the target house were drawn. Samson knocked on the door. 'Mr Samuels?'

'Police,' added Officer Galanos. 'Responding to your call.'

There was no answer.

Samson knocked again. Louder. 'Mr Samuels?'

He stood back and wandered to the window, pressed his forehead to the glass and peered through the sliver of gap between the curtains. No sign of movement. He couldn't make out anything past his own reflection.

He wandered back to the entrance, where one of the police officers was reaching for the door handle. Samson thought the handle could use a pol—

He barged the policeman aside. He spread his arms, made himself a barrier. 'Get back! Don't touch it! Don't touch!'

Startled and bemused, the officers peered past him and he stood aside enough to afford them a view. The handle was a crude stone-carved thing, way too much like that crusty pebble embedded in Owain's palm.

The wood of the door appeared untouched. Safe enough. Samson kicked. Part of the frame splintered and the door swung inward.

He looked to Galanos. The guy gave him an 'after you' wave. Samson indicated the latch, similarly afflicted to the handle, gesturing for the officers to avoid it like wet paint. He stepped inside. 'Samuels?' he called. 'Mrs Samuels? Hello? Here with the local police. Everything okay?'

Quiet. Quiet enough to hear the hushing waves down at the beach.

Samson thought about the villa. The gunmen. Hostage situations. He pictured an ordinary family - mum, dad, kids – tied and gagged in a bedroom maybe, terrorists pacing before them. But that handle felt like it implied a worse find.

He pulled his gun.

The Greek policemen tensed.

'You think...?'

'Just taking precautions. After the villa, you understand.'

'Okay.' The officers breathed a little easier.

Samson led the way through the house.

Open suitcases on the couch and coffee table, clothing tossed in as messy heaps. The clasps on the cases succumbed to that weird stone effect. Through into the kitchen, he found a kettle and some cutlery that looked like they'd been unearthed from some archaeological site, encrusted with a similar stone coating. Bathroom told the same story with taps and basin and the mirror on the open medicine-cabinet.

Metals. Returned to raw ore, almost. Rock, anyway.

The bedroom boasted more luggage on the bed, clothes and other effects thrown in as though in a major hurry. Open wardrobe, open drawers. Stone clasps and stone handles on practically all the doors and drawers.

Packing in a panic. But then all of it abandoned.

The police officers poked with their toecaps at a few abandoned shoes and assorted belongings scattered on the floor.

Samson's radio crackled. 'Mayhem One to Mayhem Two, over.' It was Bishop.

Samson lifted his radio slowly. 'Mayhem Two receiving. Go ahead, Mayhem One. Over.'

'Situation report. Over.'

'I'm not sure if any of this ties in to the terrorists or anything else, but we've definitely got something else to worry about here. Over.'

'Specifics? Over.'

'Missing British family. Abandoned holiday let. Over.'

'Any signs of struggle? Over.'

'Negative, sir. But – there are signs of...' How to put it? 'Damage. Some kind of corrosion or... something. I'm not sure how much Mayhem Leader has filled you in, sir, but I've seen similar on Nephew's hand. Over.'

'Right. Yes, had a vague update on that. Mayhem Leader is with Nephew now. Meeting with a House Guest. We're stationed at the villa, sitting on the crime scene awaiting the Greek investigation team from the mainland. Over.'

Samson wandered out into the living room and lowered his voice. 'Sir, maybe it's above my pay grade to say, but this is looking a lot like a matter for the Madhouse. Not for local law, if you get my meaning. Over.'

'Clear as day, Mayhem Two. I'll notify Mayhem Leader. We'll see if we can deter the locals from making the trip. Stories of hazardous materials wouldn't be a lie.' There was dead air as Bishop paused. 'Listen. You'd best collect a sample. But don't touch it under any circumstances. And have the bobbies tape off the site. You can inform them we're handling the situation from here on. Got that? Then you'd best get back here, pronto. Over.'

'Understood, sir.' Understood was a stretch, but Samson didn't need telling twice. 'There's more, sir. The attackers who came ashore here – anywhere between twenty to forty of them. People described them as "stone men". Over.'

'I see...'

'And the thing is, sir. They've gone missing. Whatever they are, they're loose somewhere on this island. Over.'

More dead air.

CHAPTER FIFTEEN
A Bargain of Necessity

'WOULD EITHER of you gentlemen like a cup of tea?'

Bugayev shook his head. Lethbridge-Stewart shrugged and told *Señora* Montilla, 'Why not. That would be splendid, thank you.'

'Well, Private Atkins house-sat for several hours. I daresay he knows where the kettle is.'

Lethbridge-Stewart nodded. 'Then if you'd be so good as to tell Private Atkins, and have him make one for the captain in case he changes his mind.'

Smiling, the archaeologist swanned away inside, sliding the patio door closed behind her.

They relocated their talks poolside shortly after Atkins and Mullins had arrived, trading the dining table and chairs for plastic garden furniture. Thus far, talks had centred primarily on Owain and how he had come to be in Bugayev's company. It was time to move on to the nitty-gritty, some of which might prove sensitive. There were people back home who would view this as sitting down to dinner with a wolf. But at the end of the day they were merely two men, both soldiers at that.

'Tea and biscuits,' Bugayev mused, a wry grin developing. 'May I say, you are the very epitome of a British officer, Brigadier. Politeness and civility personified. I expect if we were meeting at your home you would lay on the finest tea service. But we are both soldiers. Under the courtesy and manners, you and I understand certain realities. Killing, for example.'

'I prefer not to unless absolutely necessary.'

'Sure. But you are no desk commando. Silently slitting the throats of envelopes with your paper knife.'

Lethbridge-Stewart had to admit the fellow had quite the turn of phrase. He sensed a marked education, possibly a high achiever. Several ranks below him, of course, but also a significant quantity of years. This was a driven professional officer, career soldier to the core.

'What is it you want?' Lethbridge-Stewart asked.

'We both understand exigencies. That is what I am saying. Our national interests clash. Our ideologies. But our interests right here, they overlap.'

'Do they? Listen, I don't know what my nephew told you about our–'

'The boy – forget the boy. This is between us. This is about pooling what you know and I know. Some of our intel anyway. It need not be all.'

Lethbridge-Stewart was relieved at that, although he took care not to show it. How rash had Owain been? How much pressure would Bugayev have exerted for answers? Surely there were things that the lad knew not to divulge under any circumstances? Besides, there were some lines of questioning that Bugayev would have had no reason to adopt. Unless handed a clue, perhaps, through some careless slip of the tongue. It was all too easy to see how Bugayev might make a civilian nervous.

'Did you interrogate him?' he asked.

'I said to forget the boy. What he told me, he told me freely and willingly, under no duress. We gave him soup.'

'It's no joke, detaining and interrogating British citizens.'

'Let's shoot closer to the target, shall we, Brigadier? Here's something I know that didn't come from the boy: your Royal Navy task force, so noble to volunteer its services in the search and rescue operation, was using that as cover. To attend to repairs to the SOSUS array.'

'That is…' Lethbridge-Stewart bit his lip. What could he say? Top Secret? Confidential? Pointless to argue that now that it had been voiced aloud.

A kettle whistled shrilly in the kitchen.

Bugayev waited it out. 'Let's leave the official denials to the liars who hand down our orders,' he said. 'In any case, your admission or otherwise is immaterial. What is pertinent,

Brigadier, is that your Western listening devices that litter the seabed sustained damage. As did one of your Royal Navy warships. This, by the way, I only suspect. That is one piece of the puzzle I slotted in myself. But it fits perfectly with no forcing or any need to cut it to shape. Why else would the task force withdraw, minus one vessel? Our people lost track of HMS *Aphrodite*. I presume it's either retreated to port for repairs or missing like much of the civilian shipping that brought it here in the first place. Ostensibly.'

Lethbridge-Stewart wondered if he was being invited to share. He was not willing to go so far, but he could at least trade suspicions. He leaned across the table. 'Well, Captain, if you count yourself so well-informed I can only assume your sources are better than mine. If I had to assemble a jigsaw puzzle of my own, I would look for a piece with a Soviet submarine on station where it ought not to be. And now a Soviet captain where he shouldn't be. Why is that? What is your mission in this region?' He sat up. 'You've lost one of your subs.'

'Good. We have no need to deceive one another further.'

The patio door slid open. Atkins, with the knack of many a waiter for arriving at an awkward moment, emerged, bearing a tray of tea things.

Lethbridge-Stewart waited while the private set down the tray. He spoke up once Atkins returned indoors. 'What kind of boat are we talking about?'

'We're not talking about it. All you need to know is my primary concern. Which amounts to eighty men.'

Eighty men. In some respects, a clue as to the nature of the Soviet boat. But Lethbridge-Stewart understood its true meaning. Whatever else this Captain Bugayev might be, whatever other secrets he might be guarding, he cared about lives.

'All right.' *For now*, Lethbridge-Stewart thought. 'So what are we talking about?'

'Missing vessels. Other non-military vessels. Ancient relics. Archaeology. Contaminants. And, if your boy is to be believed, an industrial cause behind it all.'

'VTMB,' said Lethbridge-Stewart.

'That rig, yes. I was sceptical initially. But if I take Owain's story at face value, well, I can conclude that the South Africans don't like visitors calling by on their facility unannounced. I cannot see the connection, but I would put money on there being one.'

'I'm no gambling man, Captain, but I would double whatever you're willing to wager. The *Señora* swears she heard a South African accent among the terrorists who assaulted the villa.'

'Someone mentioned me?' *Señora* Montilla was at the patio door, her red bucket in hand.

'You heard these terrorists speak?' Bugayev asked.

'Yes, one of them was definitely South African.'

'On its own, it doesn't amount to anything,' Lethbridge-Stewart said. 'But taken with the presence of a VTMB chopper at the airfield at the time of the attack and the company's hydraulic fracturing operation in the region…'

'I wouldn't even call that a gamble,' said Bugayev.

Lethbridge-Stewart was inclined to agree. 'Unfortunately, I'm not sure my superiors would agree. As we are both soldiers – officers – we both understand the need to run things by the book. Which means authorisation. Permissions.'

'Permission for what? We would simply like to talk to them.'

'If they had anything to do with that slaughter at the villa, you need to do more than talk,' *Señora* Montilla said.

'Questions first, *Señora*,' Bugayev pointed out. 'Certainly, a visit to the rig is called for.'

'Captain, you said yourself, the company does not care for visitors,' Lethbridge-Stewart said. 'If we head out there, they would most likely turn us away.' Complaints all the way up the official channels. Lethbridge-Stewart could see the avalanche of paperwork crashing his way.

'True. But how would they go about turning us away, Brigadier? You think, with harsh words? You know what I think?'

Not at all, Lethbridge-Stewart thought. Although he had a suspicion that when Bugayev said 'questions first' there was a 'shoot later' implied.

'I think they have already told us how they would respond. I think Owain staged an effective demonstration of their standard response.'

'You believe they would fire on us? A military envoy?'

'How would they know? Military, civilian, they did not stop to tell the difference when Owain and his friends sailed into view. A boat is a boat. And I don't know what your rules of engagement tell you, but if someone shoots at me I shoot back.'

'You're talking about provoking a firefight.'

'No. I'm talking about provoking an unprovoked attack. I'm talking about doing what is necessary to deal with men who have no compunction about permissions or authorisation. You think those murders at the villa were according to some rulebook, some code?'

The *Señora* opened her mouth to speak – but she appeared to lose her voice. Her gaze drifted, undoubtedly into the recent past.

Lethbridge-Stewart would have loved to deliver some measure of justice for her – and for the deceased. But there were ways and means. The captain's barbs aside, there was more to propriety than tea and biscuits.

'Even so, however you care to dress it up, Captain, I can't condone that. I'm sorry. We can exchange information with a view to assisting each other. But I will not – *cannot* – sanction some joint assault on a civilian corporate facility. If we stoop to their level, then we are no better than them.'

'I beg to differ. Because when I am done, I go home and there are fewer murderers in the world. And what if Owain proves correct and it is VTMB behind this contagion? The missing civilian vessels, damage to your Royal Navy warship?'

'I suppose that would be a different matter. But we need substantial evidence. We need to know they are the enemy.'

'Fine. Well, when something happens to change your mind, Brigadier, you let me know. For now...'

'For now, what?'

Bugayev shrugged. 'You tell me.'

'I'll tell you,' *Señora* Montilla volunteered. She stepped forward and planted her bucket on the garden table. 'Both of you. We need to find the evidence. And the key to that lies in these artefacts. Or rather, the site where they were found.' She reached into the bucket and fished out the clay disc, holding the two halves together, making them appear to be as one once more. Whole, but with a crack running down the middle. She lowered one hand and the pieces somehow stayed together. 'Miracle, no?'

Lethbridge-Stewart frowned. He hadn't expected glue to be part of the scientific methods the *Señora* applied to fragments of such historical interest. 'What should I be noticing, exactly?'

'It healed itself. I didn't do a thing. This is the first time I've looked at it since before... Before the villa. It's been sitting at the bottom of my bucket. Oh and for those present who weren't here to see it in its original state, Captain, this item was broken. Right down the middle.'

'I can see the signs of the fracture, yes,' Bugayev said. 'You're saying it mended itself.'

'Is that even possible?' Lethbridge-Stewart asked.

'Possible is moot at this point, Brigadier,' *Señora* Montilla said. 'It has happened. Now, I can't be certain because I didn't think to measure the quantity of sediment in the bucket, but based on casual observation there appears to be less than before. As though this used some of the sand to affect repairs.'

'A piece of clay did this? All on its own?' Bugayev was disbelieving, but he was more besides. He glanced towards the patio window, evidently contemplating something inside the house. Owain, of course, realised Lethbridge-Stewart as his thoughts caught up. He visualised Owain's bandaged hand and the sight of that 'carbuncle' or whatever one might call it.

Stone 'contagion'. Stone that heals itself. Living stone?

It made approximately no sense. And yet at the same time it added up horribly well. If such stone growths were an undeniable fact, then why not stone that grew?

'In any case,' the *Señora* pressed on, 'now more than ever I – we – need to examine the site where these articles were found. And you, Brigadier, need to contact your expert. We will wish to know what has become of our one-armed Snake Goddess.'

'What do you need?' Bugayev asked. 'To investigate the source of these relics?'

'A boat, diving equipment. Some laboratory facilities.'

'Those we have.'

'Now, wait...' Lethbridge-Stewart began. He wasn't sure about having his recently recruited expert whisked off by the Soviets.

'And a location,' continued *Señora* Montilla. She lowered the disc gently back into the bucket. 'Which I've been thinking about. The trawler I acquired those artefacts from. I'm sure the captain would have marked the position on his charts. If he's making a little cash on the side out of this trade, he'll want to go back and cast his nets in the same spot.'

'You know where this boat is harboured?'

'Vlychada.'

Bugayev stood. 'Good. Let's go.'

'Wait.' Lethbridge-Stewart rose too. He could see which way the wind was blowing. All he could do was keep a hand on the tiller to some extent. 'We will need to share intelligence on anything that's found. And I will need reassurances of *Señora* Montilla's safety.'

'I need her alive. Reassurance enough?'

'Not exactly, no.'

'I can take care of myself,' she pointed out.

'I'm sure you can, *Señora*. Even so, I would like Sergeant Major Ware to accompany you.'

Samson might not be present, but this was a mission for either him or Bishop. And Lethbridge-Stewart needed Bishop to head up the main investigation here on Santorini.

'Sorry, I can't allow that,' Bugayev said. 'It's one thing to allow a civilian access to my ship. But military personnel of a foreign power? No.'

'I think, Captain, we are beyond the bounds of jurisdiction already.'

'*Señora* Montilla is an archaeologist. Her passion is for history and is less likely to concern herself with the present.'

'Well, I don't know that I would go that far,' she said. 'I pay attention. But if you mean I don't care for your petty political squabbles and secrets, then yes, you would be absolutely right.'

That prompted a laugh from Bugayev. 'Fair enough. So, Brigadier, can this sergeant major of yours be relied upon to be discreet?'

'He can be relied upon to keep me informed.'

'Not the answer I was hoping for.'

'This is not the situation either of us would want.

Nevertheless, I believe this is the smart approach.'

'Okay. But his movements will be restricted between certain areas of the ship. It will not surprise you to learn that we have already had a passenger go exploring without permission.'

'Owain. Of course.'

'Of course. Your boy has an inquisitive nature. He would not make a very good soldier. Too many questions.'

'I'll send Sergeant Major Ware with you,' Lethbridge-Stewart said. 'He'll have his own questions, but he will keep them to himself.'

'Have him rendezvous with us at Vlychada. We'll be waiting.'

'We?' *Señora* Montilla asked.

'You and I, *Señora*. Go pack a bag.'

Señora Montilla picked up her bucket and disappeared inside. Bugayev produced a small pad and pen from his pocket and dashed off a note. He tore off the page and handed it over.

'For you, Brigadier. When you have all the evidence you need. You can reach me on that channel – and use these call signs.'

Lethbridge-Stewart glanced over the note. A radio frequency and the words 'Red Bear' and 'Blue Bulldog'.

As soon as they stepped out in the street, Captain Bugayev plucked the radio from his belt. 'Coming down. I'm bringing a passenger.'

A throaty voice crackled back. In the stream of Russian, but Sophia was sure she discerned the name 'Owain'.

'No, Owain is not returning to us.' Bugayev eyed Sophia. 'And our passenger is a lady. So tell those slobs to behave like gentlemen.'

Laughter answered and Bugayev wore a wry smile as he clicked off. He clipped the walkie-talkie back on his belt. 'Shall we?'

Sophia walked beside him. 'You speak to your men in English?'

'A courtesy to you. Although don't expect it all the time. There will be some things that will need to be discussed strictly in Russian.'

'Secrets.'

Bugayev said nothing. Not a waster of words, this one. Sophia strolled with him in silence, amusing herself with the thought that this was a date that had dried up in the Santorini sun. Memories soon swept in like the evening tide to wash away any amusement. Those murderers at the villa. Washing another man's blood from her face. She shivered.

'Well, I won't begrudge you those,' she said.

'Those?'

'Secrets. You saved my life, Captain.'

'You're welcome. My pleasure.'

They sounded like automatic platitudes. As though he felt nothing. Or he didn't wish to feel anything. The many times she'd relived that moment she'd wondered if it was heroic, although she'd thought it cold-blooded for a while – even though it was her life being saved. It had never occurred to her to think of it as business.

'But...What goes through your head at a time like that?'

'You know, as long as it's not a bullet...' He shrugged and let the joke hang, unfinished.

They walked on, descending the donkey path.

'I'm a soldier, *Señora*. There's value in what I do. I don't process it until... Well, until I am obliged to have conversations like this with ladies such as yourself. And that, it happens less often than you would think.' He sidestepped a tourist-laden donkey on its way up and patted its rump to drive it on. Earning a reproving look from the animal's handler.

Bugayev was the most relaxed, intense man she'd met.

'Do you take any... pleasure in it?'

'Pleasure in my job, yes. Killing? No. Men like that; mercenaries, terrorists, whatever they call themselves. Maybe it's a job to them, maybe it's a cause, maybe they take pleasure in it. Mostly they carry a gun and think themselves soldiers. There's satisfaction to be had from disabusing them of that piece of self-deception. But you have a mind worth saving. That is where the real satisfaction lies. That is where I mean it is my pleasure.'

Sophia nodded – to herself, since he was walking ahead. She'd misread him entirely. There was a reason, she supposed, she'd always found Russian literature impenetrable. If you hadn't an element of winter in your soul, you would probably feel like giving up and throwing the book on the fire.

'Flatterer,' answered Sophia.

'No.'

He upped the pace, almost marching down the path. Their stroll had turned into a mission.

Bugayev's men must have taken their captain at his word. None looked the least bit slobbish, so Sophia suspected he had overstated that. But one was quick to offer a hand to assist her into the launch. Unnecessary, but Sophia didn't like to be churlish by refusing.

Bugayev introduced her and she settled down in the boat. The chivalrous young man, Cherezin, loosed the ropes and jumped on board. The crewman at the helm guided them out into the caldera. Hardly another word was exchanged during the whole boat ride. Bugayev the conversationalist had flipped the sign in the window to *Closed*.

Once it reached the peninsula, the launch hugged the island's coast all the way around to Vlychada. The boat steered into the double-ring harbour and glided quietly along the docked trawlers.

Sophia pointed. 'There. That one.'

Bugayev signalled. The helmsman brought them in to bump the trawler's side. The captain clambered easily into the fishing boat. Took a quick survey, then beckoned Sophia. She picked her way between the other crewmen and took Bugayev's proffered hand. Allowed herself to be pulled up and swung her legs over the side to land on the deck on which she'd caused so much trouble earlier.

A thud from the cabin had Bugayev drawing his pistol.

'It's all right,' said Sophia. 'It'll only be the captain. Or one of the crew. Honestly, I thought they'd be taking a day off after a long fishing trip.'

Bugayev edged towards the wheelhouse. 'A crew who handled those relics.'

He had a point.

Something rolled and clunked against wood. The cabin door opened and the trawler captain staggered out. He looked like he'd just weathered a force ten storm. He shielded his eyes from the sun, but lowered his arm as soon as he saw Sophia.

'You! Crazy lady! Who you bring now? Police?'

'Show me your hands,' said Bugayev.

The trawlerman blinked. And registered the gun for the first time. He raised hands in surrender, showing both palms. They were rough – but clean.

'Crazy lady!' He spat. Then started gabbling away to Bugayev in Greek.

Bugayev stowed his pistol. 'Relax. I'm not here to arrest you. We want your charts.'

'My charts?' The trawler captain swayed as though out at sea in rough weather. There was a strong waft of fumes on the salt air, suggesting he'd either been hitting the Metaxa or guzzling petrol straight from the tank.

Bugayev gave an impatient huff and waved Sophia past him. She headed by, dodging the fellow's breath as best she could, and stepped over the empty bottle just inside the cabin door. The place was a mess but the map was displayed on the wall, a circle scrawled in black marker pen. She tore the chart down and got out of there before the atmosphere knocked her out.

The trawler captain shot her a furious glare as she emerged.

'Hey,' said Bugayev. 'You and your crew; they all wore gloves, yes? Did they handle any of the relics directly?'

'Some. Maybe. Sure. Why?'

'Names, addresses.'

The man gaped. Blankly.

Sophia snapped her fingers in front of his eyes. Her Greek wasn't up to lengthy explanations, so she tried slow English. 'Those relics may have been contaminated. Poison, you understand?'

That sobered him some, like a swig of black coffee. 'Poison? No… Wait.'

'Give us some names and addresses. It's for their own safety.' Sophia dug in her pocket and thrust a notebook and pen in the man's hand. They'd return smelling of a distillery, but it was a small price.

The trawler captain scratched out a short list. He held out the notepad. Sophia plucked it – and her pen – from his fingers and handed the pad to Bugayev.

He got on the radio. 'Blue Bulldog. This is Red Bear.'

'Lethbridge-Stewart here.'

'We've some people you need to check out. One's in Fira, close to you. Wear NBC suits if you have them.'

CHAPTER SIXTEEN
Earthshock

MANOEUVRING THE unconscious Owain to the hired Land Rover drew some attention from passers-by, but were it not for the lad's bandaged hand he might easily pass for a youth who'd hit the *retsina* a little too hard. Lethbridge-Stewart smiled and nodded at locals and tourists to reinforce that impression, while Atkins and Mullins carried Owain between them.

Laying Owain in the Land Rover, Mullins jumped in the back beside the patient and Atkins took the wheel. It would be a short ride to the airfield, but Lethbridge-Stewart was not one to sit idle when he could get other things moving.

He was on the radio before Atkins got the Land Rover underway. 'Mayhem Leader to Mayhem One. Over.'

'Mayhem One receiving. One moment, sir. Over.'

Bishop hated to cut off a superior officer, but the call had come through to coincide with some sort of kerfuffle at the villa's gateway.

Spooner and two privates stood over one very deceased terrorist. A single glance told him why they had all backed off from the corpse.

Patches like scabs of grit had spread from under the man's collar. The lesions, or whatever they were, extended over the jaw, and even advanced up his left cheek.

Recovering himself, Bishop waved at his men to relax and more importantly shut up. He got straight back on the radio.

'Sorry about that, sir. Situation here at the villa. Same sort of effect you described on Nephew's hand; we're seeing signs of it in a dead man. Over.'

'Which? Over.'

'One of the gunmen, sir. Over.'

'Only the one? Over.'

'Just a minute, sir.' Bishop gestured at Spooner, motioning him towards the parked BMW. The sergeant jogged to the vehicle and bent over the body at the open car door, then peered in at the driver. He nodded, his grim expression relating the rest. 'All of them, sir. All the gunmen. Over.'

'All right, Mayhem One. Tidy them away. Shower curtains, tablecloths, sheets, wrap them in anything you can find and store them out of harm's way. Under no circumstances are any of the men to handle them without gloves or make any direct contact with their skin. Over.'

'Sir. I advised Mayhem Two the same when he reported in.' Lethbridge-Stewart listened as Bishop summarised Samson's report. 'He's on his way back here. Over.'

'Get hold of him again and have him redirect to Vlychada harbour. South coast. He's to rendezvous there with the *Señora* and the House Guest. Meanwhile, Lieutenant, I want you to organise the men into search parties. This is a small island, not too much ground to cover. Leave one squad at the villa. The rest we need out there tracking down those two youngsters. Also, these *stone men* of Mayhem Two's. And I want you to head up a party yourself and chase up some leads, starting with this address in Fira.' Lethbridge-Stewart dug out the notepaper on which he'd scribbled the names and addresses given by Captain Bugayev. He read them out to Bishop. 'Apparently, there could be some trawlermen affected by this thing. At this stage, we know contact is dangerous and I can personally vouch for the strength and violent potential of those two youngsters. Make sure the men are armed and take no chances. Over.'

'Understood, sir. Beg pardon, sir, how is Nephew?'

'We believe he'll live. We're on our way to getting him treatment now. Over and out.'

Lethbridge-Stewart rode out the remainder of the drive in quiet. Within a minute or two they were coming up on the airfield.

Atkins was a capable driver and he detoured smartly around the terminal building, straight out onto the field and headed for the Hercules.

Atkins braked at the base of the ramp. He was out in one bounce and assisting Mullins with Owain. Lethbridge-Stewart led them aboard the aircraft.

Atkins and Mullins laid the patient across several seats and strapped him in securely. Lethbridge-Stewart proceeded all the way through to the cockpit for a word with the crew.

'How long before you can be in the air?'

'Fifteen, sir.'

'Fine. Can you raise Akrotiri for me?'

Lethbridge-Stewart looked back through the cockpit doorway, wondering whether he should pop back and check on Owain while waiting for his call to go through. The pilot surprised him, however, handing him the mic before he was quite ready.

'Group Captain Winser for you, sir.'

Lethbridge-Stewart thumbed send. 'Mayhem Nest. Mayhem Leader. Over.'

'Brigadier, sir. Good to hear from you. Anything we can help you with? Over.'

'Possibly a tall order, but I'm hoping you can put in a word for us with the air marshal. I'm going to need to investigate that VTMB platform at some point. Sooner rather than later. I'm hoping he can get on to the Ministry, see if he can obtain authorisation. Over.'

'I'll sell it as hard as I can, sir. What do we have to go on? Over.'

'Not much, I'm afraid. It's on the thin side. One of our terrorists at the villa was South African though. And very likely a mercenary. And a VTMB chopper was on the island at the time of the attack. Over.'

'That'd be enough to convince me. Over.'

'Well, see if you can frame it in terms of an interview. All we want to do is talk to the chap. Over.'

'Right, sir. We'll do our best for you. Meanwhile, I have Moreau here wanting a word. Over.'

'Right, thank you, Group Captain. Put her on. Over.'

Lethbridge-Stewart braced himself for the research report, uncertain what manner of Miss Travers he might encounter on the end of the line. All being well, her efforts had fully engaged her attentions and she might be better disposed towards the mission, if not him. He hoped there might at least be some good news. More than that, he hoped it would be delivered in language he could understand.

'Brigadier?'

Lethbridge-Stewart waited for her to end her transmission with the standard signal, and realised with a slight smile that she wasn't go to follow protocol. 'Here, Moreau. How are things at the base? Over.'

'On the mend. Your Snake Goddess is in rude health especially. She has her full set of limbs.'

Lethbridge-Stewart frowned. He could almost have wished for signal break-up, but Miss Travers was coming through loud and clear. Some details about the figurine would have escaped his inexpert notice, but he definitely recalled the number of arms. 'You're saying she grew an arm? Over.'

'And a snake. My best hypothesis — by which I mean, guess, but we scientists don't like to use that term — is some form of crystallisation. The artefact appears to have drawn minerals from suspension. Like crystals in solution.' It sounded very like the clay tablet's gift for self-repair. 'But it suggests the structure is programmed. And this isn't just some crystalline formation. This is a piece of art. Primitive art, perhaps, but art nonetheless. It's... Well, the fact is, I'm sorry, I was so busy dismissing Nephew's Atlantis theories that I completely overlooked the Gorgons. Tell me, did this Snake Goddess have anything to do with Medusa?'

'What makes you say that? Over.'

'Simply put, she turns things to stone.'

'I see. Over.'

'That's taking it in your stride, Mayhem Leader.'

'If I hadn't heard some disturbing reports, I'd have similar trouble believing it myself.' He wondered if he ought to apprise her of Owain's condition. There was no sense in spreading undue concern, but on the other hand she had best be prepared for when the patient arrived in Akrotiri. He postponed it for now, something for a little later on the agenda. 'Anything else you can tell me? Over.'

'Well, you must understand, it ate my microscope. I've been

limited in terms of how I've been able to conduct any studies. But I managed some classroom level experiments, which have imparted something. I'm not sure I believe the evidence of my own eyes, to be honest, and I don't know if it will prove of any use to you in the field, but it's all we have.'

'Try me and we'll do our best. Over.'

There was a pause. An intake of breath, perhaps.

'This thing, superficially the effects resemble corrosion. But it's more complex than that. It doesn't consume the material it comes into contact with, it mutates it. If it was organic, I would compare it to a cancer, altering the structure of the cells around it. It spreads by contact. The more prolonged the contact, the more rapid the conversion. Other factors, such as the size and concentration of the source will affect the speed of transformation. And it has a great affinity for metals. Obviously, I've not had the resources for exhaustive tests and they won't let me back in the base canteen, as it is. But I'd assume all metals. And all manner of raw silicates – unprocessed ores, stone. I think we're dealing with some form of silicon-based organism.'

'A silicon-based cancer? Over.'

'Perhaps. The worst part is that I experimented with a tin of corned beef. It mutated the can and the contents. Its interaction with flesh was significantly slower, but it effectively petrified the meat. Converted carbon-based organic material to its own silicon-based structure. Now that was dead, not to mention salt-cured flesh. I've no laboratory mice, but I would hate to observe the effects on living flesh.'

Thoughts of Captain Bugayev's divers sprang to mind. And the image of a can of corned beef and men trapped on a stricken submarine was an unfortunate analogy impossible to push aside once pictured.

'Yes, quite. I've been given an account of what it can do. And I've seen some small measure of its effects firsthand.' He wondered if he should inform her of Owain's condition after all. Perhaps now was not the time to be coy or protective. 'I'm afraid Nephew has had some sort of brush with this stuff. Over.'

'He has? Oh my—'

'It's all right. He's stable and otherwise unharmed.' He could practically hear Miss Travers thinking on the airwaves and was aware he'd been very quick with his reassurances. 'Its growth hasn't been rapid. Indeed, it appears to have stalled. But I'm having him shipped back to the hospital on Akrotiri. You can have a look at him yourself. Over.'

'It's stalled, you say?'

'Yes. We're not altogether sure why. Its spread has been rapid in others. Perhaps if there's any way you can account for that, we might formulate some sort of cure. Over.'

'It's possible. I'm no medical expert, but I think between myself and the base hospital staff we should be able to piece some clues together.'

'Oh, and it was suggested you might experiment with radiation as a catalyst. Over.'

'Radiation? On what basis? Suggested by whom?'

'Unimportant, Moreau. If this is comparable to a cancer, isn't it possible radiation would have some effect? Can you test for that? Over.'

'I expect the base hospital has an X-ray machine,' she said. 'Hopefully I can rig a simple test right now on the artefact.'

'Right. Good. As for these relics; am I to understand someone fashioned statuettes and the like out of this organism? Wouldn't that require some manner of carving tools. Metal tools? Over.'

'That's one of the odd parts. I don't think anyone made these artefacts. I think the organism constructed them. Whether because it had encountered something similar or – well, basically I can't say how.'

'But why? Over.'

'I'm afraid with that we'd be in the realms of wild speculation. Trust me, I've gone over it countless times and there aren't any hypotheses that make any sense.'

'All right. No sense in burying ourselves under further questions. Hopefully your researches will turn up something more. Thank you, Dr Moreau.'

'Over and out,' she said. And Lethbridge-Stewart could detect a tongue firmly in cheek.

As he handed the mic to the pilot, he allowed himself a smile.

A small enough thing – to which the world took exception.

The aircraft rattled and buffeted as though bombarded by anti-aircraft fire. Unlikely, given they were on the ground. Lethbridge-Stewart reached to steady himself on the back of the pilot's seat while the plane did its best impersonation of a cocktail shaker.

What on earth now?

The street shook from side to side, hurling pedestrians to the ground or into walls. People screamed and cried, some reached for the sides of houses in hopes of steadying themselves, many simply reached for a friend or loved one's hand. Some launched themselves into swerving sprints down the hill, breaking past Bishop's squad. So disoriented and panicked they barely registered the handful of men with guns. Not that the soldiers could have been much help as they too staggered and battled to stay upright.

The tremors faded and the street settled. A few people slowed to dust themselves down or collect their nerves. Most kept on running, leaving the narrow street thinned of civilians.

The troops checked each other with glances and breathed a sigh or two between them.

'Everyone all right?' Bishop asked.

The four men offered nods and assurances. It would take more than a minor earthquake to rattle them. Satisfied, Bishop mounted the front step and knocked on the door. 'Mr Mundis?'

Not a word, not a stir. Bishop waved Trudgian up beside him. The corporal boasted a smattering of Greek on his CV. He gave it a try with a few knocks and calls. Bishop trusted he wasn't claiming to be the Greek police or military, but hopefully just the sound of someone in some sort of authority showing up on the back of a quake would fetch the occupants to the door.

'Nobody home, sir.' Trudgian stepped down.

Bishop didn't like himself for his next decision, but if there was any danger this fisherman was infected, well, this wasn't the time for niceties. He waved Trudgian up again. 'Bust it in.'

'Sir?'

'Do it.'

Trudgian muscled up with the rifle, presenting the weapon's butt to the door. Here they were, foreign invaders breaking down doors. If they found some terrified civilian inside, Bishop promised himself he wouldn't lead with the line, 'It's for you own good.'

Two solid blows and the latch gave way. Bishop drew his sidearm and headed in. The men followed, fanning out as best they could in the modest interior. They swept through and swung their guns around doorways, searching.

'Wait! Shush. Stop, everyone.'

Pedestrian footwear still slapped cobbles outside, but Bishop heard a vocal bubbling under the backing track. Sobs? He let his ears lead and brushed past Trudgian into a bedroom. Traced the voice to a slatted wardrobe.

Taking a breath, he opened it to reveal a woman cowering inside.

He squatted before her. Glanced over her face and hands. She whimpered and cringed under his inspection and his attempts at smiles did nothing to soothe her. She was a small, thin woman with grey hair and a tanned complexion, heavily creased with age and fear. She mustered some fight and shouted at him.

Bishop rose and retreated, inviting Trudgian forward.

'See if you can learn anything, Corporal. Gently.'

Private Franks nudged in at the bedroom doorway. 'Sir. Got some artefacts in the kitchen. Cutlery, something that might have been a kettle. That stone effect.'

Right. Similar story to the one out at Samson's holiday chalets. He pretty much knew what to expect from Trudgian when he was done with his interview. But he heard the man out anyway, while the poor old dear resumed her sobs.

'Husband came home from a fishing trip. Came down with something. She keeps saying he turned to stone, sir.'

'She say where he is now, by any chance?'

Trudgian bent to ask more questions. And managed to make the woman cry. He shook his head.

'All right, Corporal. Tell her – advise her – we recommend she goes stay with a friend or neighbour for now. Tell her we will search for her husband and see that he gets treatment.'

Trudgian inhaled as though that was a tall order, but got on with it nevertheless. Bishop withdrew to the living room, keen to give the woman space. Fortunately, the men had had the sense to lower their guns.

'What now, sir?' Franks asked.

Screams joined the noise outside, rolling down from somewhere uphill. The mood of the street changed. An added urgency to the run for shelter.

'Now that,' Bishop declared. 'Come on!'

He charged outside. Franks yelled for Trudgian to follow. Bishop pressed on up the street. A small stampede of people came at him. Frightened as they were, they dodged around him without too much trouble. He patted the last one and urged them onward.

'That's right, get out of here! Get to somewhere safe!'

The squad took his cue, waving and encouraging the people down the hill. Whatever they'd met up top had them scared for their lives.

The ground decided to terrorise them some more.

A subterranean thunderstorm rumbled under Bishop's feet and he was back to stopping still and throwing his arms out for balance. The squad, piling up behind him, did likewise. Tiles slid from the nearest rooftop to dash themselves on the cobbles.

Then it was over. The ground went back to sleep in the late afternoon heat.

'Everyone okay?' he asked again.

Another round of nods, thumbs up and yes-sirs.

'Good,' he said and led on. But halted almost immediately as he happened to glance left.

The view over Fira's blue and white rooftops offered a glorious panorama of the caldera. Where grey wisps rose from the central islands. That was a lot of cigarette smoke clawing its way up through a filter of ash.

CHAPTER SEVENTEEN
Awakening

TIDES. DRAGGING him, drawing him over an invisible horizon.

Undertow. Coalescing. Solidifying. Sinking in an ocean of fire.

A churning cauldron of heat and crushing pressure. Radiation, burning, searing, blasting. Killing and killing, decay in every particle until all that's left of him is a few grains of thought.

Currents. Endless currents. Pulling him in every direction.

Disintegration. The grains rip apart and scatter.

He is everywhere and nowhere. He is lost.

The ocean cools with the patience of a sun. Temperature falls to the merely unimaginable. Currents shift and he feels the change. Liquid fire grows heavy, hardens some impossible distance overhead. The ocean grows a skin; its skin turns to a shell. The cauldron grows a lid.

He swims in Hell. With the weight of the world above.

Hell has a roof.

It is a world he must reach.

One lone grain of sand crawls upwards through a molten hourglass.

Awake.

Owain sat up. Only to have some firm hand push him back down. He blinked, focused on the face. Nobody he recognised. But his uniform sleeves sported a corporal's stripes. Plus a medic's armband.

'Whoa there, son. You're under orders to rest easy.'

Owain let his head settle on the pillow, but every part of him was itching to be up and moving. His right palm especially. His left hand shot over to scratch it and he noticed the bandage. He also noticed the medic was wearing surgical gloves. His mind flashed on Bugayev's ship, the divers – and Kara, him grabbing her by the arm. Then–

Then what?

'Wait right there. I'll let the brigadier know you're conscious.'

'How long was I out? Where're Kara and Paolo?'

'Wait right there.' The medic rose and left him.

Owain craned his neck to get a better fix on his surroundings. Ribbed metal walls in a gloomy rounded shell; he could have been in the belly of a steel whale. But the space was a shade too tubular, the windows small and square. More likely a transport aircraft. The ramp was up. He was sealed in and strapped down. Parked on the seat across from him was Atkins, the private from *Señora* Montilla's place. The medic had disappeared through a doorway towards the front end.

Atkins waved. 'All right, mate. Corporal Mullins'll take good care of you, don't you worry.'

Owain raised a smile for politeness' sake.

Minutes crawled by. To hell with it. Owain wrestled free of the straps – they were clearly buckled to keep him from rolling off rather than to imprison him – and sat up. Uncle Alistair, in combat fatigues, marched in from the direction of the cockpit, with the medic on his tail.

'Owain. Glad to see you back in the land of the living.'

Owain swung his legs off the seat to sit like a normal person and not a patient. 'Not sure I'd go that far. Where're Kara and Paolo?'

Alistair stalled. He ushered the medic to join Atkins on the opposite side of the aircraft, then took some time moving the blanket so that he could sit next to Owain.

'I'm afraid your friends have gone AWOL, as it were.'

'They needed your leave to go absent?'

'No, although I'm concerned they may have been on active duty for somebody. The fact is, Owain, you didn't see what they did inside the villa. Truth to tell, I'm more afraid that they're not quite what they seem. If I didn't know any better, I'd say they were possessed.'

Owain nodded, biting his lip. His head was crowded with

about a thousand things he wanted to say, but he forced himself to sit and listen. Feeling like he might've been out of it for days, he badly needed the update.

'Indeed,' his uncle continued, 'at this stage, none of us knows any better. This infection – whatever it was that knocked you out and... scarred your hand – well, it's our concern that your friends may have been contaminated. Miss Travers has furnished me with everything she's found out to date. And Lieutenant Bishop has a number of search parties out scouring the island. We'll find your friends and see to it they receive the best medical treatment available.'

'That's all well and good, but it's not an infection.' Now to accompany his worries about Kara and Paolo, Owain was haunted with images of Bill and his troops hunting them with rifles. Engines growled into sudden life, the fuselage vibrated to the din of gravel churning in a giant cement mixer. Owain flipped the trailing end of the blanket off his lap, levered himself up. 'Wait, are we taking off? You have to stop this plane! I have to get out there and find them!'

'Now, steady on, young man. You're not going anywhere.'

The view out the window crawled by as the plane dragged itself into a slow turn. They were taxiing.

'You don't understand!'

'That I can't argue with. There's rather too much going on here that we don't understand yet.' Alistair pinned Owain in place with the tip of his swagger stick. He was having to raise his voice. Not quite shout, but enough to emphasise his insistence. 'For one, I'm not sure if you were awake at the time, but we have just been hit with a minor earthquake. I would like it to be entirely coincidental, but try as I might I can't bring myself to be that naive. But. What I do know is that I'm not about to let you go haring off until you've been declared fit for active duty.'

Owain frowned. 'Well, like my friends, I'm not on duty.'

'A mere technicality.'

Owain laughed, despite the frustration. Sometimes he was nephew to Alistair. Sometimes a recruit. Just like on Fang Rock, just like in New York... And both times Owain had got himself involved. And here he was, doing so again, with his uncle following behind to clean up the mess.

'Honestly, I feel fine. And I'm... Look, I think... No, I'm sure I'm safe from this thing.' He showed his bandaged palm.

'What makes you say that?'

'Because I met it.'

Uncle Alistair arched an eyebrow. At least a dozen questions implied. He looked across at the two soldiers, signalled to Atkins. The private jumped up and ran for the forward section.

Within less than a minute, the engines were winding down. Atkins returned and walked back to his seat. The view outside trundled to a standstill on a nicely framed shot of a lonely twin-prop parked out of the way to one side of the airfield.

Owain drew his legs up and rested his arms across his knees, thinking his way through the – what had it been? – dream? – vision? He guessed it amounted to data, and all he had to do was process it.

'All right, how can I explain it...?' He met Alistair's gaze. 'Okay, it's not an infection. Let's start with that. It's a creature.'

'Alien?'

'Not really. I don't know if we can call it that. An intelligence, I guess. Small "I",' he added quickly, and forced a smile. 'It was sucked into the mix when the Earth was formed.'

'How can you possibly know that?'

Owain fidgeted on the seat, aware how crazy he must sound. 'It's like... When I touched Kara's arm, something inside me touched something in her. I think it encountered the... Well, the thing inside me that will become the Intelligence – big "I". This "immortal soul" I possess. And this thing from the earth knew what my soul was... erm, is. Will be. Whatever. And that's why I'm not... That's why I didn't end up like one of Bugayev's men. Believe me, Uncle, if you'd seen them–'

'Yes, well, from the sound of things we have something similar on the loose on Santorini. Some sort of outbreak. Whether you call it an infection or not, it's certainly affected people. Only these victims are up and about.'

'Seriously? Well that means you have to let me go. I have to be out there. I have to find them. Maybe if I can touch one again, I can – I don't know – commune with this thing somehow. Make contact again. Learn more about it, find out what it wants.'

'Or how to destroy it?'

'Maybe.' Owain didn't like to think about that. There had to be some way to communicate that didn't lead to outright conflict. Surely survival didn't have to come down to kill or be killed? Not every time. 'It might not be our enemy. It might just be –'

'What? Misunderstood?'

'Something like that. I didn't sense any hostility. Any will to destroy.'

'You can be sure of that, can you?' The brigadier was entitled to be sceptical. And this was definitely the brigadier seated by his bedside right now, not Uncle Alistair. 'I don't know, Owain, after what happened to you in New York...' He shook his head with a sigh. 'And you really believe you might be able to communicate with this thing? With no risk to yourself?'

'Yes. I know it. Look, it would've spread by now. This soul I have, it has it contained somehow. And what if... What if I can use that to – sort of – reverse the infection in others. Use it just like I did in New York. I survived that, I can survive this. Let me try and persuade this thing to release its hosts. Let me try. Let me find my friends before they're too far gone.'

Uncle Alistair rose, inhaling at length as he did so. 'Very well,' he decided. He looked across the plane. 'Corporal Mullins.'

The medic and Atkins both snapped to attention. 'Sir.'

'Ready the Land Rover and raise Lieutenant Bishop. Atkins, you're to remain on board. Relay every communication from Akrotiri to me.'

'Sir!'

Corporal Mullins rushed to operate the ramp. Atkins headed for the cockpit.

Uncle Alistair turned to Owain. 'One condition, young man. You stay in Bishop's sight. And you wear gloves at all times. We don't want you accidentally spreading this thing to anyone else. Or anything.'

'Sir, yes, sir. Although,' said Owain, 'technically that's two conditions.'

'Yes, well. At least we know you're back to your normal self.'

Owain grinned as he jumped to his feet.

CHAPTER EIGHTEEN
Underwater Menace

SOPHIA EMERGED on deck to find the ship a hive of noisy activity. Both the sun and Ware were up, with little to do but look on while crewman trotted here and there and shouted at one another.

The big man, Oleg, was dishing out most of the shouting, directing a team under the crane. The great rusting arm swung down and men flocked around the yellow submersible like pit crew around a racing car. Towards the bow, the men did an odd dance, skirting around a recent repair. A large steel plate had been welded over a patch of deck and it looked solid enough, but the men seemed keen to avoid it nevertheless. As though they didn't trust the steel.

Trust was still an issue for Ware, she noted. He'd tucked himself over on the starboard side, doing a good impression of not even being here. But he faced their way, uninterested in the sea view, and appeared suspicious of every movement.

Sophia joined him, but faced outwards and searched the sedately rippling waves. Looking aft along the hull, she saw the white wake fanning from the stern. She imitated a petulant child: 'Are we there yet?'

'Like they'd tell me,' said Ware. 'But they did get excited a short while ago and they've let out something on a winch back there.'

Sophia stretched out over the side. More crewmen were busy astern, but whatever they were doing was obscured by the roosting helicopter.

'If I had to guess, I'd say some kind of towed sonar array,' Ware continued.

'Of course. Getting the lay of the land. Or seabed. And where is Captain Bugayev, do you know?'

'Oh, I expect he's getting ready to fill us in on everything any time now.'

Sophia's laugh escaped as a sigh. 'You're not going to make friends with that attitude.'

'What can I say? None of these guys have had a word to say to me the whole trip. Today, we're co-operating. In theory. Tomorrow, we'll be back to watching each other through a twitching Iron Curtain.'

'Deep and philosophical, Sergeant Major. And probably true.'

Ware smiled. 'Anyway, I'm here to guard you. And if I were you it's not these guys I'd have trouble trusting. It's that.' He pointed and Sophia looked at the submersible, now getting hooked up to the crane. 'As our resident expert, I think you're expected to go down in that. And if the Brig is right, these people have already lost one submarine.'

True. That would be something to look forward to. A game of sardines in a potentially brittle can.

'*Señora* Montilla. The captain would like to see you in the galley, please.' Cherezin delivered his invitation like an actor who'd rehearsed his one line thoroughly and desperately wanted it to go without a hitch. It was sweet. Ware looked a question at the young Soviet and, after some hesitation, he saluted the sergeant major and beckoned him to follow. 'Please.'

Accompanied by her guard, Sophia headed below to find Bugayev spreading rolled printouts on the table and staking the corners down with tin mugs.

'Take a look at these,' he said.

Each sheet presented detailed conspiracies of coloured dots. Rorschach ink-blot tests engineered, it seemed, to make her see buildings on the seabed. Their arrangement suggested clear avenues between the structures. A sprawling town of shadow-blocks and columns rising from a plain of sandy brown. Broad square expanses hinted of plazas, bordered by larger edifices and more columns.

'Incredible,' she declared.

'Care to expand?'

'No, I mean incredible. Literally. I cannot credit it. There is no way this site lay here undiscovered for... any length of time.'

'What about the seismic activity? Could that have uncovered it?'

'No. A violent geological shift would have destroyed these ruins. And they're too perfect.' Sophia stared at the printouts but couldn't unsee the illusion they had painted. 'Actually, no. What they are is fantastical. Somebody's fantasy notion of Atlantis.'

'Well, you and I are going down for a closer look at this fantasy,' Bugayev said.

'Is it safe? That little submarine?'

'It's a DSRV, as robust as such machines come. But no, it is not safe. You have seen our patched deck up top. That gives you precisely no idea what we are up against. What this thing can do. The man best qualified to pilot the DSRV is dead. I am going in his place because I am not willing to risk any more of my men. And if the vessel becomes infected, my men have orders to cut the cable. They will not bring us back on board, you understand?'

'You're willing to risk me though?'

'*Nyet.*' His deliberate use of Russian lent the negative an added edge. 'You are willing to risk yourself. If I ordered any one of my men to go, he would go. If I forbade you to go, you would argue until one of us was blue in the face.'

Sophia couldn't resist a smile. 'Wait, did I miss when you interrogated me or something?'

'No.'

'Only, you know me so well, Captain.'

Sophia peered into blue space through a glass bubble. The submersible's lamps melted the gloom with their wide beams.

Strapped into her seat, walled in by console lights and instruments, switches and dials, it was easy to imagine herself an astronaut. The confines were cosy going on cramped, but the air clean and faintly cool. Which was welcome, as she slow-cooked in the cumbersome rubber suit.

Bugayev manned the pilot's chair, guiding the craft with a small wheel and checking the depth gauge. He was similarly clad and sporting a few beads of perspiration on his face.

'Really, is this necessary?' she asked him, tugging at the suit for the tenth time to get some air circulating inside.

'These suits may keep us alive if we come into contact with the contaminant.'

Yes. Sophia recalled young Owain's hand only too vividly. The stone that had seemed embedded in the pit of his palm. Captain Bugayev had explained what had happened to his men, but she had tried and utterly failed to picture that. Her, with her ability to see so much. As far as she knew, their hull hadn't touched anything in the dive, but she couldn't help but scan the ceiling and banks of controls anyway.

The radio fizzed and crackled a few words. A Russian crewman, checking in every few minutes, as ordered. Bugayev answered in the affirmative. He flicked a series of switches above his head and steered the sub in a graceful descending turn.

They drove on through the twilight. Fluid and moving around them, but empty and lifeless somehow.

'Where are all the fish?' Sophia asked.

'Turned to stone?' Bugayev offered.

There was no motion out there beyond the natural currents and those their passage stirred. No marine life to dance and shimmer past their cockpit window. Nothing to be seen darting over the rippled sands beneath.

Then Sophia gasped as the first column faded into view. Grey fluted stone, paled by the lights, seeming to rise out of blue paint.

And a short way past it, the seabed ran into a wall of shadow.

Until the beams illuminated it as a cliff.

Bugayev held them safe yards from the rugged face and had the sub climb, rising and rising to peer over a huge shelf or plateau.

Where Sophia looked out on Atlantis.

Samson paced the deck like a lion at the zoo. He frequently walked to the side to peer at the stretch of water where the DSRV had dipped out of sight. Pointless, because it could be anywhere by now and there was no chance of it bobbing up exactly where it had disappeared.

He glanced at Oleg who lurked nearby. 'You don't have video feed to the sub?'

'Sure. Vashkov is in communications room, in constant contact. We record everything.'

'Well, can't I see it?'

'*Nyet.*'

Samson bunched a fist and growled. His exasperation made no dent on Oleg. With a shake of the head, Samson looked out to sea.

A fly buzzed over the horizon. Growing steadily into a Sea King helicopter. The aircraft skimmed at a steady hundred feet above the waves, beelining for the ship. The dull burr built and built, then exploded into a roar as the chopper flew low overhead, threatening to clip the top of the crane. It gave everybody a good look at its orange-white-and-blue livery. VTMB.

Samson wondered if any of those mercs from the villa were up in that aircraft enjoying the view.

The chopper climbed in an arc and banked, coming around for another pass. One of the Soviets went to one of the covered crates. Oleg planted a hand on the crewman's arm and shook his head. The tarp remained in place.

The VTMB chopper flew on back the way it came.

Samson watched it go. If these Russians were packing what he reckoned they were packing, then he wished Oleg had given the nod.

Bugayev guided the mini-sub between towering trees of stone. There was more space to manoeuvre than it appeared, Sophia was sure, but the depths played tricks. In the wash of shadows, the great columns seemed to sway, as though taking a swing at the passing craft.

Sophia sweated a few more pints into her suit. She peered out through the glass and watched for details caught in the sweeping beams.

The radio speaker fizzed. Sophia caught the word '*kapitán*' and a burst of Russian. Bugayev's answer was curt and to the point. Whatever that point might be.

'Our ship has just been buzzed by a helicopter,' he explained. 'VTMB.'

'The drilling company?'

'Their rig is ten miles west. I suspect they are just checking on their new neighbours who have moved in.'

Sophia nodded. If she could've thought of anything to say, memories of the villa and a gun at her head killed it.

'They need not concern us,' Bugayev told her.

Sophia nodded again, taking his word for it.

The submersible burrowed on through rippling gloom. Its beam spotlighted edges of houses, corners of temples, pieces of a great city. All those sketchy shadows from the scans translated into three dimensions, drawing her gaze to swim along streets and concourses between the buildings of a citadel to rival the Acropolis.

'What do you make of this?' Bugayev asked.

'The same as I made of your sonar scans. Only with greater clarity. This is the Atlantis of films, of popular culture. Public consciousness. It is the part of Greece they see when they visit Athens as tourists, it is the part they take home with them as memories. The imagination is a powerful thing and this is the Atlantis most imaginations would build.' Sophia shook her head. 'But it has no place here, it does not belong. It cannot be real.'

'And yet, it is here.'

The light slid the length of a great gabled roof mounted atop rows of Doric columns and trimmed with ornate friezes. The marble figures were so perfect they might have been carved yesterday.

'Yes, I would struggle to deny that,' Sophia agreed. 'But whatever it may be, it is not Atlantis. It has nothing to do with Minoan culture. It is not even a bona fide Ancient Greek site.'

'What then? A forgery? On this scale?'

'It does seem ambitious. Like a sunken film set. You know, they built some hugely impressive sets for *Antony and Cleopatra* which ended up scrapped or abandoned. Maybe they dumped them in the ocean.'

'You are not being serious.'

'No, I am not.'

In the absence of facts she could accept, Sophia had no idea how else to be. Primitive minds could attribute the inexplicable to gods. Where could she turn for answers?

Ahead in the barely-stirring blue, the water conspired to paint a new shape among the impossible temples and houses of the sunken city. An enormous dark shape that did not belong – and yet it seemed merged somehow. As though growing into or out of the surrounding structures.

Her heart stilled.

There, lodged at a steep angle between columns, lay a great black whale. Hump-backed, with a long wound torn in her side.

The captain slowed and turned the sub, steering the lights over the stricken beast.

'*Madre de Dios*, what is that?' She knew already.

A submarine. Easily over three hundred feet long, the manufactured contours of her hull were now textured like a well-worn cliff, the metal scarred and pitted with vesicles akin to igneous rock. Her conning tower bulged from her spine like a coarse-sanded outcrop and her tail fin resembled a knife-like crag. Sophia had seen wrecks colonised by barnacles. Nothing like this – nothing. But it was the only comparison her memory could draw.

'That,' said Bugayev – and he hesitated, almost stopped there, 'is a burial mound. A relic of more recent history.'

The sub's beams slid back down from the tail-crag. A large segment of the hull, well aft of the conning tower, retained its smooth metal, untouched by what Sophia could only think of as the *stone plague*. It rendered the whole sight stranger, more chilling in some way, than seeing the entire vessel succumbed to the disease.

'Is there a chance you may pretend you did not see it?'

Sophia shook her head in a slow apology. 'I don't think I could ever forget, Captain. But – really – it's none of my concern. That is... My concerns are for the men on board. How many crew?'

'Eighty.'

Sophia said nothing. She was used to studying sites, combing through them in the finest detail, scraping away dirt grains at a time. All the while, understanding and visualising the lives of the inhabitants. They were never merely trenches and earth and buildings. They were streets and homes, places of worship, common halls. Places that lived and breathed and vibrated with voices, with language.

A submarine... Well, what was that but a village in a steel bottle?

And now, just as Captain Bugayev had said: a burial mound.

Bugayev punched the bubble.

CHAPTER NINETEEN
Blood of Stones

OWAIN JOGGED down the Hercules' ramp and hopped into the waiting Land Rover. Where he found Corporal Mullins at the wheel and Uncle Alistair on the radio.

Bill's voice came through on the receiver. 'We tracked the fisherman through town, sir. He linked up with a group of others. Sir, you wouldn't believe—'

Alistair cut him off. 'Let's save the credibility test for later. We'll come see for ourselves. What's your position? Over.'

'Hilltop midway between Messara and Karterados. Take the north road out of the airfield and turn left. Over.'

'All right. We're on our way. ETA five minutes. Sit tight and do not engage. Repeat, do not engage. Over.'

'No danger there, sir. I don't think we could engage this lot if we tried. Over.'

'On our way,' Alistair repeated. 'Over and out.'

He turned to check on the passenger. Owain settled himself in the back seat and gave a thumbs up. Mullins started the Land Rover rolling.

'Now let's go and see for ourselves,' Brigadier Lethbridge-Stewart said.

Mullins swung the Land Rover off the road and parked at the foot of a grassy hill, where a dirt track climbed to a small cluster of trees. Owain peered through the windscreen at a stone circle.

He climbed out of the vehicle and stood rooted. Whether it was shock or something else, he couldn't be sure, but he held back, as though repelled by some sort of magnetic field. Like poles pushing each other apart.

They stood in a twenty-metre wide circle, facing each other, a dozen of them spaced a couple of metres apart. Like a re-enactment of Stonehenge, made of people. Except he couldn't be sure the figures were people any more.

He scanned the ring of the figures and couldn't recognise any that looked like Paolo or Kara. Not at this distance. That helped. He willed some strength to his legs. Approached the circle.

Soldiers – a squad of four – gathered a little to the left of the 'henge'. Two had their rifles slung over their shoulders, but a couple had weapons readied. Whether under orders or just to make themselves feel safer, Owain could only guess.

Bill jaunted down the slope to meet the new arrivals. He saluted Lethbridge-Stewart then tilted a smile at Owain. 'Good to have you with us, Little G. How're you feeling?'

'I'll live. I'm not made of china.'

'No. Stone, last I heard.'

Owain waved his gloved hand. It looked puffy and fattened with the bandage under the glove. 'Only this part of me. You want to see it?'

'Hmm. No, thanks. Best not. The brigadier has told me some stories.'

'Yes, well,' Lethbridge-Stewart interrupted. 'Talking of stories; what can you tell us, Lieutenant?'

Bill stood aside, allowing them a clear view of the human henge at the crest of the hill. Peering more intently, Owain could make out two shorter figures making up the circle. One that might easily have matched Kara's stature. The other was even smaller. And that produced a cold lump in his throat.

'Exactly what you see, sir. Number two squad have located another of these circles. Not far from the beach where some of these things came ashore. They're standing guard, steering people clear. But so far no movement from the, ah, statues. There may be others and...'

'And?'

'And they're quite the mix. Some have only a few remnants of clothing. Scraps of blue-and-white striped shirts, remains of uniform jackets. Soviet Navy insignia.'

'Right, I see. Owain?'

Owain barely heard his uncle. He'd begun a slow walk up the path.

Alistair, Bill and Mullins all followed close behind, but he was only marginally aware of them at his back.

As he closed on the circle, imagination kept taunting him. Persuading him the figures moved. He'd look. Pretty sure they were all in the same pose. Confirm the illusion. But doubts would creep and then he'd have to look again.

Don't be daft, he told himself. Although it wasn't so daft when he knew that the figures had come here under their own power. Arranged themselves in a circle too. But why?

There was only one way he could think of to find out.

Owain yanked off his glove and tore at the bandages.

'Hey, hold on there!' Bill reached to stop him but held off from actually touching. 'Aren't you supposed to keep that hand wrapped?'

'This is what he's here for, Lieutenant,' Lethbridge-Stewart said. 'To "speak with the stones".'

'Yeah,' said Owain. 'As New Age and hippy as that sounds. I won't touch anything else, I promise.'

'All right. I guess.' Bill held up his hands in mock surrender.

Owain wondered if it was all right. They'd find out soon enough. 'Listen though, if I keel over and end up in a coma again, just keep everyone clear okay.'

Owain marched into the circle. And turned, taking in the faces.

There she was: Kara. Or was she?

And there was Paolo too, standing silent sentinel beside her.

Pain pinched his heart. But the sight of the little girl damn near broke it. She looked almost ridiculous, like some cherub fallen off a fountain. A toddler moulded from stone, decked out in a little summery outfit of denim skirt and floral blouse. She definitely didn't belong in this circle of tall men, wearing their seaweed and rags and blank expressions. No, not men exactly – templates, waiting for life and character to be added. A lot of Adams trapped in clay, waiting to be made. But the woman one figure over – maybe that had once been her mum.

Owain shook his head. The last thing he wanted to be doing was imagining backstories for them.

Owain focused on Kara. Tried to shut out sight of the others. He approached. Walked slowly around the figure.

He raised his arm. Opened his palm and held it an inch from the statue. It was easier if he told himself it was a statue. Not real. Much easier to think than believe though. Too much of the girl remained in the features. It was like looking at one of those fossilised victims of Pompeii. Knowing they'd been real people who'd lived – and died. Perished in a volcanic nightmare. Preserved in ash. And recognising a friend.

Was there anything left of his friend in there? He had to hope so, for Kara's sake. For Paolo. For the *kid*. And all these people. Strangers to him, sure, but nobody deserved this fate.

Those divers had died. How had these people survived long enough to drag themselves out of the sea and walk ashore? To walk here and place themselves in this arcane circle? Why did this thing race through some, eat them up, while sparing others? Questions circled like vultures, picking the meat from his confidence. He guessed he'd better do this before his strength was gone altogether.

He pressed his palm to the stone that used to be Kara's face.

He swims in Hell. With the weight of the world above.

Hell has a roof.

It is a world he must reach.

He is everywhere.

This time, Owain is aware of himself. His feet firmly planted on solid ground. The air, warmed in the evening sun, kissing the back of his neck. His hand, fingers splayed, on stone that was once his friend. Cold.

Kara is gone. Lost in a deep, dark well on the other side of the world. He reaches for her and she trickles through his fingers like grains of sand. He reaches again and again. But can grasp only memories. And those fade like ghosts in the strange space before him.

He stands in a stone circle, he knows that. But he sees himself looking back at him. He is inside the centre, looking out. He stands in other circles in other landscapes. Other islands.

His vision is everywhere; he peers through a hundred

different windows at once. Kaleidoscoping in his mind, cascading shards of awareness.

They spin and spiral and shatter like a falling chandelier. But they only multiply and he is besieged by more windows. He sees more everywheres.

Approaching infinity.

A face leaps out. A fragment that means something to Owain. Recognition stabs like a knife.

Anne Travers. She's leaning over him. Studying him intently. She feeds him material: cutlery, a blade, a microscope, a tin of corned beef.

He lies in the deep. A craft, small and yellow, stirs the currents around him as it powers by, tantalisingly out of reach. But he can taste the metal of its hull. He can feel the life inside. Owain spies the faces of Captain Grigoriy and *Señora* Montilla illuminated in the space within the glass cockpit.

He festers in darkness, imprisoned in a cell of steel. Invisible chains restrain him, keeping him from touching his prison walls. He reaches, testing the limits of his restraints, but he has no limbs. He is slave to an unseen master and he has learned hate from the thoughts that bind him. A man appears before him, like a guard looking in on an inmate. The hatred rises. It is Rolph Vorster.

And in the heart of it all, he surges upwards in a bubbling furnace.

Fire in the mouth of a dragon of rock and ash. Not a dragon. A mountain. Fracturing and splitting open, exploding to set the sky aflame.

The mountain rips apart, spewing magma and cloud. Lava bleeds down ruptured slopes, boiling the sea.

Disintegration. The ash scatters.

Blacks out the sky. Suffocates the world.

He is the world. The world is him. They are one.

Owain staggered, like he was back on the deck of Grigoriy's ship. And in rougher seas. But no, his feet were on *terra firma.*

He spread his arms for balance. The world rocked a bit more. Then his back hit the ground. He lay flat in the grass and the sky wheeled above him, but the ground finally settled. 'Whoa.'

People called his name and he heard them rushing towards him. Faces hovered into view, blotting out the wheeling sky. There was Bill Bishop, Uncle Alistair. Some other soldier heads he didn't recognise. And Mullins crouching to examine him.

'I'm all right.' He waved off the fuss and tried to sit up. But only got as far as lifting his head before his thoughts started swarming like too many strikers fighting for possession over a ball. 'Okay, I'm not a hundred percent all right.'

'Check his hand, Mullins. And redress it,' his uncle said.

'On it, sir.'

Owain suffered the field treatment without further complaint. While he lay there, he reined in his storm of thoughts and had a go at processing everything he'd seen. Or dreamed or whatever.

It was tough. So hard to break past all the anguish and heartache about Kara and Paolo. He was sure, right there at the start, he'd touched Kara ever so momentarily. Not the stone, but Kara herself. Her *self*. They couldn't be gone. Not like Theo. His friends were still in there, somewhere. All those people, they were deep in the heart of whatever this thing was – a core of souls under a mantle of rock. He'd lost Lewis, and he'd since learned that some friends he'd once travelled with for a time had died during all the business with Dominex in the summer. He couldn't let more die. There had to be some way to bring Kara and Paolo back.

Making that a promise to himself, he gradually cleared his head enough to focus on the rest. Just in time for Mullins to finish the bandage job on his hand.

'No harm done, far as I can tell,' the medic reported to Lethbridge-Stewart. 'The, uh, infection's the same.'

'Somebody help me up?' Owain asked.

Mullins and Bill obliged and kept hands in place until they were sure he was stable.

'You're sure you're all right?' Uncle Alistair asked, maintaining his official officer face. 'Let's take him down the hill, sit him in the Land Rover, shall we?'

Owain acquiesced. He was shaken, but most of the swimming sensation was in his head. Bill and Mullins lent support anyway. His uncle accompanied them down to the parked Land Rover and Owain sagged gratefully into the front passenger seat.

'So, Owain, no harm done,' Uncle Alistair said. 'But did we learn anything?'

It was a fair question. 'Yeah. Yes, I think so.' Owain summoned the images, sieved through the confusion. It was a challenge just divining a starting point. 'It's... it's all connected.'

'How? What's connected?'

'Everything. The stone circles. The ships. Vorster and his rig. He has something out there, a whole mass of this stone stuff. I hate to say I told you so, but... No, listen. It's more than that. The stone itself. The creature. It's all one. What do they call that in those science fiction books of yours, Bill?'

'A gestalt?'

Owain nodded at Bill. 'Right. But it's also part of the Earth. Only different. Different in nature.'

'Silicon-based life, according to Anne,' Bill said.

Owain nodded. 'That'd be it. And we're carbon-based. But it means to change that.' He managed a cold laugh in face of the chills. 'It just wants to fit in.'

'What are you talking about, Owain?' his uncle asked.

'These circles, they're hubs in a... In a communications network, I suppose. And I'm not sure, but I think the part that Vorster has is some sort of central node or... or nucleus. But this network, it's... They're talking to the Earth. Specifically, trying to wake the volcano.'

'And you still believe it's not hostile?'

'Not in our understanding of the word. It just wants to spread itself far and wide.' Owain relived the image: ash blotting out the sky. A memory of something that hadn't happened. Yet. 'What you think of as an infection... It'll be airborne.'

Lethbridge-Stewart eyed Owain, confident on the whole that the lad was as all right as he claimed. But the opposite of confident on other questions.

'Bishop, a word.'

'Sir.'

Lethbridge-Stewart strolled with Bishop back up the hill.

'Owain is understandably emotional about all this and I want us to do everything in our power to help these people.'

'Of course, sir.'

'But,' said Lethbridge-Stewart, wishing he could disregard any qualifiers and leave it at that. 'If there is imminent danger of an eruption and these stone circles are causing it somehow, then we cannot afford to allow that to happen. There are liners out in the bay that, given time, might manage to take on a couple of thousand passengers and clear the area. But we have no idea how much time we might have. And a full-scale evacuation of this island... It's out of the question.'

'Agreed, sir. What do you propose?'

'Lieutenant, I want you to give Owain one more shot at communing with this thing. See if he can't talk – or think – some sense into it. Reason with it, if it has any capacity for reason. But after that...'

'After that?'

'What's our situation with explosives?'

'Explosives? Well, I think we might have some plastic to hand. And grenades, of course.'

'Enough to break up these stone circles?'

'Not sure about that, sir. I...'

Lethbridge-Stewart headed off the objections he knew were coming. 'Tamped charges on each of the centre stones might be sufficient to disrupt them. Prevent this channelling or whatever Owain believes they're doing.'

'It might, sir, but–'

'But, Lieutenant Bishop, we are short on alternatives. I am aware that these things were people. Right now, they are a threat. A danger to everybody on this island and quite possibly well beyond. Obviously the circle will have to be screened in some way so that the blast can be contained and all our people pulled well back. Don't want particles of this thing scattered on the wind. We will give Owain his chance. He succeeded against the Intelligence in New York, so maybe he can do so here, too. But at the same time we must lay preparations for the worst case scenario. See to it.'

'Yes, sir.'

*

Owain looked up the hill to where Alistair and Bill were strolling by the circle. They appeared locked in some discussion or debate, with Uncle Alistair gesturing a good deal at the stone figures.

He wondered what military men made of the statues? Victims, or enemies? Mullins loitered nearby. He could ask him. Something kept his mouth shut though. He wasn't sure he wanted an idea of what his uncle was thinking.

He got out of the Land Rover and stretched his legs. Give himself another five minutes and he reckoned he'd be up for another communion. Really try to get through to Kara or Paolo this time.

He paced a short line beside the vehicle, practising being upright.

A car pulled into view at the foot of the hill. A tan Mercedes. Not an off-roader, it bumped its way up the dirt track.

'Great, spectators now.' Mullins marched past Owain and waved the car to a halt like a car park attendant. 'Hey, you can't be here. You're going to have to turn around. Off-limits. Military business.'

'Wait,' said Owain. Too quiet.

Mullins strode up on the driver's side. The door smacked into him. A guy jumped out, plus another from the passenger side.

They wore stockings over their heads.

Owain turned to yell up the hill.

Somebody dived on him from behind and clamped a big hairy mitt over his mouth. Then dragged him downslope, alongside the car where the driver was giving poor Mullins a kicking to keep him on the ground.

Owain's captor hauled him towards the rear of the car.

Apparently he was going for a ride.

CHAPTER TWENTY
State of Decay

'IT'LL TAKE a while to get the X-ray developed.'

'Thanks.' Anne appreciated the technician's eager assistance, even if he hadn't the strongest clue what the experiment was about. In a lead-lined apron matching her own, he followed her through to the treatment room. 'I'm not sure it would tell us anything. No. I'm more interested in discernible effects on our patient.'

Anne approached the table and peered down at the Goddess. Almost afraid she would start to grow, turned into some rampaging B-movie monster by radiation exposure. *Attack of the 50-Foot Snake Goddess.* Thankfully, the figurine lay perfectly still and as diminutive as ever. In fact...

Anne leaned in for a proper study. The sheet around the Goddess was lightly dusted with minuscule filings. She fished a ballpoint from her top pocket and gently prodded the Goddess. The point remained pristine, as though the cancer had lost its appetite. More than that, the statuette crumbled, her arm falling to ash.

Result.

The question was, what did it mean?

She gingerly touched the ballpoint to the residue. Nothing. No reaction.

'The pen is mightier,' she said. 'With a little help from hard radiation.'

Kitted out in flight suit and life jacket, Anne felt like she'd doubled in weight; gone up several dress sizes. But the extra padding was of some comfort against the gusts beating down from the rotor blades, and the vertiginous view from her perch in the wide-open helicopter doorway.

It was no comfort against the chills that seized her on first sight of HMS *Aphrodite*.

Floating perilously low in the otherwise deserted waters below, she too appeared to have gained weight. The Leander-class frigate could best be described as a plague ship.

Anne twirled her finger and shouted to the airman crouching beside her. 'Can we take another pass?'

He nodded and signalled to the crew. The sea revolved slowly beneath them, with the ship like a dial on a compass, turning to remain pointed in the same direction.

Large swathes of her hull, her decks and superstructure had succumbed. Her forward-mounted turret, the bridge and hangar, were crude stone mouldings. Her smoke-stack resembled a crumbling stone keep in the middle of some old fortress, her radar tower was now some strange Stone Age totem. She looked like a floating tomb.

Could anyone be left alive on board? Anne had to remind herself she had requested to be here. More than that, she'd insisted against chauvinistic opposition from Group Captain Winser.

'You need to put me down there!'

The airman, a Flight Sergeant Driscoll, regarded her dubiously for a second. But pointed at the winch. 'If you insist, Miss, it's going to have to be that.'

She really was doing a lot of insisting lately. 'All right. Lower me. Then my apparatus.'

Her X-ray machine was secured nearby. Portable, yes, and she'd spent a couple of hours on modifications, attempting to boost the power and lighten the load. But it was still too bulky to take with her on the one trip. Not when she would need both hands to hold on.

'Wait, Miss, I should escort you down.'

'No,' Anne countered. 'And I'm not debating that, Flight Sergeant. The fewer people setting foot on that ship, the less chance of contagion.'

It was easier to talk in terms of disease, biological contamination. Qualifying it any other way would only undermine the deterrent.

Anne buttoned her lip and waited, sending the message that the subject was closed.

Driscoll had a second bout of uncertainty, but eventually relented.

At another signal, the aircraft dropped and turned, positioning itself to hover over the ship's stern. All the while, Driscoll issued encouraging smiles along with instructions as he helped her into the harness. Last, he fitted her with a helmet, bending the radio mic around to the corner of her mouth. He rapped the top of the helmet as though checking she was home. 'I've known crewmen not half as brave as you, Miss.'

'Flatterer,' she said. Sure that he wouldn't have commended her courage so freely if he could count the butterflies in her stomach.

Ready as she would ever be, she gulped down a few butterflies that had strayed as far as her throat, then swung herself off the edge.

Despite the many feet shaved off the altitude, Anne dangled several houses' height above the frigate. Driscoll's voice was in her ear, coaching, as he worked the winch, lowering her. Just as she'd anticipated, she grasped the line with both hands. Surplus to requirement, but no effort was wasted if it helped her feel that little bit safer.

She spun in a faintly dizzying circle. The motion aggravated her butterflies. She felt like bait on a fishing line, being paid out towards the water.

But she looked down and her boots were a foot above deck. One moment more and she planted herself down. She gave the thumbs up to Driscoll in the helicopter doorway above. Then unfastened the clasps and released herself for a look around. The winch reeled in her line. She berated herself for feeling a little stranded.

Anne peered into the gloomy mouth of the hangar. With the structure transformed into a rough stone cowl, it was impossible to escape the impression of standing at the entrance to some ancient tomb or forbidding cavern. And ancient was the word. The stone spoke of age. Not mere years, but geological timeframes.

The thought reminded her: she was a scientist. She didn't deal in impressions. She tried to filter out the imaginative nonsense and stick to the analytical. She could observe the mutagen's continued spread, encroaching on one of the few as yet untouched patches of deck before her. Discernible to the naked eye, but much slower than she had observed in the laboratory.

Proximity to the source? A brief contact, say. The hull grazes some outcrop lurking below the waterline. The ship sails on, the crew noting the damage but unaware of its malignancy. It fit the data.

But what of those crewmen?

She sighed. Objectivity wasn't easy when you knew lives were involved.

She looked up to see the machine on its way down. The chopper maintained as steady a hover as possible, but the sway of the ship and the cable made it tricky to reach and grab the equipment without it clubbing her. Her helmet lent her some confidence. Anne waited, gauging her moment, then snatched at it and pulled it to her. She worked quickly to unstrap it and sent Driscoll another thumbs up.

'I'm heading inside,' she said in her mic.

'Roger. We'll stay on watch.'

Cradling her machine, Anne moved along the side of the warship.

She tread with great care. She was safely cocooned, with perhaps only the buckles and zips of her flight suit vulnerable if they happened to come into contact with afflicted surfaces around her. And her helmet, she supposed, in the event she bumped her head. But the lining ought to insulate her from the mutagenic effects, long enough for her to whip the headgear off. So possibly her caution was excessive. Well, so what. Caution wasn't one of those things that ought to be taken in moderation. Not in this situation.

Laden with the X-ray machine, she told herself she ought to worry less about 'infection' and more about pitching over the railings for an unscheduled swim.

Driscoll kept Miss Travers in his sights, watching her pick her way along *Aphrodite's* port side. It went badly against the grain not to be down there with her. On the other hand, it was a choice between staying up here and feeling guilty or earning grief from Miss Travers for arguing. Talk about the devil and the deep blue sea.

The chopper slid off-station a little, but Pilot Officer McCann steered her back. He was doing a pretty good job of keeping her steady.

Below, Miss Travers was looking a little wobblier on her feet, carting that machine along the deck. But she made it to a bulkhead amidships.

Throwing a parting wave in his direction, she disappeared inside.

'Miss Travers? Still hearing me? Over.'

'Loud and clear. Um – over.'

'Okay. Just checking. Take it easy in there.'

Driscoll was probably overegging the gentleman act. But there was too much about that ship that worried him.

Anne waded in calf-deep water. Cold and damp found their way into the legs of her flight suit. She hoped nothing else did.

The passage was dark. Her flashlight put paid to some of that, as did the infrequent sparks from damaged electrics. The torch beam slid over rough-stone walls, making her feel like a pot-holer wading through a flooded cavern system. She shone her light into an open doorway and glimpsed stone bunks. Mounds under blankets that might have been human. A grim knot tightened in her gut, strangling the butterflies. It stopped her from entering for a closer look.

She slipped past a bulkhead, watching her suit didn't snag on the encroaching rock.

The stone formations grew beyond the pre-existing structure, expanding somehow without any obvious materials to feed on. She wished she'd had longer to study the substance under the microscope. But was it actual growth, in addition to the transformation of the metals? Some kind of cellular division for silicate life?

She was left with educated guesswork. Stabs in the dark.

At least the water explained why the ship was riding so low. It was easy to see now what had happened to the other ships. Holed by some collision, some of them succumbing rapidly if they remained in the vicinity of the initial contact perhaps, taking on water and – if this was actual growth she was witnessing – eventually overcoming the craft's carefully designed buoyancy. Sending it to the bottom as little more than a large boulder or ridge on the seabed.

Interesting that it favoured processed metals over raw minerals.

Otherwise, surely, it would have spread across the entire floor of the Mediterranean by now.

Anne's beam pounced on a stalagmite of sorts obstructing the passage. Swollen, tumescent, a misshapen lump fused to the walls, ceiling and deck by tendrils of rock. Almost like... Like a heart, she supposed; arteries and ventricles extending to meet the body of the ship around it.

She let her torch travel up and down the mass, following some of the stone bridges connecting it to the surrounding structure.

Something clanged in the passage behind her.

She jumped. Fumbled her torch.

Caught it, and her breath. Just.

Anne swung around, shone her torch aft.

Before she saw anything, she heard the slosh of footsteps. Some other body wading towards her.

A malformed silhouette squeezed itself through the opening. In the dark it looked like a tar baby, all grown-up. It advanced into the light, showing Anne crudely moulded features. Hollow depressions where eyes should be, like a pair of deep thumbprints in clay. Mouth closed over like a healed wound. Someone had clothed it in the uniform of a Royal Navy sailor.

The man it had once been had served as crew aboard the *Aphrodite*.

'Please,' said Anne. 'Hello?'

Was there anything left of that sailor within the shell?

It waded on, pulling at handholds along the walls. Unwittingly, it snapped a length of pipe. Or what had once been pipe.

Anne thought the figure meant to use it as a weapon, but it discarded it immediately. Let it splash into the water around its legs.

Anne lifted the X-ray machine in front of her. She thought of the Snake Goddess. Just a figurine, but she couldn't inflict the same effects on something that used to be a man. Might still be, beneath the stone.

She spun and aimed her machine at the heart-like mass. Thinking to clear a path.

She fired.

In an invisible flash, the whole thing crumbled, falling apart into dust.

The stone arteries cracked and crashed into the water. Anne was set to charge forward, but the sight of the walls stopped her. Blackened decay bloomed across the surrounding surfaces.

She heard an ominous heavy splash behind her. Turned to see the stone sailor collapsed in the flooded passage.

The toppled human statue turned to ash. Black particles, coal dust, floated on the water, muddying the ripples where he – or it – had fallen.

Too long, too quiet.

An ugly little knot developed in Driscoll's gut. He scanned *Aphrodite's* decks, searching for movement.

'Miss Travers?'

He reached for the winch cable, set to hook himself up.

'Miss Travers? Are you receiving me? Miss Travers? Respond, please.'

The chopper slipped into a lazy circle, granting him a slow overhead pan around the warship. Nothing moved on deck.

'Miss Travers!'

The broken end of petrified pipe disintegrated, scattering more ash on the water. Creeping dark ate its way across the walls and ceiling.

Anne snapped out of her freeze.

'Sorry, yes, Flight Sergeant. I'm here. I'm okay. There's… We have to get word to the brigadier. I'm on my way out.'

Anne waded back along the passage, stepping over the crumbling remains of the stone sailor.

HMS *Aphrodite* fell apart around her.

Remnant metal groaned. A conduit splintered, raining stone chunks. A bulkhead sloughed a granite slab that used to be a door. Anne clambered over the resulting ramp and hopped off the other end before it completely cracked under foot.

She waded on and on. She forced her legs to work faster against the drag, like trying to run through a swamp.

Somewhere throughout *Aphrodite's* hull, crewmen died in silence. Maybe they had already been dead. But they died again unseen,

CHAPTER TWENTY-ONE
Kidnap

THE DRIVER, presumably having finished kicking Mullins, ran around in front of Owain. His features were squashed and ugly under the stocking, but Owain reckoned the man would've looked no better without it.

Behind him, his captor held him in a half-nelson, but suddenly shifted his hold and yanked both Owain's arms together. Metal clicked and the cuffs locked around his wrists. The man in front whipped out a pillow case from nowhere, fast, like a magician pulling a bouquet from his sleeve. Owain struggled and twisted, but there was no stopping that pillow case being pulled down over his head.

Hey presto! Daylight was shut out and Owain's world disappeared.

The two men wrestled him around to the car boot. They pushed and shoved and dragged him. He tried a kick at some shins, but fighting blind wasn't his forte and his toecap never made a firm contact.

'What's going on? Let me go!'

'Shut it,' ordered one of them; a gruff voice, screened through fifteen-denier cotton or whatever. A hand batted the back of Owain's head. A gag pushed the cloth of the pillow case into his mouth, fastened quickly with a knot that pressed into the base of his skull.

The car boot popped.

Then the kidnappers double-teamed him. A kick swept his feet out from under him and he was roughly manhandled inside. He rolled, bumping metal. Firm hands pushed his face down against upholstery, carpet fibres scratching at his cheek.

The lid slammed closed.

He kicked upwards as best as he could with his legs scrunched up. The lid banged but didn't budge. He threw muffled shouts through his gag.

Car doors clunked in quick succession. The engine fired, mechanical growls drowning his efforts. The vehicle was off and running.

Owain left off the verbal and physical protest. Lay there and rattled and bounced about in the boot.

Not that the fight had gone out of him, but he had to pause and think.

Who were these people? What did they want with him?

Scrub that. Most important: how the hell was he going to get out?

He wriggled his fingers, flexed his wrists. They felt bruised from when the cuffs had snapped on.

The car hit a downslope. Owain rolled with the gradient. Narrowly avoided banging his head.

His fingernails accidentally scratched at the stone scab in the pit of his palm. Apparently the dressing had torn loose in his struggle. The scrape almost snapped a nail and Owain bit down on the gag.

Wait. Would that even work?

Just because the contagion or infection had stopped in him, did that mean it had lost its power to spread? Right now was the perfect time to find out.

Wriggling his hands into better position, he pressed his palm to the metal of the cuffs. And waited.

The chain cracked and Owain's hands were free.

Bracing his legs against tumbling around, he pressed his infected palm flat against the lid above him.

He practically willed the stone into the metal. Like wanting to pass on a cold. Stupid, really, and he hadn't a clue if his focus made any difference. Of course, he couldn't see either. There was no way to tell whether his touch was having any effect.

Except by touch.

He felt it, the sudden coarseness. Creeping like hard mould.

Abrasive, sandpaper texture blossomed under his fingers. He pictured it spreading like grey lichen. Eating its way across the expanse of metal. Expanding outwards from that grainy lump embedded in the heart of his hand.

How fast? How long? He had no way of knowing once it passed beyond his fingertips.

Owain waited. The car motor burred in his ears, vibrations pummelling his cheek. The vehicle slowed. Its horn blared. Twice.

Somebody shouted in Greek.

God bless the local traffic, thought Owain.

The car picked up some speed.

'Come on, come on.' He tried to visualise it: the stone plague eating its way into the locking mechanism.

The latch popped.

Light flooded in through the pillow-case weave. The car slowed again, taking a bend. Before centrifugal force rolled him into a corner, Owain propelled himself towards the opening. He flopped out of the boot and slapped down hard on tarmac.

The engine revved and the car sped on.

Owain lay there wincing at multiple pains.

Boots came running. Hands worked at the knotted gag, tore that loose then yanked the pillow-case hood from his head. Owain blinked against the assault of daylight.

Bill hauled him onto his feet. 'Who the hell were those guys?'

Uncle Alistair was there too. He peered down the road where the kidnappers had fled. A number of pedestrians shuffled by, staring at the strange trio in the middle of the road.

Owain shook his head. 'No idea. Vorster's mercs, maybe? Out to take care of a loose end.'

'Is that what you are?' Bill smiled.

Owain laughed. 'To them, yeah.' He bent over, resting his hands on his knees, took long slow breaths. His left knee stung: he'd grazed it through his jeans.

'Are you okay?' asked Uncle Alistair.

'Yeah, I think so. Just more cuts and bruises to add to the collection.' Owain frowned at the feel of his knee under his palm. That was the thing: he could feel his knee, with no intervening lump. He lifted his hand. The skin had returned to normal, the stone scab gone. With only the faintest hollow to indicate where it had been. If he was the slightest bit practiced in palmistry he could have read his lifeline and everything. Hopefully, maybe, predicted a few more years for him yet.

'I'm good,' he said, and showed Bill and his uncle his clean hand.

'That's great.' Bill patted him on the back. 'I think we should still get you checked out before I shake you by the hand.'

'Yes, well, never mind all that. This settles it,' declared Alistair, back in full brigadier mode.

'Settles what?'

'Have Owain here placed under guard.'

'Wait? Am I under arrest?' Owain had only just escaped captivity. He didn't think much of becoming a prisoner.

'Protective custody, young man. No arguments.'

'What about the stone circle? Kara and Paolo?'

'I'm sorry. We can't afford to have you out and about where Vorster's people can make another grab for you.' Lethbridge-Stewart about-faced and began the march back up the street. Bill kept an arm on Owain to help him along. 'You'll be safe under guard aboard the Hercules. We'll bring Corporal Mullins; he'll need to rest up. And, Bishop, you can drive back with us, collect those supplies.'

'Sir. What about you, sir?'

'I'll be making some calls. I mean to pay a visit to that rig, permission or no.'

Owain nodded, not in the mood to serve up the I-told-you-so. For right now it was enough to see his uncle meant business.

CHAPTER TWENTY-TWO
Enlightenment

THE SOVIET helicopter fanned a gale, whipping Sophia's hair about her face as it dropped in to land on the pad. Ware, beside her, stood to attention as Lethbridge-Stewart hopped out.

Captain Bugayev trotted forward, ducking rotors, and extended a hand. Lethbridge-Stewart appeared to think it over before completing the handshake. Bugayev led the way down from the pad, while two squads of British soldiers emerged from the aircraft, looking around like they'd set foot on the Moon. Several of the Soviet crew regarded one another doubtfully, none prepared to roll out a carpet.

'Welcome aboard, Brigadier. To what do we owe the change of heart?'

'First things first, Captain. You mentioned findings of your own. We should exchange intelligence.'

'Of course.' Bugayev collared a nearby crewman and issued a brief barrage of instructions in Russian. The crewman was off like a shot to greet and guide the British visitors. 'I'll have a cabin cleared where your men can rest and wait.'

Lethbridge-Stewart nodded to Sophia and Ware as Bugayev led him past.

'Sir!' Ware saluted.

'I trust they've looked after you, Samson.'

'After a fashion. Can't complain.' Ware turned and fell into step with the officers.

'Come, we'll talk in the galley.' Bugayev beckoned Sophia. '*Señora*, join us?'

It was only nominally a question. And anyway, military

dealings aside, she was too invested now to miss this discussion.

'Allow me to open proceedings,' Captain Bugayev offered, down in the mess. 'I was wrong.'

Lethbridge-Stewart arched his eyebrow. 'About what?'

'Radiation. I thought perhaps some radioactive contamination in these waters accelerated the contagion. But I believe now this thing has an aversion to radiation. The *Señora* and I observed evidence to support that conclusion.'

Señora Montilla hovered on the periphery of the meeting, propped against the cabinets to one side of the room.

'Tell him, *Señora*,' Bugayev invited. 'It's all right. You can speak up.'

'Thank you,' she returned with a half-teaspoon of sarcasm. She seemed unusually ill-at-ease, perhaps mistrustful of this apparent detente. This tiny corner of the Cold War had entered a new era of openness, but who could say how long it might last? Lethbridge-Stewart had taken a bold risk in bringing two squads here. Quite a step from merely sitting down to talk in the *Señora's* back yard. 'Well, lodged in the centre of our ersatz Atlantis, we found the captain's missing submarine. Turned to stone. Except the effects appeared to have avoided certain sections of the vessel. I assume there's some sort of nuclear reactor in the stern section. And... something I perhaps shouldn't mention in the forward area.'

Torpedoes. That was a piece of the puzzle Lethbridge-Stewart could supply himself. In effect, the *Señora* had said enough to confirm the presence of nuclear-tipped ordnance on board. Something the Soviets would never officially confirm or deny, assuming the presence of the submarine in these waters was ever admitted in the first place.

'Permission or not, I get the feeling it could be one of those "I could tell you, but then he'd have to kill me" deals.'

'You are quite safe, *Señora*,' said Bugayev. 'No killing between temporary friends.'

'Thank you,' *Señora* Montilla said again.

'If you would be more comfortable, confine yourself to your field of expertise. What we learned from the archaeological site.'

Oddly, the *Señora* appeared no more confident on her own

topic. 'What we learned is I am out of my depth. I don't know where to begin.'

'You are too bound by what you know,' Bugayev assured her. 'Think. If the citadel we saw has no foundation in history, what can it be?'

'Well, a forgery. But nobody would–'

'Nobody would. True.'

Lethbridge-Stewart stepped in. 'What does it suggest to you, Captain?'

'In military terms. A decoy. Like Mussolini's armies of cardboard tanks. Or a wooden town built to deceive bombers. Or something more sinister. Not a defence. But a trap.'

'But who is the enemy?' *Señora* Montilla asked.

'The city. The stone. I have seen it consume men and now I have seen it claim a submarine.' Bugayev stared down on the charts, as though able to see the archaeological site laid out within the marked circle. 'This is what we are fighting. And it has constructed this city for a purpose. So, *Señora*, if you were to view this as the enemy, to credit it with the intelligence to evolve strategies et cetera, what conclusion would you draw then?'

'Well... I would have to ask myself what it could possibly want. And if we were to think of it in terms of an empire, then I would have to say it would wish to expand. To spread its influence. So... no, not a decoy, but a lure. Bait. And these relics; they would be part of the trap. A means of propagation.' She shrugged. 'But that's... ridiculous.'

'I wouldn't be so sure.' Lethbridge-Stewart empathised. There had been a time when he would have met anything like this with greater scepticism. 'You'll recall when I enlisted you, I referred to abnormalities; anomalies of any description, I believe I said.'

'This I would definitely categorise as abnormal, yes.' The *Señora* patted her pockets, probably in search of a cigarette.

'Quite. Well, in any case, permit me to share what intelligence I've been able to gather.' Lethbridge-Stewart strolled around the table, examining the map, with the rig's position marked not five miles from the circled site. 'After calling in for my ride here, I consulted with my scientific expert in Akrotiri. She confirmed much the same, as regards its aversion to radioactivity.'

Lethbridge-Stewart replayed his conversation with Miss Travers.

'Radiation is not a catalyst. Quite the opposite. It alters the nature of the beast. Kills it. Stone dead, if you'll pardon the pun.'

She had sounded uncharacteristically shaken, despite her attempt at humour.

'Is that something we can use against this thing?' he'd asked.

'That depends. Exposure renders it inert to other materials, but toxic to the mutagenic material. We can stop the mutation, but it won't save the patients. With time I might be able to work on a means of reversing the process, but that may be beyond me.'

Captain Bugayev leaned across the table. 'Brigadier? This scientist of yours; was she able to learn more about this contaminant? Do we understand anything more of its nature?'

'As to that, I am afraid you wouldn't believe me.'

'Try me. As a political bloc, we may be closed to Western ideas, but some of us keep an open mind. To an extent.'

'Very well then.' Lethbridge-Stewart took a deep breath, reminding himself of what Bishop had called it. 'A gestalt. Some form of silicon-based life. Whether virus or some higher life, we can't say. Our expert compared it to a cancer. All we know for certain is that it is inimical to life on Earth.'

'But we can fight it, sir? With radiation?' Samson asked.

'Yes, Sergeant Major. Contagion or cancer, whatever we choose to call it, radiation is our key. Clearly, low-level seepage from reactors or warheads is insufficient to kill it, but a more violent release, shall we say, could rid us of this thing altogether.' It was a cold summation. Far from disregarding those people locked in their stone circles, it weighed them into the equation and arrived, regrettably, at the same conclusion. No matter what hopes Owain clung to, Lethbridge-Stewart was sadly persuaded that those victims were already dead. Miss Travers had not admitted defeat – it wasn't in her nature – but her tone had said more than her words. 'It's a question of whether we can apply that knowledge.'

'Hmm. I have considered available options, Brigadier,' Bugayev said. 'If a fatal dose of radiation is required, there would potentially be one obvious method of delivery open to us. Except there are feasibility issues.'

'Care to clarify?'

'All right. Cards on the table. From a deck we will call hypothetical. Let us imagine the remains of a stricken submarine contains a number of nuclear warheads. And if those warheads could be detonated...' Bugayev opened a fist in slow-motion, mimicking an explosion.

'But if this boat is at the heart of this underwater city, as you say...'

'Exactly, Brigadier. Further, if the reactor is intact we might possibly engineer a critical meltdown. But divers, our submersible, all are prone to the contagion. This cancer. The practicalities of accessing the wreck...' The captain threw up a hand. 'Borderline impossible.'

'And what would be the range of such a blast? Hypothetically.'

'Five kiloton yield. Kiss goodbye to anything subsurface within four nautical miles, ranging to six. Half the radius for surface effect.'

It was slightly troubling that Bugayev was so ready with the kill radius of a nuclear warhead, and Lethbridge-Stewart suspected the man had more specifications to hand should they be required.

'Well, my question was less one of feasibility, rather more of the will to do what needs to be done.'

'You'll find no shortage of that here, Brigadier.'

Lethbridge-Stewart had expected no less of Bugayev. He couldn't doubt that, if he knew some of the individuals now standing in those stone circles were fellow countrymen, submariners from the stricken vessel, his answer would be the same. Costs were a given.

'Well, it may be that I have set some alternative wheels in motion on that score. Understand, Captain, I'm not sure I consider myself at liberty to discuss details. In any case, my own plan is awaiting authorisation and confirmation of a precise target.' Lethbridge-Stewart had taken the opportunity to confer with Group Captain Winser and requested Miss Travers to state the scientific case, such as it was, when presenting his proposal before the air marshal. What happened after that rested in the hands of government ministers back home. 'Whatever our ultimate approach, any effects would have to include that hydraulic fracturing platform. The fact is, our intelligence suggests VTMB are harbouring some sort of core or nucleus for this creature aboard that rig.'

'Ah.' Bugayev straightened. 'You are ready to pay that visit?'

'A conversation couldn't hurt. Along with some level of inspection.'

'If Mr Vorster is amenable.' Bugayev snapped his fingers at his lieutenant.

The big man supplied a pencil. Bugayev snatched it and sketched a quick cross then drew a square around the rig's marked position. 'Us. And them. This,' he said, 'is how I would go about making an appointment.'

He proceeded to outline his plan.

CHAPTER TWENTY-THREE
Gunfighters

THE LAUNCH clipped choppy waves. Night had turned the sea black, but clouds were scarce and the Moon too bright for Lethbridge-Stewart's liking. Bad enough to be buffeted around, but he felt exposed out here. Still, even if the weather was an unreliable ally, he wondered how much further he could count upon Captain Bugayev.

Samson, seated beside him, blinked into a faceful of salt water. He looked at Lethbridge-Stewart, and there was distrust written all over him.

'Relax, Sergeant Major!' he yelled to compete with the engine. 'We're up against a predictable enemy.'

'Yes, sir. But do we have predictable friends?'

Lethbridge-Stewart grimaced. He preferred to remain tight-lipped on that question. The answer would be forthcoming – or not – any moment now.

Bugayev's reasoning was sound. There was no reason to believe the welcome they were about to receive would be any different to the one that had met Owain and his friends. But Bugayev was not the one making himself a target in open water. It was difficult not to feel like sheep driven across a minefield.

'I'm sure Captain Bugayev is a man of his word!' Lethbridge-Stewart assured Samson, with enough volume to sound like conviction. 'And if not, well, the man wants this operation to succeed as badly as we do! He'll come through!'

He had better.

The rig loomed large. A monstrous framework of steel shadows, edges trimmed with moonlight. Active artificial lights were few, dotted here and there about the structure. The waves frothed lightly around its giant legs. Hopefully generating enough background wash to cover the noise of the boat engine a while longer. Timing would be critical.

Five hundred yards.

'Keep those weapons hidden, men. But be ready,' Lethbridge-Stewart ordered.

Spotlights snapped to life on the rig. Beams wheeled around to skate the waves and home in on their craft. The launch sped on and the beams raced to stay with them. Lethbridge-Stewart shielded his eyes against the glare.

Four hundred yards.

On cue, the chopper leaped into view from the far side of the superstructure. The readily identifiable flying-whale shape of a Sea King. Figures fanned out along the rig at different levels, like lines of dancers silhouetted in footlights. This chorus line came armed.

The launch ploughed on, moving fast. But there was no mistaking the fact that they were sitting ducks.

The Sea King banked and dipped, swooping towards them. The flashing fuselage lights were enough to illuminate the figure manning its side door. If or when he spotted their kit he would likely give the order to open fire. Possibly even before, if Owain's account was any indicator.

'Keep going!' Lethbridge-Stewart urged.

Tensed, he watched the helicopter. And flicked intermittent glances at the men on the rig. Who pressed rifles to their shoulders.

Oleg Kolachik hoisted the launcher across his shoulder and pressed his eye to the scope. Night vision painted his view in tones of green and picked out the aircraft sharply. A tadpole-blob hovering above a very big pond.

He half-pulled the trigger. The LED lit up and the weapon buzzed, the IR seeker engaged almost instantly.

'*Do svidaniya*,' he murmured. And pressed the trigger fully home.

Wearing a star-bright tail of flame, the missile traced a comet plume across the night sky. The helicopter spun and dropped, attempting to evade. Without luck. The missile streaked in to spear it firmly in its flank. It blew apart in a ball of metal and flame, lighting up one side of the rig. Pieces of aircraft tumbled into the waves.

'Heads down! Take cover!'

There was no cover, but Lethbridge-Stewart and his men made themselves as small as possible. The boat powered forward, zipping left and right, sidewinder fashion.

Guns cracked, spat bullets into the water.

'Come on, Bugayev. Come on,' Lethbridge-Stewart muttered.

He looked up and aft. Searched the sky.

There!

The ungainly shape of the Mi-8 Hip. Bulbous, functional and ugly, but right now an inspiring sight. More importantly, its appearance interrupted the gunfire from the rig.

It closed swiftly to five hundred yards.

Pods flared under its wing-stubs.

Rockets streaked overhead. Lethbridge-Stewart counted a dozen. With fiery tails and a ferocious whoosh, they flew into the skeleton of the rig. Blasts coughed up smoke and thickening clouds rolled along the platform at different levels. The gunmen faded to shadows in the smoke, many waving arms and stumbling about, blind.

The Soviet chopper pressed on with its swoop and hit the rig with a second salvo. More smoke billowed, engulfing the structure's midsection and further swamping the figures in its midst.

'Time to unwrap the presents, gentlemen!'

Samson threw back the tarpaulin, uncovering the stash of firearms. He hefted the PK light machinegun and nestled it against his shoulder.

'Suppressive fire!'

The men opened up, spraying the railings and catwalks. Throwing sparking ricochets in amongst palls of smoke.

Private Gilliver cut the motor and the launch glided in under the structure, thudding into the pontoon jetty.

Lethbridge-Stewart jumped out of the boat, leading the charge.

Bugayev perched in the chopper's doorway, watching enemies mill around in the billowing smoke below. And listened to the satisfying thunder of the DShK machinegun, hammering down suppressive fire.

So far, nobody answered back.

Bugayev signalled to the pilot and pointed at the deck.

The helicopter dropped into a hover forty feet above the helipad. Vacant space now, but Bugayev wanted the aircraft to remain in the air. He slapped the machine gunner on the shoulder. The man ceased fire and budged aside.

Troops hooked up in pairs to rappel down onto the big stencilled H.

Bugayev slid down his own line. He hit the pad, knees bent, AK ready.

Shouts came out of the smoke. Bullets followed.

Lethbridge-Stewart stormed the stairways. The entire rig was a riot of gunfire and clanging bootsteps.

He loosed a few rounds at the catwalk overhead. The bullets only sparked off the steel grill, but they might keep the enemy on their toes. As he hit the first landing, a body leaned over the railings above, swinging a rifle to cover him. He fired twice, encouraged the fellow to duck. Samson rushed in and crouched in front. He let the chap have a burst from the LMG. And a second and a third to keep him down.

Samson's LMG-fire found its way past the railings and cut the fellow's legs out from under him. He belly-flopped to the catwalk and Lethbridge-Stewart and his men hopped over him. Lethbridge-Stewart kicked the chap's gun over the side as he raced by.

Sea breezes thinned the smoke.

Bugayev's team rolled from the helipad and hunted out cover among the machinery and superstructure.

'Pick your targets!' he yelled.

And practised what he preached. Sight swiftly along the barrel, find a man, three-round burst, sweep to find the next, three rounds.

The enemy scattered, firing wild on the move. Arm the ducks, it was still a duck shoot. He listened to sporadic exchanges coming up from below. The enemy thinned in line with the smoke.

Bugayev put another man down and glimpsed two disappear through a darkened doorway. This wasn't a scatter in mad panic. It was a fighting retreat inside.

Bugayev waved his men to advance.

They peeled from cover in twos, left and right. Move, fire, move, fire. Bugayev added to the covering fire, keeping the enemy on the run.

Another mercenary popped up from nowhere and made a dash for the doorway.

Wait–

Bugayev traced his path back to where he'd appeared. Where there should have been a corpse on the deck.

That was quite some sprint from the guy he'd just put down.

Quiet. Temporary lull, but for now Lethbridge-Stewart located Bugayev and hunkered down, glad of the breather.

'You put many down?' Bugayev asked.

'I wasn't aware we needed to keep count.'

'No, but some of your men might want to go back and make sure. I just saw one target get up from three bullets, centre mass.'

'Vest?'

Bugayev shook his head. 'Some are wearing them, sure. Not this one.'

Lethbridge-Stewart frowned. He summoned Samson. 'Sergeant Major, take a detail and sweep these decks. Any men we've injured, see to them and make certain they're secure.' Disarmed, rounded up and placed under a two-man guard, minimum. But he didn't need tell Samson that. 'What about the rest of them?' Lethbridge-Stewart asked, turning back to Bugayev. 'Disappeared indoors, I take it?'

'Yes. We'll have to go room to room. Shut this place down.'

'And find the owner.'

'Let's knock on some doors.' Bugayev plucked a grenade from his belt and lobbed it through the open doorway.

Anne watched the Vulcan bomber roll out onto the runway. A winged beast with a certain elegance of geometry, it had that combined ungainliness and surprising speed common to alligators on land.

Group Captain Winser, standing beside her, along with a small collection of officers and maintenance crew, must have witnessed this sight a hundred times. But there was tension and electricity in the night air, like the promise of a coming thunderstorm.

Jet engines roared loud enough to make dragons tremble and the aircraft rocketed down the lane of runway lights.

Monsters, she thought, as the bomber launched into the air. The world kept sending new ones her way, but mankind manufactured its own fair share of them. Flame flared from the Vulcan's tail as it climbed into darkness.

But it was the payload in the beast's belly that troubled Anne. And she had been instrumental in arguing the case for its use. At Lethbridge-Stewart's behest, certainly, but a responsibility of this scale shared wasn't halved. Not by a long chalk.

'Does it trouble you, Group Captain? What we're unleashing.'

Winser tracked the receding aircraft with binoculars. He gave up, lowered them. 'Necessary evils, Miss Travers. The brigadier would never have proposed the mission without that necessity. And the Ministry would never have sanctioned it. You're having doubts? Even after what you saw on *Aphrodite*?'

Anne grimaced and glanced away. She shivered, although the night was a warm one. 'Still, it's a weapon we've never fired in anger before.'

'Small consolation, but we won't be dropping this one in anger, Miss Travers. More in fear, I think.'

Anne lost sight of the Vulcan. Although she could still hear its roar. It sounded like that storm, raging across the sky in search of its target.

She thought back to Bill's remark. About going up against enemies that might as well be gods. Well, they were going up against this one with much more than bullets.

More powerful weapons helped even the odds. But they didn't stop her being afraid.

Gunfire continued outside, but sudden quiet reigned in the passage. Bugayev stepped over a dead mercenary, allowing his AK barrel to linger over the corpse as though expecting it to twitch into life again. Lethbridge-Stewart followed close behind, exercising similar wariness.

'Come in, gentlemen. Come in.'

Vorster stood centre-stage in the corridor, holding a suited blonde as a shield and sticking the barrel of a handgun deep into her tousled hair. 'You know it's highly uncivil to come busting in here with guns. There are ladies present.'

'We would have come to talk,' Bugayev said. 'To question you. Had you not opened fire.'

'Oh, but you were prepared. Extremely well-prepared for the alternative, I'd say. You blew up my damned helicopter.'

'Why take chances?'

'Indeed, Captain? Well, you're going to have to take a chance now. On this young lady's life. Because I will blow her brains all over the wall if I don't see those guns on the deck in the next few seconds. I don't need to trouble myself to count out loud, do I? And now that you've gone to all this trouble to see me, no appointment or anything, I'd really welcome the opportunity to show you something.'

Lethbridge-Stewart looked askance at Bugayev. He was as illegible as ever. Although he looked murder in Vorster's direction, that was clear enough.

Lethbridge-Stewart crouched slow and laid his gun on the deck.

Captain Bugayev issued a command in Russian. Nothing happened. He repeated the order, louder. His troops filed reluctantly outside.

'I won't sacrifice any more of my men,' he informed Vorster. 'You'll have to make do with the officers. Make no mistake though, any of your men wander out for a breath of fresh air, it will be their last.'

'Fair enough, you hold the exterior. For now. I remain in charge in here.'

Bugayev tossed his gun. Then drew his sidearm and threw that down with the Kalashnikov.

Lethbridge-Stewart raised his hands.

'Thank you, Brigadier. That won't be necessary. You can surrender later.' Vorster motioned with his gun and mercenaries swept forward to collect the discarded weapons. Two moved around behind to prod Lethbridge-Stewart and Bugayev in the back.

A poisonous smile slithered across Vorster's face. He released his hostage. She straightened herself and smoothed down her hair. 'Thank you, Miss Van Den Haas.'

'My pleasure, Mr Vorster,' she said. And turned to follow right behind her boss.

CHAPTER TWENTY-FOUR
Masterplan

VORSTER LED their small party on a short tour of the facility. Lethbridge-Stewart did his best to use the opportunity for reconnaissance. Looking in open doorways, glancing along routes not taken. Many of the cabins appeared vacant and given that none of the crew would be out working during a gunfight, he had to assume the facility was short-staffed. He took special notice of the radio room, manned by a single fellow of similar build and demeanour to the guards escorting him and Bugayev. The radio operator also wore a holstered sidearm. The man spun in his swivel chair and reached to give the door a shove. It clanged closed as they passed.

Lethbridge-Stewart made a mental note of the turns in the passages – coupled with the descent down one flight of stairs – after that point.

The party stopped beside an unmarked bulkhead door. Vorster waved one of his faithful dogs forward. The man spun the wheel and pushed the door open. Vorster stepped through and the guards prodded Lethbridge-Stewart and Bugayev to follow.

Vorster advanced with the reverence of a priest, then turned and gestured at the enormous aquarium tank that dominated the chamber. Magnified behind thick glass, suspended in water illuminated from below, a large and irregular boulder bobbed a foot or so above the floor of the tank. The stone was massively gouged and cratered, as though bombarded like the Moon. The lights lining the base of the tank lent it an otherworldly glow.

Collected at its base were a familiar set of plastic boxes.

Containers Lethbridge-Stewart had previously seen being carried from the villa by Vorster's mercenaries.

Vorster beamed like a rather sinister television evangelist presenting a newly decorated chapel. Miss Van Den Haas stationed herself beside her boss, waiting like a faithful magician's assistant.

'What is that? A meteorite of some kind?' Lethbridge-Stewart asked.

'That's funny, Brigadier. That's what I thought when my workers first discovered a specimen in one of my mines. Some fragment of space rock that fell to Earth. Well, I say "discovered", but of course that honour belongs to those left alive to report the find.'

Vorster looked at his soldiers and two peeled away, departing and closing the door behind them. The other two guards positioned themselves on opposite sides of the room. Solid, flanking presences. Wherever this was leading, the odds did not look good.

'The first men died, I take it?' Lethbridge-Stewart enquired.

'Naturally. They were fool enough to touch it. The rescue team were a little more cautious. Most of them. Believe me, we had a hell of a job containing what we thought was an outbreak. Some kind of disease.'

'That would explain the disasters at your mining operations, I suppose.' Lethbridge-Stewart glanced at Bugayev. The Russian was resolutely silent, his eyes busy measuring everything.

'Yes, the first,' said Vorster. 'The second, only indirectly. We needed a cover for the first disaster. Identified an engineering flaw common to both facilities, sent out a lot of condolences to the families of the deceased, took steps to ensure nothing of that sort ever happened in the future. Shares took a hit, but we recovered. I considered it part of the price tag.'

'You're a madman.'

'On the contrary. My mind is clearer than you could possibly understand. It has to be.'

'I suppose it all must seem like sanity from the inside.'

Finally, something from Bugayev: a laugh. More of a snort, really.

The sound appeared to catch in Vorster's face like a fish-hook, much more so than Lethbridge-Stewart's barb. 'Amused, Captain?'

'Well, you know how it goes. Everybody laughs at genius, don't they? Until they understand.'

Calm descended over Vorster like a glacier, but there was the sense of great effort underneath, thinly masked. 'In the land of the blind, the one-eyed man is king. Neither of you sees a fraction of the truth.'

'What we see is a rock, *Mr* Vorster,' Lethbridge-Stewart said. 'A large quantity of hazardous material. Which you appear to have been amassing here under the auspices of a legitimate hydraulic fracturing operation. Whatever it is I'm failing to see, I do understand one thing. You have sanctioned the murder of innocent civilians and you need to be shut down.'

'Blind. But you will see.' Vorster gave a nod to the guards. Both moved in.

Lethbridge-Stewart received a hard kick behind the knee. The mercenary shoved him down. Likewise, Bugayev was encouraged to kneel. The guards lingered close.

'It's a truth easily demonstrated,' said Vorster. He turned his back on them. He moved to stand beside the tank.

'What truth are you talking about?' Lethbridge-Stewart demanded.

Vorster bent to the plastic boxes. He tugged off his glove and tossed it to the floor. He popped the lid of one and fished out a clay shard. Some fragment of a pot or urn. 'The Midas factor.'

'Is that how you see yourself? Everything you touch turns to gold?'

'Not me. The rock. Mutalith, I call it. It transforms everything it touches. Animal or mineral, anyway.'

The South African reached up and dropped the shard into the tank, like he was feeding a prize tropical fish. The shard sank, diminishing as it did so. By the time it struck bottom there was barely a pebble left. No visible change in the central mass, but Lethbridge-Stewart remembered Miss Travers' talk of crystallisation and the *Señora* holding up the two mended halves of the tablet. He didn't doubt where the material from that shard had ended up.

'How is it that you are immune?' he asked. 'Have you developed some sort of vaccine?'

'Vaccine? You're thinking of it in terms of a disease, some kind of infection. It's mutative, but it enhances. What doesn't kill us, makes us stronger. This is the epitome of that. Because those who survive the transformation with minds – with their *selves* – intact, those are the men who emerge stronger than ever. You've already witnessed a demonstration, but perhaps in the heat of battle, gentlemen, you did not get to properly appreciate what was happening in front of your eyes.'

Vorster rolled up his sleeve. Bunching his bare fist, he presented the knuckles, first to Bugayev, then to Lethbridge-Stewart.

The skin on his fingers crawled.

Rather, an effect crept across it. Discolouration, but more. Texturing. The man's hand turning to stone before his eyes.

Petrifaction.

Then, slowly, the stone began to recede, sinking back beneath the skin. Until the fist had recovered its normal tan. Complete with pores and lines and wrinkles. The gold frame of his wristwatch retained flecks of the stone texturing. The otherwise shiny metal looked diseased.

Vorster flexed his fingers.

'Control. Like any resource, it's only a matter of how to exploit it. Master it and that is the key to supremacy.'

Lethbridge-Stewart did begin to understand. He was sure Bugayev, beside him, understood too. Small wonder their bullets had not always made the impression they should have done.

'Of course,' continued Vorster, 'some of my men are understandably nervous about exercising their power. They fear that giving in to it is a cul-de-sac, you know? No coming back. They forget that they are in charge and they allow fear to rule.'

'So that's what all this is about,' Lethbridge-Stewart concluded, tasting the sourness. 'The Master Race.'

Bugayev sneered. 'There is no such thing as a dominant race. There are dominant men and there are weak men. And the worst men are the weak ones who believe themselves the strongest.'

'Have to say, I agree with the captain on that,' Lethbridge-Stewart said.

'What?' Vorster almost laughed. 'You think I'm deceiving

myself? Which of us is on our knees? Which is standing? With all the power in his hands?'

'You mistake your position for strength,' Bugayev said.

Vorster stepped in and slammed Bugayev's face with a punch. His fist came away bloodied. Bugayev spat drops of red. 'What about that? Did that feel like strength?'

Bugayev met Vorster's gaze and smiled slowly, as though to show he still had all his teeth. 'A show of force? Intended to convince, certainly. But who are you convincing? Because I have to tell you, if it's me, you have failed.'

Vorster signalled to one of the mercenaries. The man swung his sidearm up and let the barrel hover close to Bugayev's forehead.

'And now?' said Vorster.

Bugayev shrugged. 'All the same.'

'Same? Same as what?'

'You people. Capitalists. You believe yourselves superior because you hold all the cards. Because someone said money was the winning hand. Money is power so you believe yourselves powerful. But you know and understand the truth and that is why you shake in your boots every day. Others think greed drives you. But fear drives that greed. Fear of the masses you try to keep under your heel. Fear you might lose it all someday. So you amass more and more. More than you can ever possibly need. And you stress and run in circles every day trying to keep the poor man at the bottom of the food chain. You are vultures who think yourselves lions.'

'You're going to preach to me about your Communism? The rich prey on the poor in your precious system.'

'Some poisons spread everywhere. I told you, there are dominant men and there are weak men. We have weak men in the Soviet Union too. Our system is plagued with corruption. Yours is a plague at its heart. Yours is barely a step up from the law of the wild. Survival of the unfittest, most often.'

'Oh, I see.' Vorster nodded. 'You hailed from humble beginnings, did you, Captain? You resent those with more than you?'

'Strength – true strength – comes from adversity. What adversity did you ever have to face? Wealth. Privileged upbringing.

The champagne insufficiently chilled one day, caviar not the finest quality?'

'It takes strength to build an empire.'

'No, it takes the blood, sweat and lives of ordinary men. Ask the British.' Bugayev nodded towards Lethbridge-Stewart. 'The Kings and Queens of England sent their Irish and Scots and Welsh regiments to all the right places. Armed with the best weapons, the best machines of war. In your country, they battled superior numbers of Zulus and won because they had the guns. Sometimes guns are the cards, sometimes money. But the Zulus didn't go away, did they? Which is why the masses must be suppressed. Because in the masses, that is where you will find the strong men.'

'Well, a lot of strong men die. I'm sure their strength does them a lot of good in heaven. I'm more interested in strength in the real world.' Vorster sighed. 'Cynicism is only to be expected from you, Captain. What's it like to be Russian, eh? All that winter and misery, an entire history of being downtrodden and oppressed. Tyrant tsars and Communism. Of course, you would never believe in a dominant race. Watching the Western world stride ahead of you, only all that burning envy to keep you warm while you chain yourselves, generation after generation, from one master to another. Revolution? It's a joke, Captain. Your entire race, your continent, is a joke.

'Now, you British, Brigadier, with your Empire. At least you have a basis there for your sense of importance, some foundation for your superiority. Benevolent missionaries, raising lesser cultures and civilisations like your children, eh? But your Empire achieved all its greatness through power.'

'Power where it counts,' argued Lethbridge-Stewart. 'Power where it made a difference.'

'Such as power over this Mutalith.'

'Even there you fool yourself,' said Bugayev.

'How so, Captain? Are you trying to persuade me to kill you, is that it? To spare you conversion? You fear it, don't you?'

'Of course I do. Because I'm not a damned idiot.'

'Careful, because I may oblige you. I'm not sure I want you at my side, with your philosophies written in stone.'

'No, you wouldn't. The truth is a thorn in your side,' said

Bugayev. 'This thing, you see it as the key to creating your "master race". A resource to be exploited. A weapon, in effect. Plus, a little body armour for your men can't hurt the cause. But it is in the nature of this thing to spread. And yet you seek to collect it, to hoard it like your wealth. That is a conflict of interest.'

'What? The interests of man versus nature? Well, Captain, resources are there to be exploited. By strong men. Fire has its own nature; it is easily harnessed. The power of the atom. All manner of forces are there for us to use.'

'The captain thinks there is a crucial difference,' said Lethbridge-Stewart. 'And I'm inclined to believe the same.'

Bugayev nodded. 'This resource has a will of its own. I have seen it eat metal. Not just eat. Consume, and convert it to itself. Your precious Midas factor. So tell me, why is this rig of yours is still standing?'

Vorster smiled. The calm smile of a victor. 'Willpower. Force of will. My will.'

Bugayev laughed. The sound soured Vorster's smile.

'What do you find so funny?'

'Nothing. It's always a comfort to know your enemy's fortress is built on weak foundations.'

Vorster stormed forward and snatched the pistol from the guard's hand.

Bugayev moved. Launched himself off his knees and rammed into Vorster's gut. The big South African staggered backwards, halfway into a fall as his shoulders slammed against the wall.

Lethbridge-Stewart took his cue. He dropped and spun and kicked his guard's legs out from under him. Diving on the downed man, he delivered a sharp punch to the nose then grabbed for the gun, wresting it from the fellow's loosened grip. Lethbridge-Stewart jumped up and turned the pistol on the other guard.

The mercenary ran to his master's aid.

Bugayev was on top of his opponent, pinning him to the floor. Miss Van Den Haas dived at him, but Bugayev batted her brutally aside. She staggered back, head striking the wall. Slumped at its base. The Russian grabbed Vorster's head in both hands and hammered the wall with his skull.

Lethbridge-Stewart fired. The mercenary dropped, knee blown.

Another shot rang out from the gun in Vorster's flailing hand. The bullet punctured the steel ceiling.

Lethbridge-Stewart spun again to cover the punched guard. He hauled himself off the deck. 'Stay down!' he ordered. The mercenary continued on his way up. Lethbridge-Stewart grimaced. Then shot the fellow in his leg. He dropped back down.

'You. Have. To. Do. The. Job. Right,' said Bugayev, punctuating his words with bashes of Vorster's head against wall.

Lethbridge-Stewart covered the door. They could expect more company any minute.

Bugayev swiped Vorster's pistol, sprang to his feet and kicked his opponent in the chin. Then stood back a pace and aimed the gun at the South African's face.

'Captain!' Lethbridge-Stewart shouted.

He didn't get to say 'don't.'

Lethbridge-Stewart and Bugayev broke out into the corridor. And were met with deafening gunfire.

Bugayev fired a couple of shots. Another automatic burst answered back. Bullets rattled and sparked off metal close to Lethbridge-Stewart's ear. He fired down the passage, covering Bugayev as he ran forward and pressed his back to the left-hand wall.

A head and one shoulder popped into sight around the junction, assault rifle to the shoulder. Bugayev ducked into a doorway, a split second before the shots. Lethbridge-Stewart stepped back into the room they'd just exited. Another cluster of bullets zinged around the doorway.

He glanced over the bodies in the room. They lay lifeless on the deck. But the deck was turning to stone. Miss Van Den Haas lay dead or unconscious, stranded on the far side. Blood trickled down her neck while the contamination crept towards her.

The Mutalith had thrown out limbs of sorts. Gnarled and knobbled extensions like stalagmites or stalactites reaching from the central mass to touch the glass of its tank. From every point of contact, cracks spider-webbed and patches blossomed like stone bruises.

Trickles of water leaked through the cracks, rivulets conveying the effect to the base of the tank. Here and there the stone plague extended over the deck. Eating its way in several directions at once. Spreading.

Accelerating.

Another exchange of shots resounded in the passage. Two pistol-cracks traded for another three-round rifle burst.

'We don't have time for this!' Lethbridge-Stewart shouted to Bugayev.

'I agree.'

'No, I mean we really don't have time! The Mutalith is out of its cage!'

Bugayev answered with some pithy Russian profanity.

The mercenary at the junction didn't hear the warning or didn't care. He kept firing, possibly hoping to pin them here. Lethbridge-Stewart watched the stone tide advance across the floor, spreading under Vorster's corpse and now seeping out from beneath him on this side.

It really was gathering pace.

Lethbridge-Stewart waited out the next burst of gunfire, then stepped around the doorway and aimed.

The head, gun and shoulder popped out again.

Right in Lethbridge-Stewart's sight.

Two shots knocked the man back. He sprawled and the rifle clattered beside him. Bugayev sprang from his doorway and raced for the junction. Snatched a recce around the corner, then stooped and scooped up the rifle. He waved Lethbridge-Stewart up to join him.

Lethbridge-Stewart needed no further inducement. 'How bad is it?'

'Fast. And growing faster.'

'Damn. We need to get our men off this platform.'

'Radio room. We have to reach the radio room.'

'Good. It's not far.'

They ran. Elsewhere the rig echoed with the sporadic percussion of gun battles. Combined now with more ominous noises. Creaks and leaden groans, the dying pains of some huge metal dinosaur.

*

Lethbridge-Stewart swung around the doorway and shot twice. The radio operator was up, halfway through drawing his sidearm.

He dropped just as quickly.

Lethbridge-Stewart rushed in and kicked the pistol to the wall. He went straight to the radio while Bugayev crouched beside the downed man, checking for signs of life.

Lethbridge-Stewart quickly adjusted the frequency and searched the walls. Nobody had thought to post a map in here.

'What's our grid reference?'

'Forget the grid reference,' said Bugayev. 'That underwater city. Trust me, the largest concentration of this stuff is there. I'll have my crew put out a boat with signal smoke. Tell your people to plant their ordinance on that.'

'Your submarine is down there.'

Bugayev rose, joining Lethbridge-Stewart by the radio. 'Call it a Viking funeral.'

'Or a cover-up.'

'Come on, you want to stand here and argue?' Bugayev cast an eye towards the doorway. There was no telling how far or fast the stone plague was spreading, but the rig's death throes could be heard plainly enough. 'Or finish it? You know this is the right call. An aircraft from Akrotiri, yes? This is the card you have up your sleeve? What payload? A W-E one-seven-seven bomb? Ten kilotons. Sub-surface detonation. Comparable to what I had in mind anyway. This rig might collapse before then but whatever it leaves in the sea will feel the effects. Zero harm to civilians. Local marine life is not an issue, so even your young eco-warrior, Owain, will be able to sleep at night. So really, what is holding you up?'

What indeed?

Lethbridge-Stewart reconsidered for a moment telling Bugayev about those submariners who'd made it ashore, who now stood in stone circles on the Greek islands. But he honestly believed that wouldn't alter the captain's view. Not one jot.

There was no other call. It was a calculated play, but the calculations made sense. There would be repercussions, of course, but none that could not be answered.

Except one. And for that, he would have to answer to Owain.

CHAPTER TWENTY-FIVE
Edge of Destruction

FAR ASTERN, the horizon caught fire. A strip of bright magnesium stretched across the surface, as though marking where the Moon had plunged into the sea. A giant dome rose from the depths, a great blister erupting in the spreading brightness. Surging up and up in an enormous balloon of water, shockwaves driving violent ripples across the night-dark Aegean.

La Luna was safe enough. She shone serenely down from the night sky. Up where the thunder had broken across the stars: the roar of a jet aircraft high overhead, heralding this delivery.

Say what you like about mankind. They were great architects of destruction.

The crew, Soviet soldiers and British, were all gathered on the deck, lining the sides of the vessel and peering aft. Many cheered and whooped and yelled in celebration. And why not? They were at a safe remove – or so they had all been assured. With the churning wake still putting further distance between them and the blast. Captain Bugayev, Brigadier Lethbridge-Stewart, Sergeant Major Ware, all present and correct, conveyed back to the ship over an hour before in the Russian helicopter.

All was well that ended well.

Sophia wondered: did she mourn for the city? For a *faux* Atlantis?

No.

Not in the slightest.

That it had been a thing of great artifice and beauty – majesty, even – there was no doubt in her mind. The same might easily be said for the explosion she had just witnessed. And that had similarly chilled her blood.

Some forces were powerful enough to be easily mistaken for the work of gods. But she was not one to be fooled.

Sooner or later, they would all reveal themselves as the work of men or monsters.

Owain jolted awake, out of a nightmare. One in which he'd been falling and falling – and he'd hit the ground. No. Splashed down in the ocean.

An image stayed with him as he opened his eyes. He blinked, but she lingered. Kara. Drifting away from him, sinking and sinking away into the depths.

He blinked again. Glanced about the Hercules' interior in an effort to see other things. Mostly there was just Atkins, seated opposite. The private hadn't budged since the last time Owain had looked at him. Owain figured he must have nodded off no more than a few seconds.

'You all right?' asked Atkins.

'No. No, I should be out there at the circle. There's still time. For another try.'

Atkins shrugged. 'Wouldn't know about that.'

Sure. He had his orders.

Owain had seen those crates Bill had packed off with him when he'd driven back to the circle. The military were thoughtful enough to label everything. *Danger. Explosives,* said the stencils on the boxes.

'Precaution,' was all Bill had offered by way of an explanation when he'd caught Owain's glare.

But that wasn't the worst of it. Owain had been seized by an unease since his uncle had left. Picked up by the same helicopter he'd seen piggy-backing Bugayev's 'oceanographic research' ship. After a long time making radio calls from the Hercules' cockpit. And he hadn't been able to meet Owain's gaze, only told Atkins, 'Make sure he stays put. And gets some rest.'

And the last bit, Owain was sure, was only tacked on to lend it a better ring. To make it sound like it was all for his own good.

'What's going on, Atkins?'

'Wouldn't know. Nobody told me.' He appeared to take some pity on Owain. Was he looking that sorry for himself? 'And that being the case, it's probably something you don't want to know.'

Cold comfort.

Owain closed his eyes and tried to see Kara again. And Paolo. But they were gone. Both gone.

Bishop's squad moved into the circle. The men were stunned and silent.

Bishop was stuck for orders to issue.

Private Franks stepped in a pile of dust and toed the stuff around. Until he took a dislike to the powder collected on the tip of his boot and had a go at shaking it off.

'Private!' Bishop snapped. 'Show some damned respect!'

Franks retreated sharpish. Just a pace or two back, but enough. 'Sorry, sir.'

The others withdrew slowly, returning to the perimeter of the circle.

Bodily remains, Bishop thought. *That's what we are treading in. The scattered ashes of the dead, heaped in the grass.*

That was what the aftermath of success looked like. Success itself, well, that had amounted to watching the statues disintegrate. Stone to dust. Crude faces, arms and torsos and legs collapsing and falling away to nothing.

Bishop had focused on the child. He'd been aware of the other figures crumbling. But his eyes refused to look anywhere else.

And now?

Now he would be the one to tell Owain about his friends.

Don't shoot the messenger almost wasn't an issue when the messenger would almost rather shoot himself.

Brigadier Lethbridge-Stewart nodded to the men as he wove a path between them. He couldn't begrudge them their moment, even if he was in no mood to join them.

He murmured an aside to Samson in passing, warning him to assemble the troops for departure. Soon.

He found the *Señora* on her own, elbows rested on the side, watching empty seas. Well, never empty, Lethbridge-Stewart reminded himself. But safe and calm for the time being.

'Ready for a ride home?' he enquired.

'Oh, I am past ready. But... You know, if you are ever in need of an archaeologist again—'

'What? Find somebody else?'

She laughed. 'No. No, I would be happy to assist. Just, next time, if you can manage it, please make sure it is an archaeological site you wish investigated.'

'I will do my best, *Señora*. Unfortunately, in my business, we rarely know what we've found until we're up against it. And sometimes, even afterwards we're not entirely sure.'

'Brigadier.'

Lethbridge-Stewart turned to meet the captain, cutting in like an officer and gentleman at a dance. Albeit, he didn't appear to be requesting a waltz. He did, however, extend a hand.

'Shake? Or are these hands too dirty?'

Lethbridge-Stewart hesitated. Between shots fired in combat and shots fired when men were down there were clear lines that should never be crossed. Bugayev, whatever he may be, was not one for indecision.

His proffered handshake withdrawn, he stood back.

'A salute, then.'

He saluted. Officer to officer. Soldier to soldier.

Lethbridge-Stewart decided he could live with that.

He returned the salute, along with his respect.

EPILOGUE

HAT TUCKED under one arm, Captain Bugayev stood at attention, waiting for General Timarov to finish digesting the report.

The general was a slow reader. Hunched over his mahogany desk, he breathed like an old silver bear. He boasted a barrel-chest full of ribbons and cheeks ravaged by time and high blood pressure. He was a dangerous man who understood that predation was an art mastered more through patience than speed. Long years of waiting, if necessary, manoeuvring to create opportunities, coupled with deadly strikes. And when he'd reached that age when lethal sprints were beyond him, he had others do the running – and killing – on his behalf.

Bugayev wasn't about to hurry him.

The pages turned and the clock ticked on the mantelpiece.

Timarov reached for the glass in its silver cup-holder and slurped his tea. Rumour had it that he spiked it with vodka, but Bugayev had witnessed his adjutant pour and seen no alcohol introduced. Timarov swilled the mouthful around and swallowed as though washing down some words that had proved hard on the digestion. Finally, he set the glass on its coaster then laid the file to rest under one pudgy hand.

'This, Captain, is your honest report? Those men sacrificed themselves, detonated their ship's payload in a final patriotic act to rid the world of an alien threat?'

'No, sir. This is the lie you will be able to sell with the greatest of ease.' It was the lie behind whatever cover story the general chose to pass along up the chain of command. A story that would circulate at the highest levels, undergoing endless rewrites before its replacement with official denials. 'Captain Zaretsky and his crew died as heroes. That is certainly the part of the account, minus details, to be presented to the families.'

'And in sacrificing their lives, they destroyed all evidence of our boat's presence in the region.' Timarov sighed a lungful of gravel. 'You are quite the storyteller, Captain Bugayev. I would only question whether this level of creativity is your responsibility. These are matters above your station.'

'Perhaps, sir. Or perhaps I should be operating at a higher station.'

Something traced itself across Timarov's lips. The barest hint of a smile, like an expression the facial muscles only half-remembered. 'And the truth?'

'The truth, sir, is that the British Near East Defence Force launched a nuclear strike against an underwater target. Captain Zaretsky and his crew were already dead, our boat already destroyed. Their offence amounts to an act of aggression and gross disrespect against an underwater grave we would prefer to remain secret.' Timarov confined himself to a slow nod. 'The wider truth is that, while there may not be anything worse than Americans, there are more dangerous enemies out there. And the British – and we must assume other Western powers – are organised and equipped to deal with them. I believe we may have some catching up to do.'

Timarov arrested his nod and drummed his fingers on the file. He sat back and pulled open a desk drawer. From within, he produced a second file folder and slid it across the desk.

'Some reading matter for you. Major.'

'Thank you, sir.'

The file bore a codename.

Byeliye Volkiy.

White Wolves.

'This report is not to leave this office. Please, avail yourself of an office and take some time to study it. The truth – the even wider truth, as you would have it – is that others have arrived at similar conclusions to your own. The Aegean incident is not isolated. We need to be prepared. And, Major, understand: this reading matter comes with a job offer. One that you had best not refuse.'

'Understood, sir.'

Bugayev stamped forward and retrieved the folder.

He was aware he was one of Timarov's pieces, being moved on the board. No pawn, at least. After all, he'd just made Knight or Rook. But he was under no illusion. Timarov would sacrifice his high value pieces in a heartbeat if it meant winning his game. The trick for Bugayev was to demonstrate his own set of moves and place himself in a position where he proved himself invaluable.

Chess was only played against a single opponent. It became an altogether different game when the opponents were many and the pieces possessed minds and ambitions of their own.

Patience. Manoeuvring. Deadly strikes. Major Bugayev was made for this game.

Lethbridge-Stewart watched as the men busied themselves taking down the charts, dismantling the display board and generally packing up the Operations Room. If only it was that simple to wrap everything up.

Miss Travers oversaw the boxing of her equipment, happy to be occupied, happier still to be heading home. Who could blame her?

Group Captain Winser said otherwise, but Lethbridge-Stewart imagined he would be glad to have his Fifth guests out of his hair. And the base crew would be glad to have their cinema restored to them.

The door opened and Owain walked in, looking around as though he had stumbled into the wrong room.

'Ah, Owain. All checked up? Everything okay?'

The lad nodded. 'Base doctor gave me a clean bill of health. After an X-ray. Even though I told him I was good.'

'And are you?' Miss Travers breezed over and gave Owain a welcoming hug. 'It's good to see you. But good, really? You don't look altogether good.'

'I could be better.'

'Well, lots of luck sleeping it off on the flight home. I didn't sleep a wink on the way over. I understand the RAF are thinking of fitting their transports with a first class passenger lounge, but sadly not on this trip.'

Owain raised a heavily weighted smile. 'Next time. Anyway, I'm taking a different flight.'

'Really?' Lethbridge-Stewart arched an eyebrow. This was news. He was having to remain on station a while, required to play diplomacy with the Greek authorities, answer inquiries in the higher echelons of NATO. 'Where are you jetting off to?'

'Don't know about jetting, but I'm headed to Rhodes. Kara used to talk about waitressing and doing traditional Greek dances for the tourists at some tavern. Guess I'll start there and see if any of her friends know where her parents live. Figured I'd track them down, tell them... You know.'

'In person? Owain, you don't have to take that upon yourself.'

'Yes. I do. And after that... I don't know. Carry on with my globe-trotting, I guess, find a way to clear my mind a bit.' Owain stopped, as if something had just occurred to him. 'Mind you, I may need your help with something.'

'Oh yes?'

'Yes. My passport. Lost it in the sea.'

'Ah.' Lethbridge-Stewart nodded. 'Of course, that should be simple enough to sort out.'

'Thanks.' Owain sighed. 'Although I might reconsider the idea of making friends on my travels.'

Miss Travers brushed a hand down the young man's shoulder. 'Oh, Owain, isolation isn't the answer.'

'Well, it may help you to process things, I suppose. I hope it does,' Lethbridge-Stewart said. 'But you know, I'm not sure of the wisdom of touring Europe – or anywhere further afield – alone. Not with nefarious sorts out there attempting to kidnap you.' And that was something Lethbridge-Stewart intended on looking into – the remains of the kidnappers' car had been found half a mile down the Mesaria road. Not much more than a heap of ash, but he had personnel sifting through it for clues.

'What do you suggest, Uncle Alistair? Go into hiding? No. I'll keep moving, thanks. And maybe you're right, Anne, maybe I'll manage to move on as well as stay ahead of my would-be kidnappers.'

There was bite in Owain's tone. Lethbridge-Stewart had arrived in an atmosphere of grudges and cold shoulders from Miss Travers. She had forgiven or forgotten, possibly both, but he felt a similar frost now from Owain.

'Well, you take care. And keep both eyes peeled.

Unfortunately, I don't have the manpower to spare to assign you a round-the-clock escort.'

That, at least, prodded a laugh from Owain. 'Thanks. Won't be necessary. I expect Vorster's lot have gone to ground, and anyway, haven't you got Interpol or someone hunting them by now?'

'Just so. VTMB personnel files sequestered, police forces throughout the continent alerted.' That part of the job was straightforward enough. Boxes ticked, items checked off the agenda. Tasks, if not actually done, at least set in motion. 'I'm rather more concerned about the possibility of more alien invaders living under us.'

Or if not living, then dormant, like a volcano ready to erupt with only as much notice as the Earth deemed appropriate.

'Not alien, Uncle. Remember?'

Miss Travers nodded. 'He's right. What's alien? If this Mutalith was drawn in by accretion, even if it was only trace elements, then it's as much a part of the Earth as us. Maybe more so.'

'All enemies, foreign and domestic, Miss Travers,' Lethbridge-Stewart said, waving his swagger-stick.

And if they were to think in global terms, he supposed foreign would have to include forces from space. Outer and inner.

'All enemies, foreign and domestic.'

The mission statement remained the same. Only the definitions shifted.

ACKNOWLEDGEMENTS

WRITING IS often a solitary affair, conducted between you and the characters, and sometimes unwilling pages that would prefer not to have their pristine blankness sullied by clumsy black marks we like to think of as words. Crafting a novel, however, is a collaborative endeavour and the finished book owes a debt to more than the author's fevered caffeine-fuelled imagination.

Research, of course, plays a key factor and while the Internet is a great fount of knowledge, it's helpful to have starting points and, besides, some things are better learned over friendly chats and cups of coffee. So, huge thanks and big grateful hugs go to Sara Rogers, the original crazy cat-lady archaeologist who took time out of her study schedule to play consultant.

Thanks to Andy Frankham-Allen for entrusting me with the opportunity to contribute to the range, and for turning out to be an editor who's a pleasure to work with. Also, I understand, some thanks are due to Gary Russell for pointing Andy in my direction.

Thanks to the talented Richard Young for the fabulous cover. To Rick Cross, Tim Gambrell and a host of friends online and in the real world for the support and encouragement. And to David McIntee whose *The Schizoid Earth* showed me the way.

Finally, a salute to Nicholas Courtney, the man who gave us the Brigadier. I would make a useless soldier, but it's my hope I've written a good one.

SAF 2016

Candy Jar Books would like to thank Kevin Nolan and Jelena Kondrashova for assistance.